FAIR PLAY

Hat Trick Book One

Samantha Wayland

Fair Play

Published by Loch Awe Press
P.O. Box 5481
Wayland, MA 01778

ISBN 9781940839011

Edited by Helen Hardt and Meghan Conrad
Cover Art by Caitlin Fry

Also by Samantha Wayland

Destiny Calls
With Grace

Coming Winter 2013-2014

Hat Trick Book Two: Two Man Advantage
Hat Trick Book Three: End Game

Dedication

To Stevie, my dear friend and extraordinarily patient tutor on all things hockey. Never could I have imagined the impact you would have in my life when I met you all those years ago. Then again, you *were* wild-eyed with sleep deprivation and dropping f-bombs in a room full of Mormons like it was your job.

Here's to overcoming first impressions.

Acknowledgements

I could not have written this story without the help and patience of many. Above all, I must thank my family, particularly for putting up with my "research trips" to Bruins games. I promise I *will* take you with me someday.

Many thanks to Victoria Morgan, Penny Watson and Bobbi Ruggiero, for hours of support, laughter, editing, and mango martinis (sometimes simultaneously!). Thanks to Dalton Diaz for delivering the hard feedback and doing it with such grace and kindness. You are a rock. And to Serena Bell. You gave me and this story a much needed shaking up and managed to improve both.

My thanks again to Stevie, for turning what started as a research project into a passion for hockey. And finally, my thanks to Mike, who answered millions of questions about his beautiful hometown of Moncton.

I've taken some creative license when it comes to both hockey and Moncton, all in the name of making the story come to life and/or protecting the innocent. Any inaccuracies or mistakes are mine and mine alone.

Chapter One

Miss Manners had never covered how to turn down a date when the lady in question already had her hands in the man's underpants. A shame, really, since it seemed to happen to Savannah Morrison with alarming regularity.

"Rhian Savage, you know better," she chided, barely keeping a lid on her irritation.

They were alone in her work room, the tight space made smaller and more intimate by the equipment jammed into every corner and the hot tub at her back. Rhian lay on her table, stripped down to skin-tight spandex shorts that left little to the imagination.

And Savannah had a wonderful imagination.

Finished with her inspection of the fresh bruises on his hip and flank, she slipped her fingers free of his waistband and let it snap back into place from a good six inches away from his skin. He flinched, muffling his snort of laughter, while she fought to keep her expression bland.

Rhian shrugged, his massive chest shifting. "You can't blame a guy for trying."

She rolled her eyes before she turned away to gather more supplies and her composure.

Rhian was one of the good guys, and more importantly, he listened to her advice. If he didn't, he wouldn't be on her table, allowing her to climb all over him to stretch out his tight leg muscles. Now that she'd checked the damage from the previous night and was satisfied it wasn't going to be an issue, she indicated he should stand up so she could wrap him for tonight's game.

She watched how he moved, searching for any sign of pain, studying the beauty laid bare before her with professional detachment. When she wasn't feeling sensitive about it, she could admit her job was a little unusual. But being the athletic trainer for a professional ice hockey team was her dream. And she took it very seriously.

Thus, Rhian was here. He didn't have a pulled hamstring, not yet, and she was determined to prevent one. A lot of the guys would have ignored her suggestions for stretches, PT, Kinesio tape, and good wrapping. Not Rhian.

Most of the time she fought what appeared to be some kind of code among the players. One that ignored thoughtful suggestions, "forgot" mandatory check-ins and flatly refused to admit to any pain, no matter how obvious it was to her well-trained eye. The question was if the code stemmed from the fact that all hockey players were notoriously hard-headed about showing any sign of weakness, or if the real issue was the Ice Cats' new trainer was a woman.

With a sigh, she worked a compression bandage around Rhian's hard thigh and up over his hip, grateful he stood still and behaved professionally in spite of his gross breach of etiquette a few moments ago.

Not for the first time, Savannah lamented the previous trainer's disappearing act to Australia the minute he'd retired. She would have liked his thoughts on some of the players—their habits, their weaknesses—and then could have used that information to determine whether there had always existed a culture of resistance to the trainer or if it was all just sexist bullshit.

Then again, if the previous trainer was an old-school kind of guy, he might have been too apoplectic over her very existence to be much help. Hell, at least four players still wouldn't make eye contact, let alone *speak* to her unless forced. The only reason she had any interaction with them at all was because their coach, Rick, would kick their asses if she didn't sign off on them to play.

In the face of all that, the last thing she needed was to *date* one of her players. The very idea made her shudder.

She ripped off the last piece of tape with a little more force than necessary and finished Rhian's wrap. Pleased with the results, she stepped back and put her hands on her hips.

His grin was adorable, unrepentant, and absolutely not helping. She looked to the heavens for patience before casting a baleful eye on him. "Rhian, I'm flattered you asked." She grimaced when his eyebrows lifted. "But you should try to remember I'm the only thing that stands between your hairy legs and a lot of very sticky tape."

Rhian winced and quickly yanked up his gym shorts. She refused to even so much as crack a smile at his antics.

Even though he'd lost his head and asked, she suspected he understood her reasons for saying no. He was young, focused and building a reputation on the ice. He didn't need any drama to fuck that up. Nor did she. The biggest difference between them was that he might get picked up by the NHL by the end of this season. She, on the other hand, expected to put in a few years with the Ice Cats before setting her sights higher.

Rhian said his thanks and slid by, careful not to brush against her as he left the room. She made quick work of cleaning up the mess, shaking off her irritation, and turning her mind to her schedule. *Who is next?* Hopefully not one of her problem children. She could use a minute to clear her head.

Loud laughter echoed outside her door and Savannah resisted the urge to bang her head against the edge of her tub. She hadn't known that just thinking "problem child" would bring the worst of the lot to her door.

In the hallway, Rhian chatted with Garrick LeBlanc. How these two men could be friends was a mystery to her. Rhian was a good guy and a rookie. Garrick was...*not*.

That Garrick was friends with anybody had to be an aberration. At the very least, she'd have guessed he'd hang out with the men he'd played with the longest, or knew from college teams, or even grew up with in the same town. Heck, how about with the other dogs who'd taken all the puck bunnies for a test drive?

Instead, he gravitated toward the men with level heads and strong work ethics. The players she liked. The heart of the team.

What she couldn't figure out was what any of those guys saw in Garrick.

She ignored another booming laugh.

If she *had* come to Moncton to find a boyfriend and a party, she wouldn't have had to look any further. Garrick LeBlanc's reputation was on the order of legend. He'd been a sensation when he started in the league twelve years ago, his handsome face a favorite with both the female fans and the press.

For more than a decade he'd been a star for the Moncton Ice Cats. Other teams had tried to woo him away, but he had grown up in Moncton and had made himself the beloved son by refusing to leave. The fans adored his antics, on ice and off. It would have been totally unconscionable if he weren't an outstanding forward.

Oh yes, she'd learned all about Garrick when she thoroughly researched the Ice Cats before coming north. She'd lectured herself to be open-minded, and when he introduced himself the day she arrived, his firm handshake and direct gaze had given her hope that what she'd learned about him would not be an issue.

Then a nanosecond after Rick—the coach, her *boss*—turned away, Garrick had asked her out. Indeed, he had the dubious honor of being the very first player to do so—though it would have been tough to beat him, since she'd only been in the arena *ten minutes.*

She'd figured she might get asked out at some point, but having to deal with it that soon had been disappointing.

No, screw disappointing. It had royally pissed her off.

Since then she'd been cool with Garrick. Actually, she was cool with all the players. She was downright *frosty* with Garrick. And he made it easy. Apparently, his ego hadn't taken well to her less-than-tactfully blurted "no," and he'd hardly made eye contact with her since.

She snorted with amusement. Even as handsome as he was, she couldn't possibly be the only woman who had ever told him no—not that she wouldn't happily accept the honor.

Fighting the sneer begging to make its way onto her face, she patiently sorted the last of her supplies into various containers as Garrick walked into her office. By the time she turned around, his gym shorts were off and another set of imagination-free spandex shorts and their contents were on display.

In other circumstances, she might have enjoyed the view. She'd always had a thing for really big guys, and at six and a half feet of toned, hockey-playing muscle, Garrick was a fine specimen. Heck, she probably *could* look her fill, since his gaze was firmly fixed on the phone he held in front of his face.

But ogling wouldn't be professional. And she'd have her hands all over him in about two minutes anyway.

She sighed. Why did he have to have a groin pull?

Why, Garrick wondered again, as he had before every game this season, *do I have to have a groin pull?*

He'd known the moment he twisted the damn muscle playing street hockey with his nephews over the summer that it would plague him. He'd never imagined it would persist this far into the season.

Months of PT, stretching, hot soaks, strengthening, ice and wraps. Months of pure unadulterated torture.

Not torture because it was hard work, or because it hurt like hell. He was tougher than that. It was torture because the only person who made a difference, who was able to help him and give him sound advice and support, was Savannah.

She was damn good at her job, a fact he often celebrated and lamented in the same breath.

Garrick wasn't stupid. If the old trainer had still been around, Garrick's career, and possibly his ability to walk normally, would have come to an end two months ago. But Savannah pushed. She fought his stubborn old body and worked magic. And what she couldn't fix between games, she shored up and protected on the ice with pre-game hot compresses, icing, and wraps.

Hell, she'd once constructed a support wrap reinforced with *duct tape* to get the job done. She was clever and tenacious, and he was incredibly fucking lucky and grateful.

Not that he dared tell her that. At this point, he was afraid to look at her. Instead, he pretended to play games on his phone like a completely rude asshole while reminding himself to breathe normally. And if that didn't work, he thought about his grandma and fuzzy little kittens and Mrs. Plum, his kindly and ancient elementary school art teacher. When times got really tough, he closed his eyes and pictured the time his friend took a line drive to his nuts in high school.

Anything to keep from getting an erection.

Not since middle school had he spent so much time and energy attempting to wrestle his cock into submission. Back then a long t-shirt and his hands shoved in his pockets had hidden a multitude of sins.

Clearly, spandex shorts under a damn spotlight weren't going to afford him the same protection, even if she wasn't bent to her task, her nose level with his navel.

She didn't have to do a hot compress or ice for him today— weeks ago he'd taken over those pre-game treatments in an attempt to show himself some mercy. Though right now a freezing cold bag pressed to his junk would be helpful. Desperate, he recalled Mrs. Plum's wrinkled visage and fought the flow of blood.

Perverse as it was, some part of him still looked forward to coming here and giving himself over to her capable hands. He'd never pegged himself for a masochist.

Firm fingers slid over his hip and he bit back the urge to shout "down boy!" He fought to focus on his game.

Why were these birds so angry anyway?

Sighing he put down his phone. Looking directly at Savannah was not the best strategy for controlling his little problem, but he was tired of being rude, and ignoring her wasn't working anyway.

"So, how are you settling in?" he asked.

She stilled, glancing up at his face before refocusing on the bindings she was working around his thigh and between his legs. Her hand skimmed along the underside of his butt cheek. He bit his tongue. Hard.

"Uh...fine." Her brows drew together briefly while nimble fingers smoothed tape along his leg. "The season has me busy enough that I don't think I'll really feel like a resident of Moncton until the summer."

A pang of guilt hit his gut. He should have offered to show her around. Not on a date, of course, but as a local. Dorky as it sounded, he considered himself something of an ambassador for new people on or associated with the team to help them get comfortable with their new home.

But after the wonderful first impression he'd made, he doubted she'd take him up on an offer for a tour of the town. He cringed, remembering his stupidity.

His only defense—and he could admit it wasn't a great one—was that he'd come to the meet-and-greet nervous about the new trainer, having hated the old guy but knowing the various aches and pains in his leg and hip weren't going to help a veteran player further his career. In fact, he'd been thinking his career might be over, and damn it, he hoped to get a few more years in the league. At least long enough to figure out what the fuck he was going to do next.

He hadn't expected to find a beautiful woman, try though she might to hide it, standing in the lobby shaking hands with the rest of the players. She'd been wearing a frumpy suit and ugly shoes. Her disguise, as he'd come to think of it. Tonight it was loose yoga pants, a boxy men's Ice Cats pullover that fell to mid-thigh, and sneakers. As always, a tight knot pulled her hair back from her face.

But Garrick saw the truth. Then and now.

The curves. The silky hair. Smoky green eyes. Long legs, swelling hips, and a little dipped-in waist. Five feet ten inches of lovely athletic grace.

Shit. Now he needed a distraction. ASAP.

Tentatively, he smiled. "I'm from around here. Is there anything I can do to help?" At her suspicious look, he continued quickly. "I just mean, I don't know...Good dry cleaner? Best pizza? Chinese take-out to avoid if you want to live? That sort of thing?"

"As far as I can tell, such a Chinese take-out place doesn't exist."

"Ah." He chuckled, delighted that she'd actually responded. Also, the idea of food poisoning was working toward his goal of total flaccidity. "Then you *have* begun to settle in. I'm sorry one of us didn't warn you about that."

Savannah made a sound that could almost be called a laugh. Garrick grinned.

Refusing to let his big mouth get him back into hot water when, for the first time in weeks, he had one leg out of the tub, he shut up. Savannah finished his wrap. As soon as she'd applied the last piece of tape, he moved away. This warm fuzzy moment could result in a spandex pup-tent if he lingered too long.

"Thanks." He yanked on his shorts—a meager defense at best.

"Let me know how that feels. I added some extra support on the side, see if it helps."

"I have no doubt it will," he said. "You're like god's gift to tape."

A grateful, albeit bewildered smile was his reward. Months of torture suddenly seemed worth it, even if he'd come across as a complete dork.

God's gift to tape? Very smooth, asshole.

Chapter Two

"Ahem."

Bobby Kramer stood in Savannah's doorway, ten minutes early for his appointment. Turning back to her desk, she rolled her eyes. "I have to go, Callum," she told her oldest brother through the phone. Callum also had to go on the ice tonight, so they'd needed to wrap up anyway. Still, her neck heated with annoyance at Bobby.

Though she tried not to rank them, she definitely liked some players better than others. Bobby Kramer would always reside at the bottom of that list.

She nodded politely as he stomped past her and parked himself in front of her table, his ass resting against the edge. He liked to stand for his visits, probably just so he could loom over her. Most of the guys who needed elbow work sat, either in a chair or on the table. Not Bobby. He stood, leaned into her, held his arm closer to his body than necessary, and recently had taken to bending his head down to hers, trying to force an intimate conversation.

Just the memory of his breath on her neck made her shudder.

She'd made it abundantly clear she wasn't interested in him or amused by his advances. He either didn't understand her not-very-subtle rebuffs or he didn't care. The last time he'd been in her office, he asked what she was doing that weekend.

She'd snapped, "Nothing with you, Bobby, and that's all you need to know."

His friends had howled at that and she'd kicked herself for letting her anger show. Not that she regretted getting her point across since it seemed he'd finally heard her. The look he'd given her as he'd left her office that night had been chilling.

The look he sent her right now wasn't much better.

Bobby Kramer was a local, like Garrick. Yet not like Garrick at all. He was the son of some big-wig businessman who owned half the bars, all the off-track betting joints, and a couple hotels in town. His father was a notorious douchebag, from what Savannah had heard, and he had obviously raised his son in his own image.

Bobby was a spoiled brat. No, worse than spoiled. *Entitled.* Entitled to his position on the team, though his only specialty was fighting and he was one of the weakest skaters on the roster. Entitled to the devotion of the puck bunnies he treated like something stuck to the bottom of his shoe. Entitled to be late to practice and ignore the advice of the trainer, coaches, and team management alike. Entitled to show up for his appointment with Savannah any time he saw fit.

At least today he was early, so he wouldn't screw up everyone else's time too. She'd scheduled him first with the hope he'd be in and out quickly. She'd love to bounce him to Steve, the very nice assistant trainer who helped out on game nights, but Bobby's elbow work took more strength and finesse than Steve's experience or seventy-year-old hands could handle.

Facing her counter, she gathered what she would need and schooled her features before she turned back to Bobby.

"How's the elbow? Has it been bothering you at all?"

"It fucking sucks."

She kept her voice neutral. "Have you been icing it after games and practice?"

Bobby's face twisted into an ugly sneer, which, actually, wasn't too different from his normal expression. "I don't have time for that shit. I shouldn't have to. If you knew what the fuck you were doing, I wouldn't have this problem."

She forced herself to move slowly, carefully placing the rolls of tape and bandages on the table next to Bobby's hip where they would be within easy reach.

"I think you'll find icing after games and practice will help." *Just like I told you the last twenty times.* "I can also refer you to a couple good PTs in town if you want to get another opinion."

"Fuck that. I don't need any ice but the shit I'm skating on." He chuckled at his own feeble wit. "Next thing you'll be telling me is I have to do stretches after I jerk off."

Oh yes, Bobby was *all class*.

She picked up a bandage and began to wrap his arm. He didn't even try to keep it away from his ribs, forcing her to reposition him repeatedly. Her jaw ached from gnashing her teeth, but she did her job and did it well.

Bandage secured, she reached for the tape, her fingers barely brushing the roll before he yanked it from her grasp. She grabbed for it, twice, increasingly furious at Bobby's asinine game of keep-away. She realized too late she was off-balance and much too close.

She had just threaded her fingers through the tube of the tape when Bobby grabbed her ass and hauled her up against him.

Oh shit.

Stomach plunging, she tried to shove him away. "What the fuck are you *doing*?"

Using her knee against his thigh as leverage, she drilled her patella into his quad and pried herself loose. He released his hold on her ass so suddenly she stumbled back, slamming against the hot tub with a clang, the scissors in her back pocket digging painfully into her right butt cheek.

Bobby immediately advanced on her.

"Stay the fuck away from me, Bobby," she said, her voice loud enough to carry into the silent hallway. *Where the fuck is everybody?*

Not for the first time, she regretted team management's decision to move the trainer's office out of the locker room when she took the position. Steve was still in the old space since this new one was so small. She could have used his help right about now.

She dodged to the right, but Bobby stopped her. He

wrapped one ham-sized hand around the edge of the tub, cornering her and killing any hope of getting between him and the door. She thrust her palm against his chest in a vain attempt to get him to back the fuck off.

He shoved his face to within an inch of hers. "You're a fucking bitch."

Adrenaline rampaged through her system and bile rose in her throat. She'd once heard one of the most effective means to deter a would-be attacker was to vomit on him. She'd thought it would be hard to force herself to barf at a moment like this. As the burn reached her tonsils, she realized it would be no trouble at all.

She cocked her leg, ready to thrust a knee up. "Back off. *Now*, Bobby." Her command was loud and firm and it didn't do shit.

"You fucking bitch. You think you can talk to me like that? You think you're better than me?"

She wisely kept her mouth shut and instead shoved both hands against his chest as hard as she could. He didn't budge. Changing tactics, she swung her leg, her toe connecting with his shin. He didn't even blink. Goddamn it, she wasn't even sure he'd felt it except that his hand came down, blocking her knee from making contact with his groin.

"Nice try, bitch."

"Back off, asshole! *Now!*" Hysteria laced her voice and she swallowed hard. She was trapped. Fear swept away the last vestiges of annoyance and she drew in a deep, shaky breath. Time to scream her freaking head off.

Before she made a sound, Bobby shoved away from her and spun to face the door while she slammed into the tub once more. A huge man charged into her office, roaring like an enraged bear.

A sharp stab in the ass reminded her she wasn't without a weapon and she yanked the scissors from her back pocket, fully prepared—*eager* even—to stab Bobby, if he wasn't ripped limb from limb first.

Never in her life had she been so happy to see Garrick LeBlanc.

Garrick hurled himself at Bobby, determined to rip his fucking useless head from his fucking useless body. Under any other circumstances, Bobby's cowardly retreat up and over Savannah's treatment table might have been funny. Garrick wasn't amused. He was about to sail right over it himself when Savannah grabbed his arm.

"Wait." She was pale, her knuckles white on the hand brandishing the scissors.

His hesitation was all the time Bobby, the fucking scumbag, needed to escape. His heavy footsteps retreated down the hallway to the locker room. He let go of chasing Bobby down for now, though he would definitely get back to him later.

Garrick spun to face Savannah. Her eyes widened as she stumbled back. *Damn it.*

Savannah's disheveled appearance set off another surge of rage but he took a deep breath and wrestled it back under control. "Are you okay?" he asked as gently as he could manage. He reached for her, freezing when she shied away. His arms dropped to his sides, his hands curled into fists.

God, he *really* wanted to hit something.

She visibly regrouped and released her death grip on the scissors to straighten her clothes, her pale cheeks turning a dull red.

"Are you okay?" he asked again.

"I'm fine. Thank you."

Her voice was remarkably steady. He might have believed she had nerves of steel if he hadn't seen her hands shaking as she put the scissors down on a tray.

"I'm going to get Mark," he said, referring to the team's manager. "Do you want to come with me, or are you okay here alone for a minute?"

She surprised him by grabbing his arm. "No. Don't."

"Rick, then?"

"No!" She took a deep breath and let it out slowly. "Let's just get you wrapped up for the game."

"What?"

"Let's get you prepped and we can figure out the rest later."

Garrick stared at her. "Figure it out later?"

"Yes." She prodded him toward her table.

He held his ground. "No."

Her hands fell away and her shoulders slumped. "You're going to be difficult, aren't you? Can't we just forget about this?"

"Can't we just...*what*?" he yelled. Loudly. Maybe he wasn't being the sensitive new-age guy he was supposed to be in this situation, but he really didn't give a flying fuck. "Are you seriously asking me to forget that Bobby just attacked you?"

He wasn't sure what pissed him off more—what Bobby had done or that she was going to let him get away with it. He would have sworn she was smarter than that.

"No, of course not," she said, clearly trying to placate him. His anger and disappointment ratcheted higher. "I'm obviously not going to forget that. All I'm asking is that I be allowed to get through my pre-game work, then I'll go to Mark and tell him myself."

Garrick was only mildly relieved. "Bobby is bad news. You should tell Mark now."

"And what? Send you and everyone out on the ice without proper prep? Pretend they'll delay the game while Mark scolds Bobby for being a colossal asshole?"

"We can live without you," he said, skillfully proving yet again his inability to prevent his foot from lodging in his mouth around her.

"Gee, thanks." She grabbed more bandages.

"That's not what I meant. I meant for one night. Tonight."

He sighed and scrubbed his fingers through his hair. He was fucking this up. She'd never listen to him if he kept insulting her, for Christ's sake. "You're the best trainer this team has ever had."

She blinked. "Thank you."

"My point," Garrick continued, "is that Bobby can't get away with this shit. And you can't think it's okay."

Her shoulders slumped and she rubbed her hand across her forehead. "You're right. It's not okay. I give you my word I'll go to Mark. But all he's going to do is slap Bobby's wrist. I'd rather minimize the drama as much as possible."

He opened his mouth to protest, but she cut him off.

"Look, I'm the new girl, right? And, you know, a *girl*. Well, a woman, actually, but that's an argument for another night. I'm pretty sure it won't shock you to learn that I get hit on sometimes."

He cringed, taking some solace that the corner of her mouth kicked up in response. Like just maybe she could find humor in his idiocy.

"The last thing I need is some huge brouhaha that impacts the entire team before a game because of some shit like this. I promise you I will speak with Mark. Tonight. And if it's okay with you, I'll tell him to verify what happened with you if he feels it's necessary."

"Please do."

"But as much as I'd like to have Bobby smacked down in front of the entire team, I would rather have this be handled discreetly."

Why shouldn't Bobby be smacked down? Handed his ass and his walking papers? The asshole deserved that and more. Though Garrick wasn't naïve. It was highly unlikely to go down that way. *Unfortunately*.

Savannah gently urged him toward her table again. "I'm asking you for a favor," she said, her eyes pleading. "I don't think I can explain to you in the next five minutes just how much this job means to me."

Sighing, he stripped his gym shorts off and stood where she wanted him. "Try."

Her lips curled, just a little, and she met his gaze. "Thank you."

"You're welcome." He tried to ignore what her smile was doing to his insides. "I'm going to talk to Mark an hour after the game. If you haven't told him by then, I will."

She nodded, looking straight into his eyes. "He'll know."

He still didn't like it, but he believed her. "Okay."

She immediately went to work wrapping his hip. *Distraction time.*

"So why hockey? Why this job?"

She didn't hesitate. "It started with my brothers."

"Are they hockey players?"

She laughed. "Yes. All six of them."

Two hours later, early in the second period, Savannah stood with Mark in the tunnel to the locker room, next to the bench. She kept one eye on the players and the game, always on the alert in case they needed her. The line change came off the ice and all sat without a glance in her direction.

Quickly, quietly, she told Mark what had happened.

She fought to remain detached as she laid out the details, only stopping when Mark moved toward Bobby, clearly furious. She put a quelling hand on his arm, discreetly pointing out the TV cameras, her smile fixed in place.

Telling him here, like this, wasn't fair, but it worked to her advantage. She deserved one after the night she'd had.

The next line change came and went. She continued to spell it all out for Mark.

She told him about Garrick, and Mark turned to stare down the bench, nodding once. She sent Garrick a weak smile over Mark's shoulder, sorry he would be dragged into this further.

By the time she finished, Mark had repeatedly promised to address it and assured her it would never happen again. She hoped that meant Bobby's ass would get fired, but she didn't think she was that lucky.

Another line change brought her attention back to the game. Garrick rose to his feet, ready to go on the ice. He was almost seven feet tall in his skates, a veritable wall of jersey, pads, and man as he moved in front of her. He tossed one leg over the boards before lifting his hand to her.

Without a thought, she bumped her bare knuckles against his huge gloved fist, grateful for his support.

Garrick threw himself into the game while she studiously ignored the looks from Mark and a couple of the players on the bench. The truth hit her hard. In all her time with the Ice Cats, she'd never done anything as familiar as a fist bump.

They all must think I'm an uptight bitch. And why wouldn't they?

She'd been hell-bent on making the right impression as a professional, as a qualified trainer. Somehow, she'd lost sight of the fact that she was also supposed to be a *team member*.

She searched for signs Garrick's groin hurt, that any of the players on the ice were having an issue, all the while wondering when she'd sucked the joy out of the game she'd loved all her life. But she loved the job, too. And when had she decided these two things were mutually exclusive?

Probably about the same time Garrick had hit on her that first day. Or when she'd turned down two more dates within the following hour. By day four she'd turned down two more players, an assistant coach, and Sheila, the lovely woman who ran the box office. She'd also determined that she was the only straight, single woman under the age of sixty who worked for the team. And that the people of Moncton really needed to get laid.

Which was most definitely *not* in her job description.

In the end, she'd erred on the side of isolation. The operative word being *erred*. Three months later, she was lonely, didn't feel like she'd ever settle into her new home, and her teammates were surprised when she engaged one of them in something as benign as a fist bump.

If not for the cameras and the crowd, she might have fist bumped her own forehead.

The next line change was in motion and she helped Mike Erdo shove his hand back in his glove as he stood. How many times had she done this for teammates, her brothers, students she'd coached? Why had she never said to a member of the Ice Cats all the things she'd shouted from the benches of countless other ice rinks?

Mike was already sailing over the wall when he called out his thanks. She responded by suggesting, loudly, that he apply his foot to their opponent's posterior. Only not in those exact words.

It felt good. Really good. Like she'd reclaimed something she hadn't known she'd lost—her spirit.

Mike shot her a quick smile as he sailed past, already in the game.

The joy returned.

Chapter Three

Garrick strode into the arena, his teeth locked together with grim determination. He was not going to limp. He was not going to limp. He *refused* to fucking limp.

A mid-week staff meeting at the beginning of a series of home games was unusual. Likely someone had been fired, hired, drafted in, dealed out or was in deep-shit trouble. He dreamed fleetingly that Bobby Kramer was getting his ass fired, as he so richly deserved, but Garrick doubted he or Savannah would be so fortunate. He'd known the moment Mark had caught up with Bobby a week ago. If looks could kill, Garrick and the team's esteemed trainer would have died one hundred times over. Bobby was in a rage, but it was a quiet rage he was keeping to himself, so Garrick couldn't do much about it.

He strode without a hint of a goddamn limp into the meeting room and scanned the crowd. He immediately caught Bobby's gaze and was treated to another death-ray stare. *Whatever.*

Rhian sidled down a row of seats at the front of the room. Garrick found Savannah when Rhian sat down next to her.

Of course the most handsome man in the room was sitting next to Savannah. His friend's ridiculous good looks didn't usually bother Garrick, but this morning they absolutely irritated the shit out of him.

He slid down the same row and sat on Savannah's other side. She acknowledged him with a glance and something that might even qualify as a smile before turning back to Rhian. "I think the increased reps will make a difference, build strength..."

Garrick shook his head. They were talking about work, of course. What *else* did Savannah talk about with anyone on the team?

Garrick glanced over his shoulder. Bobby was still at it, trying to burn holes in the backs of his and Savannah's heads.

Bobby had issues. Big buckets full of issues. Garrick worried those issues would spill onto Savannah again before this thing was done.

Mark, Rick, and the rest of the team's senior staff came into the room, and people moved to their seats. When Rupert Smythe entered the room, instant silence descended.

Rupert was a tall and slender man—and as far as Garrick could tell, perennially nervous. His hand worried the handle of his briefcase, his gaze darting around the room. Garrick would bet his last nickel Rupert's palms were sweaty and that he'd scream like a little girl if someone sneaked up behind him and yelled "boo!"

As entertaining as that thought was, Rupert's attendance at this meeting likely meant bad news. He had only met Rupert three times in twelve years. During that time, as now, the team was owned by Edwin Lamont, a notorious recluse who reportedly never left his estate on Cape Breton Island. Instead, Lamont sent Rupert as his proxy to play the role of business manager and mouthpiece.

The "someone is in deep-shit trouble" category was now at the top of the list of possible reasons for this meeting.

From the stifling silence that held the tongues of the usually bawdy and outspoken crowd, Savannah knew the stranger at the front of the room was either very important or very dangerous. The way Garrick watched the man through narrowed eyes made her think their mystery guest might be both.

He looked to be in his thirties. His bespoke charcoal suit flattered his broad shoulders and long legs, and if she wasn't mistaken, was likely more valuable than her entire wardrobe. Even the fluorescent lighting couldn't dull the gleam of his oxblood leather briefcase. Gold flashed on his wrist. His fingers shook. Her unease multiplied.

"Hello, everyone!" He addressed their group in a crisp English accent.

No one responded.

The man blinked a few times, swallowed hard, and smiled weakly. Her dread, along with the tension she was picking up from everyone in the room, grew. She looked around her. All eyes stared straight ahead. A movement in the back of the room caught her attention and she hid her wince when her gaze locked with Bobby's.

His brows went up and his smug sneer morphed into an evil smile.

She turned to face forward.

"As many of you know, my name is Rupert Smythe and I am Mr. Edwin Lamont's business manager."

That solved the mystery of his identity and the crowd's reaction to him.

He continued on, launching into a tale about how much Mr. Lamont had enjoyed hockey over the years, how he played as a boy and other drivel Savannah assumed was meant to be reassuring.

She tuned back into the details of Rupert Smythe's message when he said, "I'm sorry to say, though, that Mr. Lamont has decided to put the Moncton Ice Cats up for sale."

Murmurs rippled across the room. Savannah sat perfectly still, her heart pounding, her hopes for Moncton being the first leg of a long, successful career in hockey taking a serious hit.

"Why?" someone called from the back of the room.

Mr. Smythe grimaced. "Well—" He paused, staring out at the crowd as if searching for the answer. The silence drew out until Savannah wanted to smack the man in the back of the head to get him to spit it out. "In truth, the team has been losing money. The arena, too."

Both were owned by Lamont.

"Other teams make money. What are you doing wrong?"

Savannah almost smiled at that question. Bless Sheila's

heart. She had brass ones.

Rupert Smythe's cheeks turned red. The man was handsome, even when flustered and blushing. Almost pretty. Probably not a great attribute when speaking to a room full of alpha-male hockey players.

"Yes, well, it's long and complicated, actually. But trust me, it's not something that is easily changed."

Pretty *and* dim-witted, apparently. Insulting the intelligence of a woman like Sheila in a room full of her colleagues was going to end badly.

The players shifted in their chairs, no doubt fighting the urge to stand up and act. Hockey players weren't known for being passive. Most of the people in this room lived to come off the boards fighting.

She clenched her fingers in her lap and resisted the urge to put a soothing hand on Garrick's bouncing leg. New ownership, and possibly new management, didn't bode any better for a twelve-year veteran with a stubbornly sore groin and hip than it did for the only woman athletic trainer in the league.

"It is our hope," continued Rupert over the rumblings of the crowd, "indeed our goal, to find a buyer soon who will be interested in keeping the team intact."

The words helped silence some of the agitation.

"You'll be kept aware of the progress through Mark, your manager." As if everyone in the room didn't know who Mark was.

Mark's thin smile spoke volumes.

"And of course, all questions should be directed to him."

Of course. Mr. Rupert Smythe appeared to be fully prepared to run from the room screaming before the barbarians got hold of him. Maybe he wasn't that dense after all. Right then, she sure wanted to body check him and that shiny briefcase of his into the cement wall.

Garrick rose from his seat as soon as the meeting was over,

careful to keep the wince off his face. *Stupid fucking hip.* He and Savannah had been slowly making progress on his groin pull, but the hard work was provoking the arthritis in his hip.

Arthritis.

The word made him feel...geriatric. It didn't help that he was damn close to hobbling as he stepped into the aisle.

He caught Savannah watching him and stopped, forcing his teammates to detour around him as they moved toward the door. Her narrow gaze was fixed on his legs until it shifted to his throbbing hip.

"What?" he asked. *Defensive much?*

She shrugged. "Nothing."

Her pursed lips told him it was something, but he wasn't about to argue.

She cocked her head and moved toward the door. "Come to my office. I have something you can take and we'll do some stretching. Maybe stick you in the tub."

He opened his mouth to decline, to steer clear of the lovely Savannah and her lair. But a soak in the tub would be bliss for his sore hip and ease the tight muscles in his groin. He could only hope the deep water would disguise any other groin issues, should they arise.

"Okay, sure."

Bobby leaned against the wall just inside the door to the hallway, his eyes fixed on Savannah. Garrick stepped forward—without anything resembling a hitch in his gait, damn it—and crowded Bobby back against the wall, blocking his view. He held a hand out to indicate Savannah should precede him through the door.

He was enjoying being able to fuck with Bobby and appear chivalrous all at once—a win-win for him—until Savannah shot him a dirty look.

Right. Not supposed to treat her differently than the guys.

He smiled at Rhian instead. "Come on, Rhi, let's get going."

He fought not to laugh at Rhian's deadpan stare. Garrick

didn't often hold the door for the perfectly capable defenseman as if he were the Queen of England. Indeed, this was a first. Luckily, Rhian caught on.

With a smirk, Rhian leaned down to murmur in Savannah's ear. "Excuse me."

She hesitated, then rolled her eyes and passed through the door. Rhian shot him a quizzical look and Garrick tilted his head toward the locker room, indicating he'd explain later.

Now, though, he had a date with a beautiful woman and her hot tub.

Savannah almost felt guilty when Garrick let out a long, painful groan as he slowly lowered himself into her tub. The cistern was filled with one hundred and three degree water that reached the middle of Garrick's bare chest, which she studiously pretended not to notice at all.

Though, she'd have to be dead not to admire the heavy swell of muscle. The skin stretched over each curving pectoral appeared velvet soft, his cinnamon nipples puckered tight in spite of the warm water and steam. His shoulders were possibly the broadest she'd ever laid her hands on—professionally or otherwise. Certainly the thickest, her hand barely able to span their width while stretching him.

He'd come to her office after the team meeting earlier, pretending his hip wasn't killing him. As if she couldn't see *that* from a mile out in poor visibility. He'd eagerly asked her for "at least four" ibuprofen before promising he'd go change into something he could wear in the tub and come right back.

The crestfallen look on his face when she'd informed him he wasn't that lucky and she wasn't that careless had been priceless. She'd forced him up on the table to investigate with her own eyes and hands.

Finally, after the second wince he couldn't hide, he sighed. "It's arthritis, okay? Just send me off to the nursing home already."

She'd laughed. "No shit it's arthritis. But it's been there are all season and not bothered you this much before."

He'd been surprised she'd known. Men were always convinced of two things. One, that they should never admit to any physical ailment or weakness. And two, that this actually worked as a means of hiding these weaknesses from the women who cared about them.

Not that she cared about Garrick. Well, she did. The way she cared about all her players and their physical condition. It was her job.

They'd worked through a vigorous set of stretches together, then she'd sent him to the weight room to do more, and to get on the equipment and run through the standard program she'd developed for him at the beginning of the season, with a few modifications. In the meantime, she worked with a couple of other players, stopping by the weight room under the guise of showing Alexei Belov, the Ice Cat's primary goalie and resident crazy Russian, a leg stretch that worked best while straddling the bench press. Not that she'd really believed she'd find Garrick goofing off, but she was concerned he might cut reps or weights to ease the burden on his hip. Or worse, keep going when his body was telling him to stop.

She was good at her job, but her dictates were still best guesses on how hard the body could be pushed, and no creature was more stubborn about ignoring biological messages like pain than the hockey-playing male.

Garrick had appeared only appropriately miserable, so she'd left him to it.

Now, though, the guilt nipped at her. His arms trembled as he lowered himself into the hot water, obviously taking all his weight in an effort not to rely on his legs. Usually when one of the guys was in her tub, she would work at her desk and catch up on emails, but today she was too wound up after that damn team meeting to sit still.

She approached the tub quietly, careful not to brush the thickly muscled arm running along the edge. His eyes were closed, his head resting on the rim. Dark hair, damp with the sweat of his workout and the steam of the tub, curled over his ears and along his neck. His long lashes rested on flushed cheeks, a fringe of inky silk against his warm skin. He would have looked peaceful if there hadn't been a crease marring the skin between his eyebrows.

"What did you think of the meeting today?" she asked.

His eyes flashed open and he held her gaze. His dark amber irises deepened to chocolate as she watched, fascinated, her feet rooted to the floor.

"What do you think?" he asked.

"I don't know. I keep telling myself it will be fine and we'll just have a new owner, which won't matter much since no one ever saw the old owner."

Garrick nodded, looking down at the swirling water. "I guess that's true." He turned those chocolate eyes back to her. "But then why do I feel so damn nervous?"

Savannah sighed. "Because we're screwed."

Garrick laughed, though he didn't sound like he found it funny at all.

Chapter Four

Garrick raced back to the locker room like the rink was on fire and the showers were the only safe place to hide. Their win that night had been a long and hard-fought. But as much as he wanted to sit and bask in the glory of a good night on the ice, he had other things to worry about.

Specifically, Savannah.

For the past few weeks she'd been a changed woman on game nights. Now she moved around the bench, worked more proactively with the team, and shouted encouragement like a seasoned, slightly foul-mouthed professional. The good news was the team was starting to think of her as something other than an uptight bitch. The bad news was her growing credibility had provoked Bobby into finding new ways to harass her.

She ignored Bobby at all times, Garrick had noticed. He'd made it his habit to keep an eye on them both as much as possible. Bobby, though, always found a way to bump into her, crowd her, or just generally make a nuisance of himself. Like how after four years on the team, Bobby now used the door right in front of where Savannah stood for the games instead of jumping the boards.

To his knowledge, she hadn't complained to Mark about any of it. Garrick wanted to be mad about that, but even he couldn't point to any particular incident where Bobby had done something *wrong*, per se. He was just being an asshole in a more general sense.

Garrick suspected the cat-and-mouse routine, in addition to Savannah's game duties, was exhausting for her. Tonight, apparently, she had hit her limit.

Bobby had come sailing through the door, caught his skate, and careened directly into Savannah. He'd slammed her into the tunnel wall with sufficient force to bounce her head off the concrete while pinning the rest of her with his full weight and equipment—hockey and otherwise.

Garrick had leapt to his feet, heart pounding, not knowing how badly she was hurt. He'd wanted to leap the length of the bench and pound Bobby, the stupid fucker, into the floor mats.

But Savannah had yanked herself free at the same moment Mark's hand landed on Garrick's arm. She'd stared Bobby right in the face, bright color in her cheeks, and shoved him, repeatedly and with all her weight, forcing him to stumble toward the bench while she tore into him.

"You're a fucking baby who needs to learn some manners. Go home to your momma if you want to cuddle. I'm here to work."

Her last shove had nearly dumped Bobby on his ass. Heads had spun and Mike Erdo's loud guffaw was audible above the noise of the crowd.

Before Bobby could react, Mark was in his face. "Sit there and shut the fuck up, or you're out of the game."

Bobby's innocent exclamation of "what the fuck?" didn't fool anyone, but everyone went back to what they'd been doing, preparing for the next line change.

Mark had checked on Savannah, but she waved him off. She hadn't spared Bobby another glance, so she hadn't seen the glare he'd drilled into her back. The death-ray was going nuclear and so, Garrick suspected, was Bobby.

Garrick dashed out of the showers, a towel barely clinging to his hips, and jogged back to his locker. He ignored Rhian's raised eyebrow, only cocking his head toward Bobby's locker before throwing on his clothes. He'd told Rhian about what he'd walked in on in Savannah's office, as well as the ridiculous staring contests and bench antics, so Rhian merely nodded and got out of his way.

Garrick's hip twinged, a bolt of pain shooting down his leg as he thrust it into his pants, and he smiled grimly. He even had an excuse to go visit the trainer.

Five minutes later he was dressed and outside her door,

waiting while she cut tape and unwound bandages from the last of her customers. He entered her office as she scribbled some notes on what Alexei told her, while Mike listened in with interest. Garrick smiled. Savannah was growing a respectable fan club.

Fortunately, there was still no sign of Bobby.

Once she sent his teammates out, he dropped his wraps in the bin and went to her medicine chest.

"Mind?" He indicated the ibuprofen bottle. He was eating the damn things like candy these days.

Savannah smiled. "Sure, help yourself. No more than four though. And only two tomorrow until *after* you work out."

He sighed. "You're mean."

She laughed. "I'm careful. And you're trouble. The last thing you need is to dull your body's myriad messages telling you to stop."

And isn't that the sad fucking truth?

Savannah saw his no doubt pathetic expression and cocked her head. "What?"

He shook his head, feeling stupid. And old.

"What?" she asked again, coming closer. "Did I say something to upset you?"

She didn't usually care if she did or did not say something to upset anyone, but she probably didn't often see grown men hanging their heads like sad puppies in her office.

"It is telling me to stop, isn't it?" He hadn't intended to ask the question. At least, not out loud—to Savannah or anyone else. Silently, he asked himself every day.

She drew up short, her eyebrows pinched together. "Your body?"

He sighed. "Yes. My stupid, beat-up, crappy old body."

One side of her lips quirked up. "It's not a crappy body." A hint of a blush crept into her cheeks. "It's a strong body, Garrick. It's a body that's in better shape than ninety percent of the men on earth, and probably ninety-nine percent of the men your age."

Garrick winced. "Holy crap, you just said *men your age*."

Savannah laughed. "Stop it. You're what? Thirty-four? I'm sorry if it's hard to accept, Garrick, but the truth is you can't play hockey forever. Not professional hockey."

"Ouch."

Savannah fell silent He was being ridiculous. But how could he *not* play hockey? It was all he knew.

Rhian's arrival spared Garrick attempting to explain any of that. Rhian looked back and forth between them in the growing silence until Savannah jumped in to ask him some questions. Rhian gave her all favorable reviews, even claiming had never felt better.

Of course. To be young and at the top of his game again. Garrick remembered how easy it had been.

A few nights later, Savannah buttoned her coat and tried to ignore the itch between her shoulder blades as the players walked past her door on their way out of the arena. When she was suitably bundled up to face the New Brunswick winter night, she turned to find Bobby standing in the hallway, talking to a friend, his eyes fastened on her.

Shit.

Even as her heart sped up, she held firm to her resolve not to be intimidated. Bobby was a serious problem that could not be ignored, but that didn't mean he was allowed to run her life. She was determined to be cautious. Not cowed.

Steeling herself, she stepped into the hall and closed her door, keeping her movements slow and precise to not betray her nerves. As the deadbolt locked into place, she promised herself she'd find Mark tomorrow and tell him about the stares, the hovering. She hadn't yet because she didn't want to sound like a baby, and it was hardly against the rules to stare at someone. But Mark had seen Bobby's childish stunt a few nights ago—she had a nice bruise on her shoulder blade because of it, too—and Bobby wasn't letting up. Not being a baby was one thing. Being stupid was another.

Bobby's friend said goodnight and moved away. The next sound was a footstep drawing closer to her.

Shit. Shit. Shit.

"Savannah!"

Garrick's voice made her jump. She spun toward it, not bothering to hide her relief.

Bobby stopped just a few feet away. He glared at Garrick then moved quickly in the opposite direction. The smile Garrick sent in his wake was more a baring of teeth.

Garrick stopped at her side. "Are you okay?"

She shrugged. "Yeah, sure."

"Okay, good," Garrick said quickly, not making her explain. She was grateful. Again.

She sighed as they walked toward the doors to the arena parking lot. "I'm going to talk to Mark tomorrow."

"Good idea. If there's anything I can do to help..."

She smiled ruefully. "You've already done more than I can possibly thank you for." He didn't look at her, his eyes constantly scanning the passageway, then the parking lot.

He'd been hanging around her office and had walked her to her car a couple nights before, after the incident with Bobby. And, mysteriously, Rhian had shown up and walked out with her last night while Garrick had done photos with the scout troop who had won tickets to last night's game.

She wanted to be irritated. Wanted to be tough. Independent. *Unafraid.* Unfortunately, her previously stated policy against being stupid prevented her from objecting to Garrick's rather unsubtle orchestration of her nightly escorts.

"So—" She broke the silence. "Do you think there will be a buyer for the Cats quickly?"

Garrick glanced down at her before returning to his

diligent surveillance of their surroundings. They left the bright halo around the arena and moved into the darker rows of cars. "I hope, but I'm doubtful. They'd be buying a bit of a mess."

"They would?"

They stopped in the orange glow of the parking lot vapor lamp nearest her car. The night was cold, but not unbearable— the wind that had been whipping in off the Atlantic for the past few days had died down at last.

"Lamont has been mostly ignoring the team and this arena for years," Garrick explained. "I think before the economic downturn, it was easy enough to make his profit and he didn't care about the margin or the size of the return until they went into the red."

She nodded. "Ticket sales are down, but you all still pull in a good crowd."

"We do, fortunately, but we could sell more. And even with sales down, Lamont's missed a lot of opportunity. To start with, the arena should be retro-fitted to allow parquet to go down quickly, leaving the ice below. Good management could arrange the basketball team's game around ours and move the poor basketball team out of the convention center. It would also facilitate more concerts. More events. The University could use it too, I'm sure. And then there are the concessions." Garrick's waving hands jerked with frustration. "He's had the same fried dough, cheap pizza, and watery beer stands going for decades. Microbrews like Picaroons and even bigger local companies like Moosehead would easily outsell at least half the Bud and Molson taps. And don't get me started on the lack of corporate sponsors and season ticket holders. I could—" He stopped abruptly, shaking his head. "Listen to me ramble on about shit I know nothing about."

"I am listening. It's interesting."

"I'm easy-chair quarterbacking. I don't know what I'm talking about." He stared down at his boots, his hands stuffed in his coat pockets.

"It *sounds* like you know what you're talking about."

He shrugged. "Not really. I just have lots of ideas."

"Have you told Lamont your ideas?"

He looked at her. "Lamont?"

"Yeah, you know, the guy who could actually make money by listening to you?"

Garrick's eyes widened. "I couldn't. I mean, I'm just a hockey player. I don't know anything about running a team or an arena."

Garrick had struck her as a lot of things, but never insecure. His lack of confidence surprised her.

"Seems to me you know plenty. Everything you just said makes sense and jives with what I've seen other arenas do. And don't give me the *just a hockey player* crap. The smartest men I know are hockey players, so that doesn't mean shit to me."

She couldn't be sure in the strange light, but it was possible Garrick LeBlanc was blushing.

"Yeah, well anyway, to answer your actual question," he said, obviously avoiding a response to her outburst, "I think the Cats and the arena need to find a buyer with good ideas and a willingness to invest. And given the current state of the economy, no, I don't think that's going to happen quickly."

She nodded. He was right. He was also a hell of a lot smarter than she'd given him credit for.

She stood, head tilted to the side, and stared up at this new Garrick, aware of the bemused smile on her face. He blinked, slowly, and his eyes darkened, going black in the dim light.

She licked her suddenly dry lips. His gaze darted down. Otherwise, he didn't move. Not a muscle.

I could kiss him.

The thought—which she never should have had to begin with—held way more appeal than it ought to. Not because she felt sorry for him, or because she was grateful for his help these past weeks. But because he was gorgeous and kind and smart and funny and *holy crap.* When had she stopped pretending he wasn't smoking hot?

Of course, none of that mattered. He was a player on the Ice Cats.

"Goodnight," she said abruptly.

"Goodnight." His deep voice drifted over her skin and made the little hairs on the back of her neck stand up beneath her scarf.

She yanked her keys from her pocket, unlocked the car, and practically dove into the driver's seat. Screw waiting for the engine or the frigid air around her to warm up. She slammed the car into gear and hightailed it out of there.

She looked back in the mirror, once, just before she turned out onto the highway. Garrick stood exactly where she'd left him, watching her drive away.

Chapter Five

Savannah was all business the next morning when she saw Garrick, which, for some reason, he seemed to find amusing. She doggedly ignored his failed attempts to hide his smile while she resolutely spoke of training, conditioning, his hip, and his groin pull.

That she wanted to smile back was another issue, one she refused to acknowledge. She hadn't meant to befriend one of the players, but she had, and it didn't mean she'd lost her ever-loving mind and would do something colossally stupid.

Once she'd sent Garrick and the rest of the players off to run through their training programs, she stopped by the gym to check in on everyone. Then she went to see Mark.

It sucked to bring him more shit to deal with the day before they left on a road trip to Nova Scotia, but she'd promised herself, and more or less promised Garrick, that she would address it.

Standing outside Mark's door, she watched how his hands tugged at his hair while he reviewed whatever numbers were on the spreadsheet before him. She considered leaving it until the bus ride tomorrow.

Tempting, but she'd need that time to get organized for the days and games to come. Now was her best chance.

She left Mark's office a half hour later, sealing off his stream of muttered curses as she closed the door behind her. Mark was a nice man, but his hands were tied. Bobby hadn't laid a finger on her since that day in her office, and the "accidental" body slam the other night, about which he had professed absolute innocence.

She sighed as she made her way back to her office. It was going to be a long season if she couldn't figure out a way to get Bobby off her ass. She didn't know where to begin and had no one she could ask. If she called her parents for advice, they'd have a seizure. And any one of her six brothers could be counted on to drive to Moncton and attempt to remove Bobby's black heart. Through his nostrils.

Settling in at her desk, she took a chance her best friend, Grace, would answer her phone in the middle of the day. She hung up a while later feeling immeasurably better. Grace didn't have any answers either, but it had been good to tell someone what was going on. She'd even managed to deftly deflect all suggestions and innuendos regarding Garrick.

Now, sitting alone in her office, a few of those suggestions wandered through her mind. She cursed Grace for giving her imagination so much fodder. She hadn't slept well last night as it was, and now her tired body felt twitchy and hot.

She just about jumped out of her skin when Garrick said "hello" from no more than two feet behind her.

"Hi!" Leaping from her chair, she yanked her fleece down over her butt and thighs.

He lifted one brow. "You doing okay?"

"Sure. Why wouldn't I be?"

His warm brown eyes met hers and she struggled not to do something ridiculous like squirm or try to push her fleece down to her knees. Her face was warm, no doubt flushed, and the rest of her body felt sensitive. Swollen.

"No reason," he said, watching her closely. "I just came in to see if I was allowed to have two more ibuprofen now that I've been a good doobie and done all my work."

She laughed as she moved to the cabinet, grateful for the distraction. "You make me sound like a grade school teacher."

Garrick cleared his throat. "You definitely don't remind me of any grade school teacher I ever had."

She was about to ask what he meant by that but bit off the question when Bobby stepped through her door. She shot Garrick a look to warn him.

"What do you want, Bobby?" Garrick's cold stare and arctic tone couldn't possibly have been less welcoming. Savannah smiled into her medicine chest.

"My elbow hurts, and *she* said I should have it wrapped before practice."

Savannah turned, speaking before Garrick could. "Yes, of course, Bobby. Please have a seat."

Bobby eyed Garrick, who stared back. Tension hovered in the air around them, climbing until she worried they would come to blows. She couldn't relax, even when Bobby relented and flopped into the chair he hadn't deigned to sit in for months.

She went to Garrick and dropped the two pills in his palm. "Here you go." She smiled up at him, her back to Bobby, and mouthed *thank you.* "Let me know how you're feeling later and we can talk about what's next."

He dutifully moved toward the door. In truth, she wanted to beg him to stay, but she couldn't hand that kind of power over to Bobby. Confirming she was afraid of him would only make him worse. Hell, just the hint that she and Garrick were friends gave Bobby too much.

Garrick shot Bobby another hard stare on his way out.

She gave him a little push. "Come use the tub whenever you're ready."

His eyebrow went up, silently giving her one last chance to change her mind. When she said nothing, he left her office and disappeared around the corner.

Savannah stared at the empty door longer than necessary, but by the time she turned to gather what she needed to wrap Bobby's elbow, she was composed.

She moved quickly, keeping as much distance as possible without being obvious. She didn't ask him any questions, which was unlike her, but she didn't want any more contact than was absolutely required.

Bobby was uncharacteristically cooperative, holding his arm as she needed and keeping his hands to himself. Too bad he spent the entire session staring into her face from mere inches away. His breath brushed her cheek when she bent to cut away a loose string and she forced herself not to jerk back. She did, though, hold her breath.

Garlic for breakfast?

By the time Bobby stood to leave, a continuous trickle of cold sweat slid down her back. She left her supplies where they were, not cleaning up as she would usually, choosing instead to stand back and let him go. He smiled at her from the door and her fingers tightened around the scissors still clutched in her hand.

His laughter echoed in the hallway as she slumped into her desk chair, tossed her scissors onto the pile of paperwork, and wiped her clammy hands on her pants.

Holy shit. How the hell was she going to fix this?

Garrick bolted out of the coach's office, barely calling a goodnight to Rick and the rest of the forward lines with whom he'd been forced to sit and review strategy for the upcoming away games.

As he jogged around the arena toward Savannah's office, his hip protested the unforgiving concrete beneath his feet. It hurt like hell.

There won't be many more than twelve years of hockey for me.

It was scary shit to think about. Almost as scary as coming around the bend to find Savannah's door closed and locked, her lights off. She'd already left.

Hoping he might still catch her, he took off at a run, ignoring the increasingly sharp pains from his hip. Bobby had left the locker room right after practice, and from there, Garrick had no idea where he'd gone. Maybe out with the sycophants he called friends. Or home with an unfortunate puck bunny who didn't know which players should be avoided.

Or maybe he was waiting in the parking lot, knowing Garrick was tied up in a meeting. Knowing Savannah would be alone.

Shit. He ran faster.

He should have asked Rhian to walk her to her car, but he hadn't thought his meeting would take long. Christ, Rick would have dissected the best shot strategy for another hour if they'd let him.

Running on concrete sucked for his hip, but when he pivoted to go down the hall to the doors, his groin pull protested too, a line of fire dropping into his nuts. He frowned and moved through the pain. He wasn't an idiot. It was time to move on from hockey. The question was, *to what?*

To whatever you were going to do when you went off to McGill and got that shiny degree in finance and economics.

Trying out for the McGill team, joining up and playing all four years had all been a lark. Something to keep him busy between classes and studying and partying. A way to keep fit. When the Eastern Hockey League scout had first approached him, he'd been astounded. And, of course, flattered. But some sane part of him had been tempted to send him packing.

Hindsight was a bitch.

Not that he'd do it any differently if he could go back. He was glad for the opportunity to play for his home team. He just couldn't figure out how he'd launched a career that could only last a dozen years and not given any thought to what would be next. Now *next* was bearing down on him like a freight train.

He swung around the last corner and stumbled to a halt. Savannah stood a few feet away in the little lobby, bundled up against the weather, her phone in her hand. The squeak of his sneakers on the smooth floor brought her head up.

She's waiting for me.

His heart beat harder and it wasn't from the run. "Hi," he said, trying not to grin.

"Hi." She smiled almost shyly.

He resisted the urge to clutch at his chest. Christ, she was adorable when she was prickly. But a shy smile? If she flirted with him, he just might collapse on the spot.

"I hope it's okay." She gestured to the door.

"Of course." He shook himself out of his momentary stupor, opened the door and walked through first. She'd broken him of the habit of trying to hold the door for her, but it still felt wrong.

She moved to his side in the glare of the fluorescent lights ringing the arena. They didn't say anything as they made their way toward her car in the far corner of the nearly deserted parking lot. Garrick burrowed his face under the collar of his parka, feeling like a love-struck fourteen-year-old when their arms brushed and he got a little zing. She didn't normally walk this close to him, did she?

They were passing under the last row of lights, almost to her car, when a pickup truck roared to life at the end of the aisle. Wheels squealing, the huge truck peeled out of its parking space and gunned toward them. Garrick leaped forward and yanked Savannah between two cars. The truck accelerated past them, gravel spitting from beneath its tires, before careening through the main exit and disappearing around the corner.

Savannah stood frozen, her mouth hanging open. "Holy shit. Please tell me that wasn't Bobby's truck."

Garrick tried to bring his blood pressure back down from the stratosphere. He'd been so preoccupied with Savannah's arm brushing his, he hadn't seen a fucking thing until the truck had practically been on top of them.

Savannah turned to him, her eyes wide.

He blew out a breath, trying to think. "To be honest, I'm not sure. I don't think so. He has that awful canary yellow one, and that truck was a darker color."

Savannah paced a few yards away from him, back into the bright orange glare of the sodium vapor lamp, before coming back to the patch of shadows where he stood.

"Regardless, that was Bobby's work, wasn't it?"

Garrick grimaced. "Yeah, I think so."

Savannah paced another circle. He watched her, helpless.

"What the fuck am I going to do? I can't complain that someone peeled out of the parking lot. Just like I can't make a stink about him standing so close to me, the stupid creep, especially since my job requires it half the time!"

Garrick was torn between his need to comfort her and the desire to rant and rave right along with her.

"Shit!" She strode faster, her hands jammed in her coat pockets. "Never in my wildest dreams would I have guessed Bobby Kramer would be so good at stalking. He's such a dumb fuck. He must have read a manual or something."

Garrick was surprised he could laugh. "They have a manual for that?"

She threw her hands in the air. "They must!"

He put out a hand with the intention of stopping her maniacal pacing so they could talk, so they could make a plan. He was completely unprepared when she threw her arms around him and buried her face in his parka. Whatever he'd been about to say left him in a quiet "ooof."

He stood, stunned, until instincts and months of repressed desire kicked in. He wrapped his arms around her and held her close.

"I'm sorry," she said, her voice muffled against his chest. "You're the only friend I have here. I just need..."

"No worries," he whispered, ridiculously pleased that she thought of him as a friend. It felt like a huge victory.

She started to pull away, but he held fast, rubbing a hand down her back, trying to offer what comfort he could. Her arms tightened around him again, her hands fisting in the material at the back of his parka as she clung to him.

Lots of victories tonight.

She sighed, her breath warm on his neck as she relaxed against him. He cradled her closer, her soft hair teasing his cheek, her legs bumping into his.

He was disappointed when she finally released him, but he let go too, ducking his head to peer into her face in the dim light. He blinked, slowly, mesmerized by her warm gaze and slightly parted lips. Uncertain. Wondering if perhaps the vapor lamps were playing tricks on him.

Her soft hand touched his cheek and he closed his eyes, his heart leaping in his chest. He wanted to press his cheek to her palm, but held himself in check. He thought about Savannah. Discreet. Driven. Fully capable of opening the door herself.

She had to be the one to make the first move. Even if it fucking killed him.

She traced her fingers over his skin, her light touch igniting his every nerve ending. His hands trembled where they gripped her coat as the soft pads of her fingers bumped over the corner of his lips.

He wanted to pounce. To leap. To *beg*. He didn't.

Her touch was hesitant. As if they stood on the edge of a cliff, teetering. So close. He would gladly hurl himself off into space, into the unknown. But would she?

He jolted at the brush of warm, soft lips along his, accidentally jerking away as his entire body clenched with need. His eyes flashed open to see her upturned face, her eyes closed, long lashes shadowing her cheekbones, lips seeking his.

He watched her approach with a mixture of hope and elation. Her mouth rubbed against his once more, her hand cupping his jaw to hold him still as she nibbled along his lips. God, she was really kissing him. And all he could do was stand there, heart pounding, brain stuttering as blood poured south, the sweet ache of arousal burning through him.

He'd let her lead, let her take the leap. Then her tongue tentatively brushed against his lower lip and he knew he had to charge after her. He *had* to.

Groaning, he captured her mouth and wrapped his arms around her until her feet barely touched the ground. His lips and teeth worshipped the full lower lip he'd dreamed about for weeks. His tongue danced into every corner of her mouth. God, he'd wanted this. He wanted her. He shifted his legs and she immediately slipped between them. He was so enamored with her taste, the feel of her writhing in his arms, he was totally unsuspecting when she checked him back against the car behind him.

Uh oh.

He grunted as his ass slammed against the cold metal, his mind reeling, prepared to apologize, though he felt no remorse. He'd no sooner opened his mouth when he was lost to another kiss. She slid her hip forward until it nudged his aching cock, pinning him to the car. He gripped one firm, lush ass cheek and held her in place as she undulated against him. He wanted to double over as the rush of blood left him lightheaded, but he held fast. Nothing was going to drag him away from the silky texture and cinnamon taste of Savannah's sweet lips.

She brought his head closer with a tug of his hair, danced her mouth along his jaw, the stinging nip of little teeth setting his skin ablaze. He tilted his head, granting her access, delighted by her aggression. She fearlessly took the lead, and he relished the outright honesty of her passion.

His cock was engaged in a pitched battle with his zipper, one he ached to end, or at least ease, but he couldn't unwind his arms from Savannah. Wouldn't.

She used her long legs and his position against the car to plaster herself against him. He could feel her heat through parka and wool and bitter cold. He couldn't remember any woman so determined to take what she wanted from him. What he freely, happily gave.

She writhed and whimpered. He damn near whimpered back. She licked and teased. He coaxed her mouth back to his and bit into the soft pillow of her lip before sucking it into his mouth. Every parry, every return, took them higher. Her fingers traced over his face again before threading through his hair to clasp his head. His cock ached with every responsive jerk of her hips.

He'd spent hours imagining what it would be like to kiss

Savannah Morrison, and the reality blew his best fantasy out of the water.

He smiled, breaking the kiss, the cool air slipping into the cocoon of heat they'd created between them. And with it came the reassertion of his true nature.

Being taken was nice. Fun. Interesting. But good god, he liked to *take.*

Spinning, he used the hand grasping her gorgeous ass to lift her, pulling her up to his height. She wrapped her legs around him, welcoming his hips as he slammed her back against the car.

She groaned when his hard cock dug intimately against her. For the first time he really appreciated those damn stretchy yoga pants.

Gasping for air, for control, he glimpsed her flushed face, her swollen lips. He rubbed his nose against hers, then captured her lips again. Now his hand skimmed *her* jaw, his thumb traced *her* wildly fluttering pulse. Her low moan vibrated along his spine before setting up a hot, teasing echo in his balls.

He pushed closer, rolling his hips. Threading his tongue through her lips, he took complete possession of her mouth. Her response was instant. Her acquiescence absolute.

If he hadn't been so intent on kissing her, he would have thrown his head back and howled. Holding her was like trying to wrap his arms around the sea, her response surging up against him, washing over him. She liked to play at taking control, but judging by her response, he suspected Savannah would much rather relinquish it.

Which suited him just fine. Perfectly, in fact.

His heart hammered, his ears pounded with his blood, and his cock leaped against the jerk of her hips. Images filled his head. Of what he wanted to do. What he would do the moment he got her alone.

The bang of the heavy metal service door was a rude reminder that he *didn't* have her alone. Yet.

With a gasp, Savannah shoved him back and practically fell out of his arms, staggering two steps away before catching herself on next car. Cold air swept over him, chilled where her warm body had been. His arms hung empty at his sides. *Shit.*

"Savannah, I—"

She held up her hand. "No. I'm sorry. That was my fault. I don't know what's wrong with me. I shouldn't have done that."

He couldn't agree *less.* "Please don't apologize. I wanted—"

"No!" she said quickly. "Please, don't say anything. I'm so sorry. That was a huge mistake."

Not one single second of that had been a mistake. *Not one.* He wanted to argue with her, the words choking him, but he couldn't ignore the pleading, the horror, in her gaze.

Just as she was capable of opening the door herself, she was equally capable of slamming it in his face. And as usual, he was at a loss how to deal with her.

"I hope we can still be friends," she said quietly.

He couldn't possibly be any more confused by this woman. "What? Of course we can. Why wouldn't we be?"

She grimaced, clearly not convinced. "I guess I should go before I fuck this night up any worse." She sighed. "Thanks again for the escort."

"Anytime."

When she turned toward her car, he put a hand on her arm to stop her.

"I mean it, Savannah. *Anytime.* Don't let what just happened make you uncomfortable or hesitate to reach out. I'm still your friend. I still want to help."

She studied his face in the dim light. "Okay." She nodded. "Thank you. Goodnight."

"Goodnight." Or at least it had been for a while there.

He stayed where he was as she ran to her car, got in, and drove away. The sting of the cold air seeped into him while he waited for his heart rate to return to normal for the first time since her lips had touched his.

He didn't have a clue what the hell had just happened, or why, but he couldn't help thinking it was a step in the right direction, even if she was running scared.

Chapter Six

Savannah sat on the bus, absurdly grateful the seat next to her was empty, and stared out the window as the beautiful countryside of the Canadian Maritimes flew past.

What the fuck was I thinking?

She'd asked herself that question a dozen times in the last five minutes alone, and too many times to count since the night before when she'd totally lost her fucking mind.

Three months. Three whole months in Moncton before she'd thrown sanity out the proverbial window.

She'd called Grace in the middle of the night, after she'd stumbled into her apartment in tears and tried to lock out the world beyond her slammed door. Grace had calmed her down, or had tried for the first five minutes of the conversation until she'd gleaned enough details to figure out what Savannah had done.

Then she'd been no help at all.

"What's wrong with you kissing this Garrick guy? You said he's your friend."

"He's on the team!" Savannah had wailed, desperate to make Grace understand.

"So? If he's your friend, he's not some blabbermouth asshole, right?"

"No, of course not."

"So, what's the problem? I mean, I agree you don't want to advertise to the entire team, let alone management, that you're in bed with the guy, but if you're discreet..."

"I'm *not* in bed with him!"

"Yet."

"Never."

And from there it had been twenty minutes of trying to get

Grace to understand the impossibility of the situation. Grace had relented on some points, but when they'd gone to hang up, she'd ended the call with, "At least think about it, Sav. And if you decide to do it, do it wholeheartedly."

Savannah rolled her eyes. There was nothing to think about. And there was definitely no wholeheartedly. She wasn't going to embarrass herself again with Garrick or anyone else. Ever.

Savannah dug her fingernails into her palms, forcing herself not to turn around and look at Garrick, four rows back and on the opposite side of the aisle. She swore she could feel it every time his eyes brushed along her back.

Which, in reality, was probably happening far less often than she was letting herself believe. When she'd bumped into Garrick while they were loading up the bus, he'd acted as if absolutely nothing out of the ordinary had happened last night. For which she should be grateful, not irritated.

He was doing the right thing. Again.

Big, dependable Garrick, who wasn't at all like his awful reputation. In fact, now that she thought about it, she'd never once seen him with a puck bunny, or any other woman in or around the arena. Or at any event. And he always did those scout events with the pictures and the autographs. She'd watched one once, and he'd been as patient and attentive to the twenty-fifth scout as he had been to the first.

He was—she was galled to admit—a good guy. A good guy who had apparently had one bad moment about fifteen minutes after she arrived in the arena on her first day. His presence in the parking lot last night made up for that ridiculous indiscretion about ten times over.

Her indiscretion last night made his initial misstep pale by comparison.

Once she'd stopped replaying that kiss in full Technicolor detail, her imagination had kept her up half the night picturing a thousand grim scenarios of what might have happened had Garrick not been there. But he had. And she'd kissed him. She could still taste every lick, feel every touch, hear every groan, whimper, and gasp.

God, was she ever going to stop thinking about it?

With an exasperated sigh, she threw herself back in her seat to stare at the carpeted ceiling above her. She was being stupid. She'd made a mistake. A huge, stinking mistake. She couldn't change it, so she would have to let it go.

She was about to give in to her compulsion to look back and see if Garrick was, in fact, looking at her again, when she picked up on the low murmur of conversation from the row in front of her.

Normally the team's management sat at the front of the bus so they could hold impromptu meetings and various people could give out marching orders as needed. If they weren't talking business, they generally weren't talking at all. Today, though, Mark and Rick sat with their heads bent together, and from the tone of their voices, the subject was serious.

The gap between their seats was small enough that she couldn't really see them, but with their heads turned toward each other, she could hear their conversation clearly.

"Smythe called to tell me himself," Mark muttered.

"Did he give you a timeline?" Rick asked.

Savannah had never heard the coach sound so anxious. She leaned forward in her seat, hoping no one would notice she wasn't really tying her shoe.

"No, no dates. But he was clear that if the Cats don't sell soon, Lamont is going to shut them down."

Rick whispered a heartfelt f-bomb but Savannah barely heard him as she slumped back in her seat.

Shut down the Cats? Kill the team? How soon was soon? Today? Next week? The end of the season? All of those were too soon for her. She didn't have a full season under her belt yet.

And what about everyone else? Garrick wouldn't get picked

up by another team at his age. Rhian wasn't drafted yet, but she was sure he was close. And Sheila? No team meant no box office.

Without a thought for the previous night's debacle, Savannah leaned into the aisle and looked back at Garrick. He was looking right at her.

Hell, she didn't even have to say a word or make a gesture. Whatever he saw in her face must have been enough. He immediately stood.

Shit. He couldn't come sit with her on the bus. And even if he could, she couldn't tell him what she'd overheard when the two people she'd been shamelessly eavesdropping on were less than two feet away. She stared out the front windshield and racked her brain for a means to get the message to him.

His broad frame blocked the light from the windows on the other side of the bus and she darted a glance up at him, shaking her head as subtly as she could before turning to stare out the window.

She held her breath, afraid he hadn't understood her admittedly mixed signals and would sit down next to her. Though, his going back to his seat with no explanation as to why he'd come to the front of the bus in full view of the entire team wasn't going to work much better.

She jumped when he put his hand on the seat back in front of her and leaned forward.

"Excuse me, Coach?"

Mark and Rick immediately stopped talking and spun to face Garrick. "Yes?" Rick asked.

Garrick's smile didn't falter. "I wanted to ask you about the best shot again. I was thinking about the clips we watched last night, and I think high and left is the way to go."

The coach immediately entered into a debate with Garrick about something that—judging by tone and the coach's exasperated, "are we really going to go through this *again*?"— was a sore issue.

At one point, Garrick casually glanced down at her and she sent him grateful smile.

Garrick had to stare at his coach's teeth, generally noted for their grayish color, until the tingle in his balls that had kicked in when Savannah smiled at him went away.

It took a few minutes, during which time he completely lost the thread of Rick's lecture. Something about beating horses to death and trusting in his coach. Garrick felt bad about poking at him, particularly since he'd already agreed to go with Rick's wishes on this, but the endless argument from the night before was all he'd been able to come up with on the spot.

And now, with the ball tingling issue, he was just as happy to have Rick railing at him. It was a semi-effective countermeasure.

Once he had himself under control, and while Rick continued his endless soliloquy on the merits of blindly following your coach's advice, he glanced down at Savannah again. The look she'd sent him a few minutes before had pulled him from his seat without thinking. Now he was stuck.

She lifted one eyebrow in sympathy and mouthed, "later."

Any excuse to spend time with her was entirely okay with him. He nodded once, then returned his rapt attention to Rick and waited for him to wind down. It took another five minutes, but eventually he made it back to his seat without too much of his ass chewed off. Now he just had to sit tight until they got to Halifax and he could get a minute alone with Savannah.

Longest two hours of his traveling career.

Fortunately, he didn't have to wait once they'd unloaded at the hotel. He was keeping one eye on Savannah, another on Bobby, and all the while trying to retrieve his bag, when Mark came up to him.

"Hey, I need you to do me a favor."

In the eight years Mark had managed the Cats, he'd never once asked Garrick for a favor. "Sure. What's up?"

"Savannah needs to check out the facilities here and at the

arena. Wants to do it all before dinner."

Garrick kept his face perfectly straight, careful not to let any of his internal happy-dance show. When Mark looked at him as if he should be able to intuit what this information meant, he stared back.

He was still trying to get the hang of this friendship thing with Savannah. Until he had it nailed down tight, he wasn't giving one damn thing away.

Mark sighed. "So I need you to go with her, because I don't want her running around alone. For now. Though, if anyone asks, it's because she's never been here before and as a veteran, I thought you'd be the best person to show her."

Garrick pursed his lips, fighting his smile. "You tell her all this?"

Mark grinned. "No, I'm giving you that job, too." With a laugh, he walked into the hotel.

An hour later, Garrick stood next to Savannah in the sultry air of the pool room, staring down into the rather small, oddly-shaped, azure-tiled pool.

Savannah sighed, her hands on her hips. "This pool sucks ass."

Garrick's laugh echoed in the tiled box. It was good to feel something other than the heavy dread that had been dragging at him since Savannah had revealed what she'd overheard on the bus. She'd managed to relay the entire conversation and have a passionate, albeit professional, freak-out in the course of one elevator ride. Since then, neither of them had said much at all.

Until the pool observation anyway.

"I think it's nice." Garrick pointed to the faux-teak chaise lounges and white and cobalt tiled walls. "Very soothing. And the hot tub looks good."

Savannah glanced at the huge octagonal tub. "Yeah, well the good news is I can probably fit three defensive lines in there." She paused. "If they still have their jobs tomorrow."

Garrick put a hand on her shoulder, trying to give comfort when there was little to be had, and ignored the zing of awareness when his finger brushed her bare neck.

She allowed it for all of ten seconds before she shrugged him off and got back to business. Kneeling by the pool's edge, she dipped her hand in the water. "Yikes!" She yanked her hand back out. "You get in there and you won't have to ice anything. Stay in too long and things might fall off."

He laughed again, but this time his heart wasn't really in it. Frustration gnawed at him. *There has to be a way.* A buyer. Someone who could be convinced to give the Cats a chance. *We need more time.*

Staring down at the pool water rippling from Savannah's touch, Garrick didn't even notice her come back to his side until she put a hand on his arm.

Even with his thoughts on the future of his team, he enjoyed a bolt of pleasure that she was voluntarily touching him for some reason other than her job.

She patted him, taking a turn at offering comfort. They were both doing a lousy job at it. "Maybe there's a buyer in the wings. Maybe someone will come forward soon."

"Maybe." *But I doubt it.*

"In the meantime, I'd like to find Lamont and kick his boney old ass."

Garrick smiled, still staring into the water. "Yeah, well, you'll be in his neighborhood in about three days. Maybe you should do that."

"What?"

Garrick stopped day dreaming and looked at Savannah. They *would* be in Lamont's neighborhood later that week. The next game on this road trip was on Cape Breton Island—home of the Sydney Snow Dogs, the Cabot Trail, and Edwin Lamont.

"You're a genius."

"I am?"

He smiled. "Yes, you most certainly are!"

She was watching him like he was a few cards short of a full deck. "Care to tell me why?"

"Nope," Garrick replied, his mind already racing to what he'd have to do to make it work. He grabbed Savannah by the upper arms, hauled her up to him, and kissed her on the forehead before she could do more than squeak out a feeble protest.

"Hey!"

"You *are* a genius though. I'll explain the rest later." He let her go before she could even think about shoving him away.

"You better!" she called as he jogged out of the pool room, dialing Rhian's number to ask him to meet Savannah in the gym and escort her to the arena.

She wouldn't like it, but she'd survive. And so, maybe, would the Ice Cats.

Chapter Seven

Four nights later, Savannah stood outside the Sydney Harbor Hotel, the blistering cold, damp wind coming off the Atlantic chilling her to the bone. Of course, her bones were a lot more exposed than usual, which didn't help.

Shifting, she stomped her heels on the red carpet, trying to find some warmth for her virtually bare legs. She might as well have been naked from the knee down for all the protection her thin stockings offered.

In hindsight, how she'd come to be standing outside the team's hotel dressed in a skirt, blouse, and actual high heels was a complete mystery to her. In the days since Garrick had declared she was a genius, she'd seen very little of him except to prepare him for the games against the Halifax Thunder, while he was on the ice for those games, and when they'd taken the team bus here to Sydney for their series against the Snow Dogs. Not during any of those times had they had a chance to speak privately.

Not that she'd missed him, of course.

She shivered and burrowed her chin deeper into the lapels of her wool coat, wishing she'd left her hair down and that the hem of her coat went a hell of a lot closer to the ground than mid-thigh.

Okay, she *had* missed him. Mostly because without him to keep her company, she'd been foisted off onto Rhian, Mark, and even Mike and Alexei at various points. Having Garrick as her shadow was frustrating. Having all these men aware of her situation and forced to traipse around after her was humiliating. She'd been ready to call Garrick and leave him a scathing voicemail about his big mouth until Mark made an off-handed comment about having to call Rhian for his shift. With horror, she'd realized that Mark was now the one arranging her constant escorts.

Somehow, no matter how annoying Garrick had been with his attempts at subtle machinations, it had never pissed her off like learning Mark was doing it. If he thought Bobby was that fucking dangerous, why didn't he *fire* the asshole?

Guess it paid to have a father who owned half a city.

Another shiver shook Savannah and she looked longingly at the warm lobby through the glass doors. What she wouldn't give to be in there by the fire.

Actually, she knew what she wouldn't give. Her reputation. The escorts were bad enough. Being spotted dressed up in a skirt and heels and going out with a teammate would be a disaster.

So here she stood, freezing her buns off after having sneaked through the lobby like a truant teenager. She stomped her feet again and prayed for the car Garrick had promised would pick her up. Soon.

He'd called her hotel room at midnight two nights ago to ask if she had anything she could wear to dinner.

"What?" she'd asked, astounded. After all this time, he was asking her out again?

"I have an idea. A way we might be able to help keep the Cats going for a while longer."

"You do?"

"Yes. Now do you have anything you could wear to a business meeting? Something like that?"

"No."

"Damn."

She'd hated the disappointment in his voice and responded without thinking. "But I can hit the Halifax Shopping Centre tomorrow before the game." As soon as the words had popped out of her mouth, she'd wondered what the hell she was doing.

"Great! I'll see to everything else." And with that, he'd hung up on her.

Irritating bastard. What "everything else"?

Damn lucky for him she'd actually enjoyed her sojourn to the mall—a few minutes alone without a hockey-player-sized shadow or the constant fear of bumping into Bobby. She'd found some great shops and even better sales—the only reason she'd splurged on the silk thigh-high stockings and a lacy bra and panty set. Really, she could have worn her serviceable cotton bikinis under her new tweed wool skirt, but no way was she going to wear a Lyrca sports bra under the white silk blouse she'd purchased to go with it. And the bra and panties came as a set. And they were on sale. And the stockings felt *so* good.

She sighed and stomped her feet again. She had spent the last day making excuses for wearing such outrageously sexy, feminine things. The truth was simple, though possibly perverse—it tickled her to wear a little secret under her conservative clothes. No one would ever know. And they were cute. And comfortable. And a good price.

And if she kept telling herself this, she might convince herself it made sense.

The shoes, on the other hand, had been nothing but an indulgence. Brown, round toe, high stacked heels and soft leather with the classic details of a pair of men's wingtips.

Somehow, wearing shoes that reminded her of every stodgy old man who'd ever told her girls don't belong in hockey made the silk against her skin feel even softer. Made her feel bolder. Standing a little over six feet tall didn't hurt either.

Of course, *why* she should feel bold was another mystery. All she knew was what Garrick's note—which she'd discovered upon returning from the arena at midnight the night before—said. A car would pick her up in front of the hotel at six o'clock tonight, and she should wear the clothes she'd bought.

So here she was, like a well-trained lap dog, too curious to know what the man had up his sleeve to worry about whether this was a good idea. As much as it galled her to admit it, she trusted him and was more than willing to go along for the ride.

Her feet began to feel warm, a very bad sign when standing in twenty degree weather with an even colder wind chill coming in off the ocean. She had no choice but to go back into the lobby. She had the door handle in her grasp when headlights streaked across the glass, the soft hum of an engine drawing near.

A black town car glided to a stop under the portico. The driver immediately opened his door and stood to look at her over the roof of the car.

"Ms. Morrison?"

She blinked at the trim man in black. "Yes?"

"I'm sorry we're late, ma'am." He hurried around the nose of the idling car. "Please get in and warm up."

She hesitated, then moved to the car. Bottom line, she trusted Garrick.

She slipped a leg through the door held open for her and caught a glimpse of grey flannel trousers. It was too late to try to get in the car in some way that wouldn't hike her skirt so high.

Her ass landed in the soft leather seat and she came to two conclusions. One, heated seats were heaven. Two, Garrick cleaned up well. *Really* well.

Shifting against the warm leather, she clipped on her seatbelt and gave herself a few seconds to adjust to the effect Garrick was having on her senses. A hint of his cologne teased her nose and made her think of the woods and lemon and something muskier, like hot sweaty sex. His hair had been trimmed, the dark curls tamed by a clever cut. He was wearing a well-fitted blue shirt, his sports coat cut to accommodate his broad shoulders. His grey slacks hinted at the strength in his thighs, the fit accentuating his height. His tie pulled everything together perfectly—from his perfectly polished wingtips to the twinkle in his amber eyes.

He was smiling at her, amused, and she was gawping at him like some kind of rube.

"Hi." At least she hadn't stuttered.

"Hi." His voice seemed deeper than she remembered. Or maybe her raging hormones were affecting her hearing.

The car quietly slipped out into traffic and turned north. She sucked in a deep breath and collected herself as they drove out of the heart of the city and into a neighborhood with large homes and quiet streets.

She opened her mouth to ask Garrick where were they going, but words stuck in her throat when she caught his gaze trailing over her new shoes and slowly devouring the length of her legs.

Her heart gave a funny beat. The logical, professional side of her brain screamed at her to object. Maybe kick him in the shins. The rest of her body insisted there was nothing wrong with putting that look in a smart sexy man's eyes.

Garrick was transfixed. Mesmerized. *Bamboozled.*

Never once in all the time he'd spent studying Savannah, watching her, walking with her, seeing her in the gym and at her office—not even when he'd held her in his arms and kissed her—had he imagined those legs.

Holy Mary, Mother of God, they went on forever. His palms itched with the desire to run over her firm, muscled calves and softly curved thighs. When she'd stood outside the hotel, her skirt had brushed the top of her knee. Now the hem rested mid-thigh, a delight to be sure, but not quite as completely heart stopping as the glimpse of lace and bare skin he'd been granted when she'd first slid her leg into the car.

He shivered, reminding himself he was her *friend*, and while he was still trying to figure out what the hell that meant and how the soul-searing kiss in the parking lot fit into it, he was ninety-nine percent certain that fantasizing about wrapping his friend's long, lean legs around his waist was a violation of the rules.

Though, god help him, he was only human.

A soft cough, more of a gentle throat clearing, startled him. He yanked his eyes up to meet Savannah's amused gaze.

"Where are we going?" she asked.

He couldn't process the question through the buzzing, jumbled thoughts banging around his head. Mostly he was thinking he was going to buy some ZZ Top on iTunes later tonight. *Legs.* "What?"

"Tonight? A business meeting? You said something about saving the Cats."

"Oh, right. Yes. We're having dinner with Edwin Lamont."

"What?"

He grimaced. Maybe he shouldn't have sprung that on her as they turned into the recluse millionaire's driveway. "I called from Halifax and explained we were with the Ice Cats and wanted to talk to him about the sale."

A massive stone and timber mansion rose above them as they crested the hill that hid it from the street.

"Tonight? *Now?*"

Garrick sighed and ran his hand through his freshly cut hair. He missed the curls but had to admit he looked more like a business man and less like a hockey jock this way. He didn't think Edwin Lamont would give him the time of day either way, but Garrick was determined to put his best foot forward, regardless.

A gentle hand on his arm brought him back to the more immediate issue.

"I'm sorry," he said. "I was so focused on the invitation and getting us here, I didn't give you time to prepare."

Savannah looked around. "Whose car is this?"

"I hired the car. I didn't want to show up in a taxi, plus I didn't think a taxi would be willing to pick up two passengers at two different doors of the hotel."

She cocked her head. "Two different doors?"

"So you wouldn't be seen going out with me all dressed up." He paused. Had he blundered again? "I thought you would be more comfortable with that."

He tried to gauge her response. It would be fucking terrific if someone would write down the male/female friendship rulebook for him. This playing by feel thing was a bitch. Every time he—

Her smile brought his thoughts to stuttering stop. She put her hand on his arm again. "Thank you. That was very considerate." She hesitated, frowning. "I imagine I seem paranoid to you."

Two months ago, Garrick would have said "hell yes" without a thought. Two weeks ago, even, he might not have understood. These days, though, he was getting the hang of Savannah.

"No, not paranoid. Careful. Smart. I get it."

"You do?"

He smiled. "I do." The car came to a stop and Garrick watched over Savannah's shoulder as a solemn older gentlemen opened the front door.

"Holy crap. He has a butler."

Savannah glanced behind her before turning back to him. "What the hell are we doing here?"

"We are going to convince Lamont not to shut down the team until he finds a buyer."

"How the hell are we going to do that?"

"I don't know," he confessed, watching her eyes widen, her mouth dropping open, "but it's going to work."

The door opened behind her and the driver's hand appeared, ready to help her from the car.

"Are you insane?" she asked in a furious whisper.

It was a fair question.

"Not insane." He wrapped his hand over hers where it still gripped his arm. "Determined."

"Are you insane?" Edwin Reese Lamont III asked Garrick

before looking at Savannah for confirmation.

"He prefers the term *determined*," she said.

Garrick flashed her a quick grin and she couldn't help but smile back. Whatever the two of them had thought they were getting into that night, it certainly hadn't been this.

For starters, she'd assumed Edwin Lamont, recluse millionaire, heir to a family fortune and Ice Cats owner, would be a crusty old miser with grey hair, rheumy eyes, and maybe even one of those silver-handled canes rich people called "walking sticks".

Instead, here stood a thirty-something year old man, chestnut hair perfectly coiffed, clear green eyes so direct they could look right through a person and see into her heart. He was tall, slim, fit. Built like a swimmer, with good shoulders and strong hands.

The strong hands part she knew after watching him and Garrick play pool for the past half hour. His long, lean fingers worked the cue like a seasoned pro, his smirk at the beginning of the game warning her he was about to hustle Garrick.

She hadn't expected Garrick to be so good either.

They'd retired from the stuffy formal dining room as soon as the last course was cleared. The food had been amazing, the service frighteningly efficient. But the biggest surprise had been the company.

Reese, as he insisted they call him, had been nothing but surprises. As had his companion, the estimable Mr. Rupert Smythe. From the moment they shook hands in the foyer, it was clear Mr. Smythe wasn't just Lamont's business manager. He was also Reese's best friend.

So here they were, in the Billiards Room—she hadn't known those existed outside the game of *Clue*—watching Reese and Garrick try to whomp each other, both now long past the realization that no one would be hustling anyone.

Savannah stood next to the bar with Rupert, sipping her beer and laughing at the banter between the two men and Rupert's dry commentary on his friend's strategy. The atmosphere was friendly, though an undercurrent existed that she had been trying to put her finger on since dinner.

Garrick smiled up at Reese, his cheeks pink from wine and laughter, and winked at their host. She almost choked on her beer as she finally figured it out.

Garrick was flirting. With *Lamont.*

Their host didn't seem to mind in the slightest.

She laughed at yet another surreal twist to their evening. Rupert grinned. She was more uncertain than ever about what the hell was going on, but she couldn't deny she was having a good time.

When Garrick's intended—and supposedly insane—double-banked shot struck the twelve and pocketed it in the corner, Savannah whooped.

"Determined is right. Reese, my friend, you're going down," Rupert said.

"Thank you so much for your support," Reese said dryly.

Rupert lifted his wine in salute. "What friends are for?"

Reese harrumphed and stepped out of the way as Garrick walked around the table to take his next shot. He took aim, but Reese leaned against the bumper, putting himself in the way. Garrick stood, the cue sliding through his fingers to rest on the floor, and cocked his head.

"Why are you here?" Reese asked, not unkindly, but with a hint of suspicion.

Garrick opened his mouth, twice, before snapping it closed.

Rupert put his glass down on the bar and muttered, "Always was a bad loser."

Reese waited patiently for Garrick's answer.

"I'd like to speak with you about the Ice Cats." Garrick's voice was calm, but she knew him well enough to know he was nervous. He wasn't moving.

"I'm selling them, as I'm sure you know," Reese said coolly.

Savannah stepped forward. "I heard you were thinking

about shutting us down."

Reese and Rupert exchanged a quick look and her heart sank. It was true.

"It seems your management hasn't been discreet." Anger heated Reese's voice.

"No," she said quickly, "it was me. I mean, I was eavesdropping and I overheard a conversation I wasn't privy to."

Reese's shoulders went down a fraction, but he still looked pissed. His face remained neutral. Rupert's too. But there was something there, the flirtation gone, their gazes narrow.

"Why would you shut us down?" Garrick asked, sounding more curious than angry.

She had to give him credit. It was difficult to reconcile this stone-faced Reese with the warm and funny host they'd laughed with not two minutes prior.

"I don't really have a choice. We've been losing money for a while. I had hoped Mark would be able to turn things around, but there has been little improvement." He went on to detail what they'd tried. The marginal successes, the outright failures. His recitation was clinical, though not without compassion. Savannah found little comfort that he obviously didn't want to put people out of work, since he wasn't going to let that change what was, to him, a business decision.

Garrick listened, nodding occasionally and giving Reese his undivided attention. Then he started asking questions.

Savannah smiled, silently cheering on Garrick as he tacked Reese down at every turn. *Just a hockey player, my ass.* He countered each issue with a suggestion. If it had been tried, he offered an alternative. If it was glossed over, he picked it apart. Reese took it well, rising to the debate, his responses getting more passionate. He referred to Rupert for facts and figures. Rupert was not just a business manager in title, but an absolute wizard with numbers and statistics. His memory for the details was impressive, bordering on frightening. The man could quote, with confidence, the smallest minutia about the team and its finances.

During one of his recitations, Savannah realized Rupert was subtly supporting Garrick's arguments, not Reese's.

"Do *you* think the Ice Cats can be made profitable?" she asked Rupert, cutting into the conversation.

All eyes turned to him. He glanced at Reese, who rolled his eyes but remained silent.

"Yes," Rupert admitted, his voice quiet compared to the heated debate seconds before. "I do."

"How?" she asked.

"He doesn't know," Reese said, his smile kind. He turned back to Garrick. "He actually had already argued most everything you have as far as the arena and how to expand its markets."

Garrick smiled at Rupert. "Great minds."

"But," Reese continued before the men could bond over their shared ideas, "he admits that in order for the team, as well as the arena, to be more profitable, there would need to be some changes."

Garrick's brows drew in. "What kind of changes?"

"You need to win more. A championship."

Garrick winced. The Cats did all right, but they hadn't won a championship in all the time Garrick had been on the team, nor for almost a decade before that.

Reese nodded, smug. He clearly believed he'd just dealt the *coup de grâce*.

Savannah couldn't let it stand. She stepped forward.

"That's completely doable."

Chapter Eight

Everyone turned to Savannah.

She crossed her arms and tilted her chin defiantly in the face of three disbelieving stares. When she shifted her weight over one leg, the other stretched endlessly to one side. *God*, Garrick thought, *those legs are amazing.*

He tore his gaze away before he rightly earned the caveman label.

"The team could win more, but you'll have to invest," she informed Reese. She lifted one eyebrow and pinned Reese with her bright green stare, daring him to dismiss her.

Garrick smiled. The legs were great, sure, but they weren't the best part.

Reese shifted, crossing *his* arms and returning her challenge. "Every time I invest in someone new and expensive, I lose them to the NHL or one of their feeder teams, Ms. Morrison. It can be profitable, but not sustainable for building a championship team."

"You don't need better players, *Mr. Lamont.* You need better talent management. You need to cut your dead weight and invest in better training, management, and coaching."

"*Excuse me?*" Reese's eyebrows disappeared beneath his perfectly trimmed hair.

"You're counting too much on the raw talent," she explained, "and not enough on the people who can and will develop that talent if you let them. What you need is discipline. If you get it, you can build a winning team that also generates NHL talent—two profitable outcomes for you."

Reese's huff of laughter was somewhere between patronizing and insulting. Garrick forced himself to remain silent, confident Savannah could still fight and win this battle.

"You don't believe me?" Savannah said with a little smile.

"Fair enough. How about an example? You kept the last trainer on board even though he did jack-shit to strengthen your players, and in some cases made systematic errors that probably shortened their careers."

Rupert's mouth fell open.

Garrick grinned. He was actually getting a little turned on. She was magnificent.

"Look at Sanders," she went on. "He was gold in the net and gone by twenty-five because he had no stamina. No discipline. And Gorensky, who practically limped out of Moncton, only to go on and kick ass in Vancouver after proper rehabilitation and a move to special teams to maximize his talents."

Rupert and Reese appeared slack-jawed as they continued to stare at Savannah. If either of them so much as insinuated that a woman shouldn't be taking them to school about how to run a good hockey team, Garrick would happily punch them in the nose.

Savannah glanced at him, her eyes widening when she noticed his wide smile. He winked at her. Her lips twitched before she turned back to their hosts.

In the blink of an eye, she launched into a complete breakdown of the current team—each player, their strengths, their weaknesses. Then the coaches. She strode across the room and they parted like the Red Sea before following in her wake, gathering in front of the dart board. She used the scoreboard chalk to draw out special team weaknesses in crisp white on green.

Garrick wanted to laugh. Fuck, he had a raging hard-on now.

Reese and Rupert were a rapt audience, asking questions that proved she'd long-since dispelled any doubts about her acumen for the business. She had them hooked and was slowly reeling them in.

Arguing with Lamont had been exhilarating and Garrick could see the same thrill in the flush on Savannah's cheeks, the light of determination in her eyes. He knew what he and

Savannah argued made sense. These were sound options. Maybe he didn't have the business-side experience, but he'd watched the business of hockey for a long time and done his homework. Read the articles, the analysis, watched which teams flourished and which failed. He'd always been curious why and tried to find the answers.

He could only hope Reese Lamont would listen to what he'd learned.

Savannah was winding down her arguments, having now fully detailed the weaknesses of their key rivals—and damned if Garrick didn't feel stupid for not seeing so much of this before now—when she turned back to her audience and paused.

Rupert immediately went to her side. "That was fantastic!"

She smiled.

"It certainly is a lot to consider," Reese allowed, thoughtful.

She shot Garrick a nervous glance.

"Are you thirsty?" Rupert asked.

She put a hand to her throat. "Yes. I left my beer on the bar."

"It's gone warm by now. I'll get you a fresh one." Rupert strode to the bar with Reese close behind.

The minute their backs were turned, Garrick threw his arms around Savannah and lifted her into a great big bear hug. He didn't even care if she felt the steel bar in his pants.

He let go and she stumbled back, blinking.

He just grinned and jammed a hand in his pocket to hide the evidence of just how fond he was of her at this moment.

Reese called from behind the bar. "What are you having, Savannah?"

She looked at him blankly.

"What do you want to drink?" Garrick prompted softly, trying not to chuckle at her bemusement.

"Oh. I uh...I love Moosehead."

Garrick looked at the ceiling, schooling his features, but a snort still escaped.

"What?" she asked.

Reese's groan carried from behind the bar. Rupert rolled his eyes as he delivered the beer.

"What?" she asked again.

Garrick sighed, resigned, and smiled down at her. "How can you tell that someone loves Moosehead?"

She looked at him, adorably confused. "How?"

"Antler marks on their thighs."

Garrick held Savannah's jacket for her. She didn't bother to protest the chivalry. Sliding her arms into the sleeves, she looked around the Lamont foyer one more time before she turned back to Garrick and buttoned up.

"Really? Moose head?" She shook her head.

"It's a rite of passage," Garrick said. "Every New Brunswicker has to tell someone that joke at least ten times in his life or his citizenship is revoked."

She chuckled. "Oh really? I'll have to bear that in mind as the single most compelling reason I've heard to date for *not* applying for citizenship."

Garrick was still grinning when Rupert and Reese arrived to say goodnight. They all shook hands. She genuinely hoped to see them again—and not at the official sale or dismantling of the Ice Cats.

"Will you think about what we said?" Garrick asked, his hand still clasping Reese's.

Reese nodded. "I will. Though, to be fair, I should tell you that if a reasonable offer comes in, I'm going to take it."

Hope and frustration were a familiar mix of emotions tonight. He wasn't talking about shutting them down, at least, but Savannah wanted more. A renewed commitment from Reese. A new owner would bring a host of unknowns, though at least it would mean jobs for them and a lot of other people for a while longer.

"Thanks," Garrick said.

"Yes, thank you," she added. "For listening. And for a lovely night. I hope we see you again soon."

Reese's warm smile slipped, his brow drawing down. Her heart ached at his obvious confusion, and only then did she remember that this man reportedly never left his house. They had been having such a lovely evening, and he'd been such a gracious host, she'd completely forgotten. *Why ever would a man as handsome and charming as Reese sequester himself?*

Reese regained his composure, his momentary lapse only evident in the now-visible lines around his eyes. His smile returned, albeit tentatively. "I hope you'll consider coming to see us again next time you're in town."

Rupert abruptly stopped speaking to Garrick and peered at Reese as if he'd grown an additional head.

"We'd like that," she said.

"Wonderful," Reese said, shooting a dirty look at the still wide-eyed Rupert before ushering them to the door. "Hodges will see you back to your hotel. Good luck at your game tomorrow night."

They'd accepted the offer of a lift back into town from Reese when the hour had grown late and their town car had been ready to go off-shift. She hadn't really thought Reese would drive them himself, of course, but the sleek black limo and liveried driver hadn't been expected either.

With a final wave, she and Garrick slipped through the door and into the waiting car. She climbed in first, sliding across the soft leather seat to make room for Garrick. The door clicked shut behind him and sealed them into a warm cocoon.

Garrick turned to her in the intimate darkness and something tightened deep in her core. She'd been harmlessly flirting with all three men most of the night and hadn't given it a moment's thought until Garrick had hugged her in the billiards room. She'd felt his erection against her hip and her blood had heated, running thick through her veins. She'd struggled to recover her composure, grateful for jokes about fellatio-performing moose to distract her.

Until now.

"Thank you." His voice was soft, rough along her skin.

She clamped down on her body's betrayal and scolding herself for being foolish.

Crossing her legs, she shivered as her bare thighs skimmed over lacy stocking tops. The press of her tightly clenched legs did nothing to stop her growing need.

God, what is the matter with me? She stared at her hand clutching the leather seat between them and counted her breaths.

The heat in the car was high, forcing back the bitter cold outside and carrying the scent of Garrick's cologne. She wanted to bury her face in the crook of his neck and inhale deeply, until she was dizzy from the heady musk hiding beneath the smooth hint of pine.

He watched her, no doubt waiting for her response, hopefully unaware of how ferocious it truly was.

She met his gaze, determined to say *you're welcome* or something equally inane and nothing like *touch me please*. The words wouldn't come. Not even the plea, though she suspected he could see it written in every line of her face.

She felt drunk, but her spinning head had nothing to do with the two beers she'd sipped, and everything to do with her pounding pulse and swelling body. Warm liquid arousal pooled between her thighs.

He was forbidden fruit. Untouchable by her own rules, and yet had proven more desirable than any man she'd known. He was her friend. Trusted.

And fucking beautiful.

She saw the questions in his patient eyes. Was aware of how unlike his nature it was for him to sit so still. It didn't take a glance at the increasingly poor fit of his trousers to know he held back. It was just there, on his face, in his gaze.

She turned away, her eyes fixed on the blank wall of the privacy screen. They were alone, behind dark tinted windows and thick sound-proof barriers, shielded from the rest of the world.

A small pocket of time and space all to themselves.

It was this thought, this reckless belief that she could steal a few minutes from a life, a career, a friendship that should prevent her from stealing any such thing, that made her turn back to Garrick.

Chapter Nine

Garrick watched, wide-eyed, as Savannah slid across the bench.

His hands shook with the need to take, to claim, to feel her touching any part of him with any part of her. He was already delirious with the hint of her arousal in the still, hot air of the car. Drunk on her scent. Intoxicated by her heavy-lidded eyes—smoky green flashes in the pale street lights before they fluttered closed.

Her lips touched his and he opened to her. His heart thunked wildly against his ribs while his cock strained ferociously against his briefs and the zipper of his dress slacks. He wanted to free his erection. He wanted to haul her up over him and grind her down on top of him. He wanted so many things, he could do little more than let her kiss the breath out of him as he tried to figure out what the fuck was happening.

Good God Almighty, he wanted this so badly he would gladly yowl at the moon from the pent up need, the desire he'd swallowed down every time he was near her.

He knew her taste, the flavor of her uninhibited kisses unforgettable as her tongue danced with his. She groaned, long and loud in the quiet dark, and her hands fisted in his shirtfront.

Every sound, every yank on his collar, ratcheted his desire higher.

He drew the knee she had crossed toward him higher, turning her more fully into his body, the warm length of her leg draped across the tops of his. He worried his touch would spook her, but she only wriggled closer, moaned louder, when his hand wrapped around one sleekly muscled calf.

He would have smiled had his mouth not been fully and delightfully occupied. He skimmed his palm up the back of her thigh, over thin silk and the rough lace edge at the top of her stocking. He forged on, desperate to know more than the touch of her lips. At last his fingers met hot, satiny skin, and he sighed into her mouth as she whimpered into his.

When she shifted, he held on, prepared to beg her not to back away. Instead she rolled over him, almost straddling his thigh, until her knee nudged his zipper, teasing his aching cock. His hips surged, searching for more pressure. Relief.

She growled low in her throat, and he fought back a laugh when he figured out she was stuck, her tight skirt preventing her legs from spreading any farther.

She stopped feasting at his mouth and turned her attention to his jaw. He arched his neck, eager for the tickle of her lips and tongue. He dragged in a deep breath, an attempt to think straight that failed miserably when he inhaled the musk of her arousal.

He needed her closer. Now.

"Come here." He slipped his arms around her and hauled her over him. She gasped into his mouth and came willingly. Eagerly. She relinquished her death grip on his shirt to yank at the material at her hips, forcing it higher so she could spread her thighs wide and straddle him properly.

His hands tore at the buttons of her wool coat, her fingers brushing his as she untied the belt. The moment it came loose, she shucked it off and tossed it into the shadows on the far side of the car.

He had a few seconds to process smooth skin above lace stockings, a flash of matching lace at the juncture of her thighs. Then she slid down, her breasts rubbing along his chest until their mouths met again and her soft heat pressed down on his cock.

God, he was going to embarrass himself. His balls tingled, and his rigid shaft swelled further. She writhed in his arms, on his lap. He was damn close to coming in his pants.

It wasn't just her kiss, though he eagerly drowned in another of those. Or her taste, or the press of her body. It was that it was so unexpected. *She* was so unexpected. This woman, who was so controlled at work, so completely buttoned down. Never in his wildest dreams had he imagined she hid this responsive, demanding wanton within her.

He wanted to wallow in the joy of his discovery. Make heathens of them both. Not an easy task in the back of a limo only miles from their hotel.

They had so little time. He tore his mouth from hers, rolled, and tossed her onto the soft seat. He dropped to his knees on the floor before her, pinning her to the leather with his hips, his hands. His cock.

She threaded her fingers through his hair and rocked against him, jamming swollen folds and lace against his shaft as she pulled him close. Her lips brushed his when she whispered his name.

"Garrick."

He shivered, sucking in an unsteady breath. The tight grip in his hair anchored him to her. Their mouths met and she plunged her tongue into his mouth. He kissed her back. Madly. Desperate to imprint himself upon her in the little time they had left.

Clasping her thighs, he spread her open, lifting her knees higher as he changed the tenor of the kiss. His tongue danced into her mouth and took control while he mastered her lips with his, taking complete possession. His cock twitched and leaked when she acquiesced beautifully beneath him, her body pliant. Her hum of approval buzzed down his spine.

He did not retreat, he led. His hands began a slow, torturous slide down her legs, from the backs of her knees and under her thighs, across those precious inches of bare skin.

Gasping with the need for oxygen and the skin-tingling pleasure of finding her thighs wet, he tore his lips from hers. He nibbled along her neck, behind her ear, giving extra attention to the places that made her groan loader, writhe harder. He hoarded the knowledge he teased from her body. He was an able pupil, eager to learn. Hoping to bring this knowledge to bear another time, but knowing this might be his only chance.

His thumb brushed over the lace covering her pussy and she jolted beneath him. He pressed harder and his heart stuttered at how wicked, how *incredible* she looked with her head thrown back, her thighs splayed wide, her skirt around her waist as she gasped out his name.

It was a plea for more. He could not refuse her.

Dragging himself away from her long neck, her tempting mouth, he turned his head and licked a determined path along the inside of her left knee.

Now she shouted his name. Loudly.

It was unlikely the chauffeur couldn't hear at least some of this, but Garrick didn't care. He craved her uninhibited reactions. He nibbled higher, delighting in her gasps, a giggle, her frantic groan when he hooked his thumb in the lace stretched between her splayed thighs. He tugged it to one side. She was wet, swollen. The head of her clitoris rose from her folds and begged for his attention.

City street lamps flashed outside the window. Their time was short.

With a groan of hunger, he danced his thumb over her clit, slicking through the thick cream and across the hood again and again. Holding the thin lace barrier aside with his fingers, he eased the other thumb deep into her body.

She rocked against him. Repeatedly. He adored her abandon. Her brutal honesty. He wanted to laugh with the sheer joy of it as he desperately held on to the woman writhing without restraint in his arms. He couldn't get enough, so he pressed harder, stroked faster. It wasn't enough. He withdrew his thumb.

"No!" she cried.

He thrust two fingers high and deep and she whimpered, rolling her hips again. He was frantic to give her the pleasure she sought. He tortured her clit with a thumb and her hot channel tightened against his fingers.

"Garrick. Garrick!"

Fuck, he loved hearing his name from her lips. Gasped. Hollered. Panted. Moaned.

She planted her hands on the seat and used her arm to gain leverage, lifting and thrusting against him.

"Oh god, Garrick. Please. I need... I need..."

She was begging. God help him, she was *begging* as she bucked against him. The sound raised the hairs on the back of his neck, his need growing with every whimper.

He pushed her leg back farther, held her open so he could thrust harder, twisting his fingers, rubbing them the length of the front wall of her channel until he found the spot that made her whimper louder.

"Oh my god!" Her mouth dropped open and wide eyes locked on his.

She held herself suspended above the seat, frozen in pleasure. Gorgeous.

With deep satisfaction, he rubbed harder, surged farther, and with a last great cry, she blew apart in his hands.

Savannah keened Garrick's name. She was loud, too loud, but she had so completely lost mastery over her own body, all she could do was let it out as the waves of her orgasm rolled over her.

Arms shaking, her elbows gave way and she fell back to the seat, gasping in delicious pain and bliss as Garrick's fingers jammed hard into her clenching body. Another swell burst within her and she threw her head back, quaking as another long groan tore from her chest.

God, it was good. So fucking *good*.

For a long time she floated there, collapsed against the soft leather behind her, beneath her, panting as she regained something resembling consciousness.

Then the limo drew to a slow rolling stop.

Snapping her eyes open, she jerked back in the seat, shocked by the sudden departure of Garrick's hands from her body and horrified to see the front door of the hotel out the window.

Holy shit. What have I done?

Garrick knelt before her, his hands on his thighs, his breath coming in deep drafts. He stared at her, his chest heaving.

The slow burn of mortification bled into her cheeks, heating her neck, her entire face.

The driver's door shut with a soft click and she jumped, panicking. Her skirt was around her waist. Her legs still spread around Garrick. One of her shoes had somehow tumbled clear to the other side of the car to land by her coat.

In desperation, she cracked the back window, clamping her legs together and hoping the dark interior would hide the rest.

"I'm so sorry," she said quickly, not even sure what she was apologizing for. The inconvenience? The screaming? "Can you drop us off in the garage? By the elevator?"

"Yes, ma'am." He said it without blinking, not giving the slightest indication anything was amiss. Savannah's face flamed hotter.

God, what is wrong *with me? How could I do that?*

With a quick jerk of her hem, she straightened her skirt, ignoring the tangle of lace and cotton between her legs. She could fix that later. She looked over at Garrick, who was slipping his sport coat off his shoulders.

"You're going to freeze when we get out of the car," she said foolishly.

Garrick's slow smile made her stomach lurch, even as it rejuvenated the burn in her face. He gestured downward and she dropped her gaze despite her better judgment.

His erection was huge. But not nearly so obvious as the large wet spot she'd left along his zipper and across the front of his pants.

And here she'd thought it wasn't possible for her face to get any redder.

"Oh god, I'm sorry. I'm so sorry. I, ah, I don't—"

He stopped her rambling with a gentle touch to her cheek. She was surprised his fingers didn't sizzle, her skin felt so hot.

"Hey," he said gently, "there is nothing to apologize for."

He sounded so sincere. But she'd had men laugh at her before. At how crazy she got. She'd lost her head. Again. *And with Garrick.*

Another stroke to her cheek. "Are you okay?"

"I'm fine."

He frowned, no doubt aware she was lying. She couldn't bring herself to explain.

The limo dipped down into the brightly lit concrete parking structure and eased to a stop at the elevators. Garrick slid her shoe back on and helped her into her coat. By the time the door opened and the driver's hand appeared to help her out, she felt reasonably intact.

She stood by and watched Garrick climb out behind her, biting her lip when he carefully held his coat folded over one arm in front of him, as if the balmy fifteen degree night were too warm for a jacket.

They thanked Hodges for his service, and he left.

The elevator came almost immediately and was blessedly empty. She prayed it would stay that way, that the rest of the team was in their rooms for the night. She hit the buttons for the fifth and seventh floors. Garrick stood beside her without comment.

When the elevator stopped on her floor, she braced for the worst and turned to Garrick. He looked concerned, possibly alarmed—which was hardly a surprise after her behavior in the car. She slapped her hand on the door when it started to close. She ought to say *something*, but what?

"Are you embarrassed?" he asked.

Oh god, here it comes. She cringed. "Of course."

"Because of me?"

She looked into his face, confused. "What?"

"Are you embarrassed because you were with me, specifically?"

What the hell was he talking about? "No. Of course not."

"You keep saying *of course* like you're making sense."

Clearly she wasn't, but loathed having to explain. She took the coward's way out. "I'll talk to you tomorrow before the game."

She lurched from the elevator, then strode toward her room as quickly as she could without actually breaking into a run.

As post-orgasmic goodnights went, it left a lot to be desired. She heard the elevator doors slide shut behind her and, with that final thud, felt a world of regret.

She squeaked, barely swallowing her scream when a big hand wrapped around her elbow and turned her around.

Garrick.

"What are you doing?" she whispered furiously.

"Honestly? Trying to figure you out. Just when I think I'm getting the hang of it..."

Could this night get any worse? A fresh wave of shame heated her cheeks. "I'm sorry."

His jaw clenched. "Stop saying that."

She searched the hallway, watching for anyone from the Ice Cats and trying to make sense of his anger. They were still alone but they were pushing their luck. With a sigh, she yanked out her key, opened her door and, with bitter resignation, lifted an arm in welcome. He stepped in and closed the door firmly behind him.

He seemed inordinately large in the tiny hallway.

"What are you apologizing for?"

She looked down at her feet and studied her new shoes. They were cute. And her feet hardly hurt at all.

"Savannah?"

She sighed and moved farther into the room, giving herself space, some time to try to sort out her words. His coat landed on the corner of her bed with a soft thump. She kept her back to him.

"For being so crazy." She hoped he would leave it at that.

"Define crazy?"

So much for that hope.

"You know...yelling. Thrashing around." She waved her hand vaguely, not sure how to put it into words without making her mortification worse.

"Who told you that was something you should apologize for?"

She really didn't want to get into that.

"Savannah?"

"A few people."

"Who?" he demanded.

He wasn't going to let it go, damn it. "A boyfriend in college. A man I dated for a while a few years back." She shrugged, wondering how many others had thought it and not said anything. "I sometimes get...I don't know. Ridiculous."

She jumped when he spun her toward him.

"At no time have I ever seen you ridiculous. You're one of the most dignified people I know."

She gave him her best *bullshit* look. "Really? What just happened in the limo? You call that dignified?"

Rather than answer, he started to pull off her coat. *What the fuck?* She batted at his hands, trying to get him to stop, but he wasn't deterred and stripped it from her quickly.

He reached for her again and she opened her mouth to protest, but stopped when instead of trying to divest her of more clothing, he turned her to face the mirror over the dresser.

He met her gaze in the reflection, his hands gentle on her

shoulders.

"You're beautiful."

Forcing herself not to look away, she shrugged, uncomfortable with his fierce regard.

"And you have terrible taste in men."

She laughed despite her embarrassment. "That's a strange thing for *you* to say."

His slow smile made her acutely aware she'd just admitted to something she hadn't intended to reveal. *Damn.*

"I'm proof your taste is getting better. But those other men? The ones who chastised you for the most beautiful, uninhibited, *honest* response to lovemaking I've ever seen? Those guys were a bunch of complete assholes."

Chapter Ten

Savannah smiled sadly and shook her head. Garrick told himself to be patient, even if every particle of his being wanted to shake some sense into her.

Ridiculous? Someone—some stupid fucking *boy*—had told her she was ridiculous?

"That's very nice of you to say, Garrick. Thank you."

He grimaced at her formality. Funny how good manners were sometimes as effective as a good *fuck you*. She held herself rigid, her arms locked to her sides, her chin high. He fought a sigh. The buttoned-down professional armor was back in place. As if she could pack away the passionate woman he'd held in his arms a few minutes ago.

That was how he wanted her. Always. Anything less than her true, uninhibited reactions, her honest response, would be selling herself short. Even if he couldn't be with her again after tonight because of her stupid rules, he wanted her to believe her passion was glorious. Not *ridiculous*.

He slid his hands down her arms and back up again, the touch meant to be reassuring, comforting. A reminder he was there.

"You're beautiful."

"I'm not saying I'm ugly or anything. Just..."

"Every second of what happened in the car was beautiful."

She sighed. "Okay. Thank you."

"Don't placate me," he warned, utterly failing to keep his tone gentle. *Stubborn woman.*

Her eyes narrowed but he avoided her icy stare, skimming his gaze over her neck. Her shoulders. The hint of lacy bra through her blouse. His hands explored, running over her ribs, around to brush her belly. He could only imagine how soft the skin still hidden beneath her clothing would be.

His gut tightened. His cock, having abandoned its enthusiasm sometime around the fourth apology, started to regain interest. Quickly.

He held himself away from her, mere inches separating his growing erection from the long curve of her spine. Once again, he waited to see if she would make the first move. If she hadn't been watching his face in the mirror, he might have laughed at them both. He was generally a take-charge guy in the bedroom, and here he was with a lovely woman who seemed to enjoy giving over control. Yet he did nothing.

They had a knack for making things complicated.

He shoved back the growing compulsion to take. To touch and taste. And focused on making her see the truth. Making her believe it.

"You are beautiful."

A little line formed between her eyebrows. Was it so hard for her to accept? He stroked his hands along her hips and belly again and her gaze focused there. He let his fingers play for a while, holding her attention while he spoke softly into her ear.

"You should see yourself when you're in the moment. When you let yourself go."

She shook her head, though her gaze never left his hands.

He drew them higher, skimming her torso until his fingers rested just beneath the curve of her breasts, his thumbs pressing the sides of her ribs.

Her nipples beaded to hard points, the pull of his hands on the thin fabric of her shirt emphasizing her reaction to his touch.

She shifted and he held his breath, certain she was going to move away and send him from the room. His heart skipped a few beats when she brought her hands to his and pushed them higher, lacing her fingers through his so that together they cupped her breasts.

His breath locked in his chest as the heavy weight settled against his palms, her hands warm beneath his, her long fingers offering herself up to his gaze. He slid forward as she leaned back, their bodies aligning and coming into full contact.

She gasped and arched her back, rubbing against him like a cat. The brush of his cock against the top of her ass tore a grunt from his chest.

She might hate her lack of inhibition in the moment, but she could not tame it. *Thank god.*

He whisked his thumbs across her nipples until the hard beads punched through the confines of her bra and begged for more. His fingers slipped from hers to pinch and tease. She left her hands where they were, holding her breasts up to him, bold and without shame. As she should be.

Her face was beautiful, lips parted, her eyes heavy-lidded and fixed on his fingers as they worked her nipples. Her hips worked in a slow, rhythmic roll against the tops of his thighs, as if searching for the answering press of his erection, which throbbed with the need to reciprocate. He grasped her hip, responded to her whimper of protest with a hard pluck to her nipple.

"God, how is this anything but beautiful? *Gorgeous.*"

He drew her back, higher, using his hands to cradle her closer. His cock lodged against the firm swell of her ass. She jerked, her eyes fluttered shut and she ground herself back against him.

Jesus, it was so *honest.*

"Open your eyes," he said softly, his lips brushing her ear.

She stilled and he waited. His thumb lazily skimmed one nipple.

She slowly lifted her lids, her gaze locked on his. The dilated pupils ringed in deep glowing green caught him. The pinch of worry around the edges of those sultry eyes punched into his gut.

"Look at yourself," he said, his hands roaming over her body once more.

He slid her blouse from her waistband and ducked his

head to suck the sensitive spot behind her ear.

"Take it off," he whispered. His tongue rasped over the gooseflesh on her neck.

"What?" Her voice was breathless. The husky timbre rubbed along his skin.

"Take your blouse off. I want to see you. I want *you* to see you."

She looked at him, so damn uncertain. Her hands lifted tentatively.

He held his breath, his body locked against hers, as she slid the first button from its hole.

Yes.

She worked quickly, as if once her nerves were conquered, she had to act before they returned.

The moment the last button came unfastened, he stripped the blouse from her, then yanked his tie over his head and shucked his shirt in record time. The cuffs almost gave him a problem, but he managed. He could sew the buttons back on later.

He turned his attention, his absolute focus, to absorbing the sight before him.

"Your skin is incredible," he murmured. Though he'd seen hints of it in the passing lights of the street lamps, he hadn't known she was this fair—a warm mix of pink and cream. The dusting of freckles surprised him and he wanted to kiss each one. He started at her throat, his nose rubbing under her chin, his lips moving over the sensitive skin where neck met shoulder.

"Lovely," he murmured.

He pursued each spot with zeal, all the while watching in the mirror. She was staring down at her hands, her fingertips resting on the dresser. The high color on her cheeks increased with every word of praise. Every kiss. She was not unaffected by his touch, but he could practically hear her brain working.

He brought her idle hands back to her breasts, fascinated

by the sight of her long fingers framing her white lace bra. The dark circles peeking through hinted of cinnamon and rose.

"I like it when you touch yourself," he admitted gruffly.

She shook her head and he sucked harder along her neck. Bending his knees, he pressed his cock into the valley of her ass.

He couldn't tell whose moan was louder.

Savannah's, though, was cut off with a strangled gasp.

He ground against her again and brought his lips back to her ear. "You can be as loud as you want. As loud as you need to be. I want to hear it. I *need* to hear you."

She shook her head, her lip caught between her teeth.

"Yes, Savannah," Garrick groaned, arguing with her and encouraging her all at once.

She gasped when the force of their frottage tipped her off balance. He caught her hips as her hands planted on the mirror. She stared, wide-eyed, at her own imagine within the frame of her fingers.

"Do you see how lovely you are?"

She studied her reflection as if looking at a stranger.

He tugged the teak pins from her hair and let it tumble down around her shoulders.

He wanted her to see herself. To see her true face, not the professional mask she wore all day. He was transfixed by the glossy mahogany mane flowing halfway down her back. The thick fall of silk framed her face. Its rich, dark color and her pale skin emphasized her bright eyes and soft pink lips.

"How can you not see how stunning you are?"

He hooked a finger around the heavy curtain of hair and drew it away from her face, her ear. He began another exploration of her neck, the freckles on her shoulder he hadn't worshipped yet.

She held perfectly still and he closed his eyes, afraid to see her shutting down. He was determined to bring her back into the moment.

She jumped when he pinched a nipple. His other hand drew down her side and skimmed over her hip to slip beneath the hem of her skirt and stroke up the inside of her thigh.

She still didn't move. His anxiety grew, his mind spinning with ways to entice her back. To make her let go. He stroked higher, lifting her skirt.

Her leg shifted and eased into his hold. He smiled against her skin.

Taking shameless advantage, he brushed his fingers over her panties. Her whimper rang in his ears. His other hand gathered more of her skirt and forced it higher, until he could hook his fingers into the strings running over her hips.

He looked at their reflection and saw how she stared down at his hands and the delicate fabric covering the junction of her thighs.

"May I?"

"Yes." The word was barely more than a soft exhalation.

He tugged down on the tiny scrap of lace and she wriggled her hips, helping him ease them lower. He stroked his palms over every inch of skin and stocking, admiring her strong calves, the soft curve of her knee.

"Your legs are incredible."

She made a soft sound, a laugh of sorts. He grinned. Not a denial. Progress.

He bent to pull her panties off and thought his heart might explode when she daintily stepped out of them. She left her shoes on, which was hot. And helpful. The height gave her, them, an advantage he had every intention of pressing.

He knelt at her feet and she flattened her hands to the mirror, her ass canted toward him. She looked down at him over her shoulder, her gaze hot and without inhibition or shame. Damn good thing he was kneeling or his legs would have given out.

He stroked his hands up her legs, trying to retain what

little grip he had on his control. He was unbearably tempted by the sights before him—the smooth curve of her ass, the hint of labia in the shadow between her legs, the shine of arousal on her thighs.

Need gnawing at him, he leaped to his feet, placed his hands over hers on the mirror, and wrapped himself around her. She was still turned to look at him and he captured her mouth, thrusting his tongue against hers, the erotic dance a precursor to what his body clamored to do. For what he prayed might come next.

Groaning, he broke free of the kiss and used his cheek to turn her face back to the mirror. Smoky green eyes met his.

"Do you see it?" he asked.

"What?"

"That this—" he rolled his hips against her ass "—is not ridiculous?"

"No."

He ran a hand down one arm and cupped her breast. "No, what?"

Her mouth fell open, her eyelids fluttered as he pinched her nipple and snugged his erection into the crease of her bare ass.

"Not ridiculous," she breathed.

He smiled and rubbed his face against her neck, burying it in her silky hair.

"This is beautiful." He dropped his hand to her hip and rocked against her.

She thrust back. Their teasing quickly took on a rhythm.

"Beautiful," he whispered into her ear.

"Yes," she groaned.

He pressed his hands back over hers on the mirror. "Keep your hands here. Don't look away."

She nodded. His heart stuttered as he took in the tops of her stockings accentuating pale, smooth skin, the damp curls in a little V covering her mound.

His cock lurched. His stomach clenched.

Now. He needed her *now*.

"Please, tell me you have a condom," he said hoarsely, regretting his lack of foresight and the blunt question.

She moaned and rubbed her ass back against him. If she kept that up, he'd go in his pants and the question would be moot.

She shook her head. Garrick's heart plummeted.

Then her head snapped up. "Wait. Yes!" She plunged her hand into the girly make-up kit on the dresser in front of them.

She pulled out two strings of condoms taped together with the words GET LUCKY IN MONCTON written with one letter on each little foil packet.

Garrick laughed.

"Oh god," she groaned in obvious embarrassment. "It's my friend Grace. She's kind of a nut." Her cheeks heated to a deeper pink, even as she planted her hand back on the mirror and thrust her ass back, forcing another grunt up from his chest.

Garrick tugged the chain of condoms from her hand and tore a packet loose. With it clenched by one corner in his teeth, he shucked the rest of his clothes, leaving them in a heap by their feet. He ripped into the packet, rolled on the condom, and turned back to Savannah as quickly as he could.

But not fast enough.

In the twenty seconds he'd taken to prepare, to protect them both, she'd gone from confident to cautious.

He wrapped his arms around her and brought them back into complete contact. His cock glided along her ass before coming to rest in the crease, his thighs framed hers, tickled by the lace of her stockings. He curled his arms around her ribs, pushing her breasts together and enjoying the rough rub of the lace cups against his biceps.

He looked into the mirror. They made the picture he'd

hoped. Her hair was tousled, her skirt around her waist, stocking-clad thighs and high breasts in lace. With him wrapped around her. Naked.

He adored her. Not only in thought, but in action. He worshipped her with his lips, his hands.

He fought a smile when her wary look bled away. Her skin glowed, her chest blushed pink, high color staining her cheeks. She caught his eye.

Her little smile was the sexiest part of all.

His index finger dipped into her navel, and her ass bumped back into his groin. He sucked in air through his nose and wrapped an iron fist around his control. Her smile faltered and faded altogether when he traced his fingers through her soft curls. The little sound in the back of her throat was music. The roll of her hips back against his, the rub of her skin against his cock—heaven and hell all wrapped up as one.

He slid his hands south, through the soft down and slipping between her legs. She opened for him, sliding her legs apart, eager and honest once more.

He wanted access almost more than he wanted his next breath, but his height was going to be a problem. With the breathtaking lack of inhibition he prized, hungered for, Savannah lifted one knee and propped it onto the surface of the dresser. Now when she spread her legs wider, she remained at the perfect height.

God, Garrick thought as his knees wobbled, *who is seducing and who is seduced?* It didn't matter. Not anymore.

His finger slid into thick hot cream. She was drenched, her arousal coating her labia, slicking her thighs, the scent wrapping around them as he stroked the pad of his finger over her clit.

He delighted in how she watched his hand, her body, with abject fascination. Her moan was long. And muffled.

He flicked his finger back and forth over her clit, driving her up, loving the grind and roll of her ass against his cock.

She whimpered. And again. Never releasing what had to be the painful bite of her lips.

"Let it go," he begged. "Don't hold back."

She gasped when she finally opened her mouth. "I can't!"

His finger worked her harder, mercilessly battering her clit. Determined. He used his other hand to spread her open, letting them both see the bright reds and pinks hidden within her folds.

She bit her lip again, the desperate sounds coming from the back of her throat almost painful.

"Say it. Scream it if you have to."

She clamped her mouth shut.

He slid his middle finger into her pussy, sinking in to the hilt.

"Oh god," she groaned.

"Yes, tell me."

She shook her head. He thrust his finger, his other hand still working her clit. She ground against him, forcing herself down on his finger, and he added a second.

She groaned again. Louder.

"Yes, that's it."

Savannah shook her head again, her hair shimmering around her face, her mouth open, her breathing hectic as he took her higher.

Her next groan was louder still. Truer.

She stared at him wide-eyed. "No."

"Why can't you? Why can't you scream it until the rafters shake?"

Savannah looked like she was desperate to do exactly that. "Because Rick is in the next room!"

Garrick faltered. *Oh shit.*

Savannah started to laugh, her entire body shaking. He dropped his forehead to her shoulder. How had his plan had gone so terribly wrong?

Now they were both laughing.

He met her sparkling green eyes in the mirror and his heart did something funny in his chest.

"You are beautiful."

Her smile didn't falter. "You are too."

His brows went up and he glanced at his reflection. He was the same as always, though maybe a little better. He looked really good wearing nothing but Savannah.

Clever woman had backed him right into a corner. How could he refute her claim and expect her to believe his?

He smiled at her again, hoping this wasn't the only time they'd play this game. He could win it eventually. "Thank you," he said graciously, albeit gruffly.

He resumed a slow stroke across her clit. She sucked in a deep breath through her nose. He shifted his fingers, still lodged inside her body, and rubbed the sensitive front wall of her channel, hoping to find the right spot.

The flood of arousal and jerk of her hips told him when he had.

"You're welcome," she gasped.

He moved his hand faster.

"God, Garrick. Keep doing that." Her hips kicked in little circles, her leg shaking against his thigh.

He worked her clit harder.

She bit her lip hard enough that he feared she'd draw blood. He didn't let up, and was rewarded when with a shudder and choked-off cry, Savannah came. The tight muscles of her pussy pulsed around his fingers. His cock ached with the need to thrust inside the rippling heat, but he didn't slow, his fingers relentless until she slumped, her head hanging between her outstretched arms.

He buried his face against her neck, desperately trying to walk himself back from the ledge.

"I don't know how you're going to do it," he said, his voice rough after what felt like hours of need riding him hard.

"What? Do what?"

"Keep quiet while we do this." He eased back and pulled his fingers from her pussy.

She gave a long, low groan. "Do what? I think I managed that pretty well."

"Yeah," he murmured, his lips to her shoulder. Hands shaking, he guided the head of his cock through the slick folds of her pussy. "But how about now?"

He thrust up, his swollen, exquisitely sensitive crown stretching into her body.

"Oh God. Oh God, Garrick."

He surged farther, slipped deeper, his eyes bulging at the heat clenching around his cock. God, how he'd wanted this. *Her.* But it was more than he'd imagined.

She suited him perfectly.

Physically, though, the fit was a little tight.

Short, sharp thrusts took him farther. He fought for every inch. His ears rang with the roar of his own blood and the almost constant noises from Savannah. She thanked him, cajoled him, her words and jumbled phases whispered hoarsely and punctuated by whimpers and moans.

Wide green eyes captured his in the mirror. His arm slid up, across her chest, to curl a hand over her shoulder. His other hand returned to its work tormenting her clit.

He drove himself forward, sinking into her to the hilt.

In return for her absolute honesty, he could give nothing less. The moment was shockingly intimate. Their gazes locked together.

He slowly withdrew from her welcoming depths and stopped when only the head of his cock remained clasped within her. Then he slammed all the way back in. *Heaven.*

He did it again. At some point her eyes fluttered shut, or maybe his did. She tilted her hips, urging him deeper as she ground back against him.

"Harder. *Please.*"

Sweat broke out over his entire body. Not a problem. Harder and faster were about the only speeds he had left. Within seconds, he was powering in and out of Savannah's body, and she was slamming her hips back to meet his.

Above the litany of muffled sounds from Savannah was the hard slap of bodies, the rasping of panting breaths. Garrick's heart raced. His balls drew up tight and hard to his body. He was close. Too close.

He pinched her clit between his fingers and plucked it hard. Again and again. He fought to keep up with the twitch of her hips, rocking together in a rhythm designed to blow off the top of his head.

But not without her.

Her eyes fluttered and when they opened, they were no longer looking at him, but lower. He followed her gaze to his hand dipped between her spread legs, the hint of movement behind.

Holding her against his chest, he stood straighter. Not enough to unbalance them but enough so that when he lifted his hand away from her clit, they could both see his cock driving in and out of her pussy.

"Oh my god," Savannah gasped. Her hips jerked, once, twice, then all those glorious muscles clamped down on his cock like she wanted to pull him up into her tight wet heat and keep him there forever.

It was right where he wanted to be.

With Savannah's moan ringing in his ears, he slammed himself as deep as he could go and let the fire brewing in his balls consume him. His climax roared over his body, arching his spine, and tore a strangled howl from his lungs. His hips pumped uncontrollably against Savannah's firm ass, bumping in tight circles until every ounce of his release had been yanked out of his body by hers.

Chapter Eleven

Savannah stared at the complete stranger in the mirror.

Not Garrick. Indeed, he was becoming all too familiar a face in her life. But the woman with wild hair, glassy eyes, flushed face, and the strangest little smile on her face. Savannah had never seen her before.

She tore her gaze away from the confusing sight when Garrick gently eased out of her body. She couldn't contain the whimper of loss. God, how she loved the ache of really good sex. Mind-blowing sex. His lips twitched as he stumbled back, his legs as weak as hers, apparently. Another moan escaped as she slid her leg off the dresser.

Not that it would be something she could indulge in again, but tonight had been...she was having a hard time coming up with anything other than *amazing*. She was also having a hard time reconciling the ache in her chest at the thought of him leaving.

She shouldn't ever do anything this stupid again. But since she'd done it, she couldn't treat it like some fuck-and-go one night stand.

When he returned from cleaning up in the bathroom, stark naked and a damn vision to behold, she took a long look.

Six and a half feet of hard muscle, thick cock, curly brown hair going in every direction on his head, eyes that had turned from amber to chocolate in the mirror.

He stopped and smiled. She laughed.

He can be smug. He's got a right. And I'm still looking.

If he was the least bit disconcerted by her inspection, it didn't show. He did, though, shift his weight to the left. His tell.

"How's your hip?"

He scowled. "Fine."

She stared at it with narrowed eyes before studying his

face. "Oh, yeah?"

He sighed. "No, it's sore. And not from sex. I will never be too old and broken for sex, goddamn it."

She chuckled and held out her hand. "Of course you won't. I'm assuming it's from your practice and conditioning today. No hot tub. Not enough ice?"

He laced their fingers together and shrugged. "Probably."

"Definitely," she said, towing him over to the bed. "Lie face down."

He looked at her for a moment before complying. She could imagine his thought process departing from *argue with the meddlesome trainer* and arriving at *mostly naked woman asking me to her bed, say yes!*

While he folded down the sheets and got comfortable, she got completely naked. It wasn't like the proverbial cat—or was that pussy?—wasn't out of the bag.

She grabbed lotion from her kit and climbed onto the bed and right over Garrick. He lay still, his cheek on his folded arms, and watched her over his shoulder. He didn't ask what she was going to do, just let her perch naked on his gorgeous bare ass. She warmed some lotion in her palm then began working it into his back.

By the time she got through his back, glutes, and thighs, he had his eyes screwed shut. The work on his hip had likely hurt, a lot, but he'd kept quiet after promising her he'd tell her if she hurt him "too much". In hockey, that generally meant dismemberment and nothing less, so she wasn't surprised he'd remained silent.

She returned to his upper back and shoulders and methodically worked the lotion into his firm skin, soothing her palms over the broad expanse of his warm muscles. The smooth motions quieted her own jangled nerves and, for a time, she didn't worry about what she'd done that night.

Garrick clearly wasn't worried about it either. His slow, deep breathing was the first hint, but it wasn't until he made a soft snoring sound that she was certain he'd fallen fast asleep.

She sat there, her naked ass once more perched on his, and stared at his handsome profile.

It had been a mistake, but she didn't regret it. She couldn't repeat it, but she could live with it.

She only hoped he could live with going back to being her friend. *Just* her friend.

Though even she had to admit it was a singularly unsatisfying thought.

Savannah woke to a pitch dark room and couldn't remember where she was.

Cape Breton Island. Sydney Harbor.

Garrick.

He was curled around her back, his face buried against her neck, his arm under her head put to use as her pillow. His other arm curled around her ribs, his big hand splayed across her belly. He was warm. Close. She had the insane urge to cuddle deeper under the covers and purr.

She should have tossed him out of her room hours ago. Hell, she shouldn't have let him in to begin with. Crawling into bed and pulling the covers over them had only been one more questionable decision in an evening loaded with them, and she didn't give a shit. She was enjoying it for the approximately six hours it was going to last.

She snuggled into the wall of heat at her back and settled her ass more firmly in the cup of Garrick's lap. His soft cock brushed her butt cheek, and his coarse leg hair tickled the backs of her thighs.

Six whole hours to feel like a normal woman, with a remarkably normal man, sharing a bed.

The only question was, why were they wasting their six hours *sleeping?*

Easing away from Garrick, she lifted her head off his arm and carefully rolled over. He reached for her, tried to hold on, but she urged his arm back to his side.

His breaths were steady as she slid under the covers and ran her hand along his ribs, his hip, gently nudging him to roll over. He was less than halfway there when she reached her goal. Without further ado, she sucked his limp cock into her mouth.

His breathing definitely changed then.

"Oh my god, Savannah."

She smiled when he flopped onto his back. She worked her mouth over his cock, running her tongue over and under, around and around as it grew.

She nuzzled the soft skin, pulled it with her lips, and let the edge of her teeth gently tug up under the crown. She loved giving head like this. From scratch, as she liked to think of it. To feel every physical manifestation of a man's desire against her sensitive tongue and lips. To witness his control slip and eventually leave him all together. It was powerful. She wanted to give Garrick this gift, even as she took her own pleasure from it.

Clearly, he was appreciating her gift quite a bit. His erection pressed against the roof of her mouth. At six foot five inches and two hundred and twenty pounds without an ounce of fat on him, proportional was a very happy thing. Her jaw would ache tomorrow and she looked forward to it.

She planted her hands on his thighs to still his thrashing legs. His hips twitched, practically vibrating in her hold. She didn't stop her careful ministrations when he tossed the covers off her and over the end of the bed.

She looked up at him, his thick shaft stretching her lips.

His stare in return was satisfyingly wild-eyed.

"I had to look. To see..." His words drifted off.

She sucked harder and bobbed her head in a steady rhythm. Blood surged into his shaft, widening her jaw, straining her lips, and she hummed around him.

"Fuck!" He threw his head back onto the pillow, his hands fisting in the sheet.

She drew off him and smiled as she licked her way down his shaft and carefully massaged his sac with her tongue. She kept it gentle, waiting to see his reaction.

He drew up one leg to give her better access.

She accepted the gift of his trust and coaxed his entire ball sac into her mouth. Her lips gently tugged and her tongue rolled his testicles against the roof of her mouth.

Garrick lifted his other leg and spread himself wide.

Unfettered access. What more could a girl want?

Releasing his balls, she returned to the base of his cock and worked her way up until she could tease the divot under the head with the tip of her tongue. He'd lasted longer than most men would without forcing her to wrap a hand around him to guide him as she wished, but now his hips bucked without control and she curled her fingers around his thick shaft.

God, it had felt good as he'd slowly worked his way into her body. He was big enough, and she'd been celibate long enough, that he'd had to fight for every inch. The stretch had been amazing. But not as incredible as when he'd fucked her properly, how they'd crashed into one another, his hot voice in her ear telling her she was beautiful.

And she'd felt beautiful. Like she could have done anything—screamed, yelled, beat her fist against the wall—and he would have been delighted with it.

Rick, her boss, his coach, and the man just one thin hotel wall away, might not have been as happy. So they'd kept the noise as contained as they could manage, but the rest had been no holds barred.

She'd done it wholeheartedly, she thought as she swirled her tongue around the head of his penis, enjoying his mumbled praise.

Grace would be so proud. Too bad she was never going to tell her friend a damn thing about it. There would be no end to the haranguing about being with Garrick more than once.

Not possible.

She closed her eyes against a wish she wasn't going to bother making and plunged down on Garrick, taking as much of him as she could into her mouth before retreating with a tremendous upward suck.

He roared his approval so she did it again and again, stopping on the retreat to tease the flange, or tickle the tip of her tongue into the little hole. He definitely preferred when she focused on the divot, but she kept trading them off.

She wanted this to last. She wanted him to stagger out of her room on weak knees and with his eyes still mostly rolled back in his head. She couldn't offer him anything more than this one night but, goddamn, she wanted it to be memorable.

Her hand followed her lips up and down his shaft, twisting and untwisting. His knuckles were white where they gripped the sheet. His breath rasped in and out of his lungs in gusts. She stroked the fingers of her free hand over his sac, finding it high and tight. When the cadence of his moan, the tenor of his voice when he said her name again was just a little higher, she gave his balls a firm tug.

His moan was choked off and his eyes snapped open.

"I'm not done with you yet," she said, surprised by the husky timbre of her voice. She'd always thought vixens had to practice to achieve that. Turned out, it was all about the motivation.

His eyes drooped, heavy as he stared at her face hovering above his glistening cock. A bead of pre-come pearled on the tip as her hand continued its relentless rhythm.

She leaned in and licked the little drop away. His narrow stare, the parted lips were all as she had expected. The quirked lip on one side, the tiny smile, was pure Garrick.

Another pearl of pre-come appeared immediately.

Her tongue darted out for that one too.

Her hand pumped steadily while she licked spots here and there around it. The divot got another tickle. She traced a vein from root to crown with the tip of her tongue, then danced the broad flat around the soft velvety head. The tang of his pre-come grew stronger, more frequent, as it continued to leak.

He showed admirable restraint. The quiver in his thighs was the only betrayal of the amount of control he was exerting over his body.

Which didn't seem right at all.

She took him fast and held him deep, using her hand to cover the rest. She wished she could take him deeper, deep throat him, but her gag reflex would never let her even close.

She decided to try something different.

Setting up a steady rhythm of plunge and retreat, lick and suck, she started him on the climb to his release. She didn't have long, she could tell. She slipped one finger into her mouth alongside his cock for one round trip, then ran her fingers over his sac again. She didn't tease, tug, or even test their weight—though it was tempting—but kept going, dropping her hand lower to press her wet finger against the seam beneath.

"Yes. Savannah, yes!"

He didn't have to ask twice. She rubbed the tight skin of his perineum, massaging gently.

His arms flew over his head to clutch the headboard as he writhed against her finger and thrust up into her hand and mouth.

One, two, three frantic jerks and he hit the peak, his body shaking with the force of his climax. His cock pulsed long jets of come into her waiting mouth. She took it all as he quaked beneath her, his face smashed to his arm, his mouth open, gasping for air between long moans.

She rejoiced in every long, drawn-out stroke until he collapsed back against the bed, then she sat and watched him try to pull his shit back together. She glanced over at the clock.

4:25 AM.

Still time for a little more sleep. Would it be totally shameless if she asked him to spoon himself around her again?

She smiled as she dragged the bedding up off the floor and over them, nudging his shoulder until he scooted back down in the bed where he belonged. With a sigh, she wriggled backwards until her ass was planted in his lap, and then wrapped his arms around her.

Who cares about shameless?

Garrick preferred her that way, anyhow.

Chapter Twelve

The first hints of light peeked around the edges of Savannah's hotel room curtains and Garrick's arms tightened around her even while he accepted the truth. It was time for him to go.

Not that he had any desire to leave. He'd have gladly stayed right where he was until they had to run to catch the bus to the arena.

But he wasn't foolish enough to ask for that. He wasn't even hopeful enough to try to make love to her again this morning. The sun was coming over the horizon and their team mates, and Rick right next door, would soon stir.

He looked down at Savannah and smiled. Her face was pressed to his chest, her hand curling over his right pectoral muscle like she was feeling him up. His chuckle shook her, but she remained asleep. Giving a man a mind-altering blow job in the middle of the night was no doubt exhausting work.

He'd never stop thinking about—*dreaming* about—last night. Nor would he stop feeling guilty for allowing her to tuck them both back under the covers and promptly falling back to sleep.

He could have spent the rest of the night giving her a taste of her own wicked medicine. He *should* have spent the rest of the night memorizing everything he could about her.

Her eyes eased open. Her sleepy smile made heat curl low in his belly. Then she glanced at her bedside clock.

"Shit!" She bolted upright.

He rose more slowly, sliding from the bed as he did. She put out a hand to stop him.

"You have to go."

"I know." Even though it sucked.

It wouldn't be easy to convince Savannah to let this happen

again—no way was he going to give her any fodder for her arguments against it. It was critically important he get the hell out of this room and back to his without being seen by anyone on the team.

He got up and tugged on his clothes, trying to pull himself together and not look like he was doing the walk of shame.

Grey flannel slacks and a sports coat at 6:15 AM. *Yeah, who am I kidding?*

He turned back to Savannah sitting in the middle of the bed, the covers pooled on her lap, her hair in wild disarray around her face. Leaving just might kill him. He congratulated himself on his supreme control as he backed away from the bed.

"I'll see you later? On the bus or at the arena?"

Her brows knitted. "Yes. Come early, so I can stretch your hip and groin, okay?"

He thought about arguing, but he wanted to see her and his hip *was* sore. Though probably not as much as it would have hurt if she hadn't given him that massage. And maybe the blow job. Everything in the world hurt less after that.

"Okay, I'll see you there." There was so much more he wanted to say.

The sound of a slamming door down the hall was like a gun shot in the room.

Without another word he turned and left, checking the hallway before speed walking to the nearest exit and running up the two flights of stairs. He checked his hallway, too, before sprinting the length of the corridor, not releasing his breath until he shut his door behind him and locked himself into his virtually untouched hotel room. He'd changed in here last night without so much as sitting on the bed.

He should probably get more sleep, but was too twitchy to go to bed. Instead he changed into his most comfortable workout clothes and set up his laptop at the small desk in the corner.

He had a brilliant plan. He would see Savannah at the arena later today and act as though *absolutely nothing* had happened.

It was the only way to prove it was possible to have earth-shattering sex with him and not have a single person treat her one iota differently. No one had to know except the two of them. And if it worked once, maybe he could convince her it was safe to do it again.

It was a long shot, but he was starting to understand Savannah and her position with the team—as trainer and as the only woman. He might have preferred to woo her, to court her openly, but it was out of the question.

So he had his plan, and come hell or high water, he was going to be patient and let it unfold.

He adjusted his cock in his shorts, trying to stem the erection that bloomed at the mere thought of Savannah sitting in her bed, rumpled from sleep and sex. Patience was going to be pure agony.

Shaking his head, he put thoughts of his lovely friend away and set his mind to their meeting with Reese and Rupert. They'd heard some of what Garrick had said, and they'd listened carefully to what Savannah had told them. But it had been late, with wine and beer and betting on pool games. He couldn't be sure how much of it had stuck—let alone resonated.

It had been years since he'd been in school, since he'd drafted anything like the document he was considering crafting, but he thought he could find some good examples on the internet and make a go at it.

Maybe Savannah would be willing to read it, give him some feedback and edits. If she had time. His goal was to get something messengered over to Lamont's estate before they left Cape Breton Island in two days time.

Savannah didn't know what to expect after spending the night with Garrick, but she was mighty put out that he seemed to be avoiding her.

Maybe he got what he wanted and was done with her?

She let that idea rattle around in her head for all of ten minutes, trying to build up a good head of pissed-off steam. All she ended up with was a headache and guilt for thinking so shabbily of him. Maybe she would prove to be a poor judge of character, but she really didn't think he would do that to her. To any woman. But particularly to her.

They were friends. *Right?*

They had to be, because why else would he have slid his *Business and Marketing Plan for the Moncton Ice Cats* under her hotel door last night?

Not exactly a love note—not that she wanted one—but a pretty cool surprise.

She had no idea when he'd found time to pull it all together. It was everything he'd talked about for saving the team, turning the arena profitable, and her ideas for how to improve the team management, coaching, and fitness. They'd met with Lamont the day before yesterday and in the meantime, he'd spent a night in her room, done his training and fitness work, played hockey, stayed late for a fan event and, presumably, slept. Though she would bet, based on the business plan, that the sleep had been mostly sacrificed.

Now it was time for a midday Sunday game and the long bus ride back to Moncton. She was about to leave her temporary office and head out to the rink, her kit packed up and ready for the game, when a shadow at the door caught her attention.

"Hello, Bobby," she said, irritated at how her pulse sped up. She slid her hand into her kit and gripped her scissors. "Did your wrap come loose?"

Bobby's smirk was mostly sneer. "Elbow's fine. How was dinner Friday night?"

Why the fuck would he want to know about her dinner Friday night? Then she remembered where she'd been. Lamont's house. Shit. He couldn't know about that.

Could he?

"It's none of your business what I do with my free time, Bobby," she said flatly.

Bobby laughed, his chuckle grating on her nerves. "It will be my business soon enough."

What did that mean? The loser couldn't possibly believe he would win her over. She studied his face, his mean little smirk. Actually, he probably was that fucking crazy. And stupid.

Bobby jumped when a hand landed on his shoulder. He moved out of the door so Mark could step through.

"Ready?"

She smiled gratefully. "Sure am." She hefted her equipment and followed Mark from the room without another word or glance for Bobby.

An hour later, Savannah stood by the bench, eyes on the game, still trying to shake off her creepy encounter with Bobby. She was starting to worry that he wasn't just mean and dim-witted, but actually insane. Had he followed them? The idea gave her the chills.

More so, even, than the thought of him telling the rest of the team she'd gone out to dinner with Garrick. So much for her sterling reputation. All that hard work, and Bobby would no doubt gleefully destroy her standing in the eyes of the rest of the team, even if all he had was conjecture and bullshit.

Then again, if he'd seen them get out of the limo in the garage that night, it might not be entirely conjecture.

She was so screwed.

And as if that weren't enough to think about, she also needed to find a way to tell Garrick. He'd been doing a really bang-up job of avoiding her these past few days.

Hell, maybe he could make sense of it.

Her free time would be Bobby's business? She shuddered at the thought.

Over my dead body.

She was so engrossed in trying to decipher Bobby's cryptic bullshit, she failed to keep an eye on the game. Her head snapped up when the piercing shriek of the referee's whistle rent the air and stopped play.

Shit!

Savannah shot to the boards, her heart nearly stopping when she saw a red and blue jersey down on the ice. One of hers.

She was over the wall and out on the ice without a thought.

Shit, shit, shit. Was it a head injury?

She almost lost her footing when she realized it was Garrick. She picked up speed, sliding the last foot on her knees, heart pounding.

"I'm fine!" he said from flat on his back.

She might have believed him if he wasn't bleeding all over the damn place. She looked at the ref. "What happened?"

"High stick. He stopped it with his face mask and..." The ref paused, peering down at Garrick. "Maybe his right cheekbone."

She studied Garrick's face, assessing the damage, and smiled at his thoroughly disgruntled look. "That's using your head, LeBlanc."

"Har har." He tried to sit up.

"Stay." Her hand on his shoulder kept him still. "You didn't get right up. Did you hit your head on the way down?"

"Nah, I caught myself. I was just stunned for a second. He clipped my nose before he hit the cheek."

With quick economical movements, she released his chin strap and tilted his head back. Not that she didn't believe him...actually, wait. She *didn't* believe him until she saw how his eyes reacted normally to the bright lights above. She took her first real breath since leaving the bench.

"Looks like you'll live." She stood. "But first you'll come with me and get that cleaned."

He easily got to his feet. Spending time down on the ice was considered a sign of weakness. She'd seen men with broken limbs get up and skate off. A simple face rearrangement wasn't going to keep him down.

"No stitches," he muttered as they passed his replacement and stepped up into the bench.

"What, you don't trust my sewing?"

He gave her a bland look, sat on the bench, and yanked off his helmet. The puck and several players moved past them, but she focused on her patient.

Garrick's eyes followed the game. His line came back and she was afraid she was going to have to tackle him to get him to stay put when they went out again.

Working quickly, she cleaned up his face and neck, confirmed no other injuries hid beneath the mess, then leaned in to examine the wound.

"Did you read it?" Garrick asked quietly.

She grabbed a couple butterfly bandages to help keep the cut closed and clean. "I did. I'm impressed. I had no idea you knew how to do something like that."

Garrick's head swung as the puck moved to their goal, his gaze narrow. "I didn't."

Now she was confused. "You didn't write that plan?"

"No, I did. But I didn't know how. I looked it up the other night. Figured out what to do. At least I think I did."

She leaned in close, her face inches from his as she applied the first bandage. "I'm even more impressed."

He grunted. "Is there anything I should change? Anything I got wrong?"

"Not that I saw." She applied the last bandage. "I thought it was perfect."

At last he looked away from the game and pinned her with his soft brown eyes. "Thanks."

She smiled a little. "You're going to save this team."

His crooked smile and pink cheeks made him look younger. He slammed his beat-up helmet back on his head and at last gave his blood-stained jersey a cursory glance.

"I'm sure as hell going to try."

She didn't think before she tugged on his chin strap. He cooperated without so much as a blink, tilting his head back and not making make fun of her for acting like his mom. She considered stopping mid-process, but it would only exacerbate her stupidity.

"Bobby caught me alone in the training room before the game," she said softly, filling the awkward silence.

His sharp look made her rush on. "He didn't touch me. Didn't even come in the room."

Garrick only relaxed marginally. "And?"

She let her hands fall to her sides, his helmet secure. "He asked me how dinner was Friday night."

Garrick digested that for a second before muttering a heartfelt "*fuck*" under his breath.

"That's just what I was thinking," Savannah said as Garrick cleared the boards with the rest of his line.

Chapter Thirteen

Garrick sat on the bus, watching the moonlit winter fields of New Brunswick fly by, and tried to rein in his chaotic thoughts.

How could Bobby possibly know about Friday night? And more importantly, who was he going to tell? Had he had seen them return? Had he seen Garrick go into Savannah's room? Scrubbing a hand over his face, he slumped back in his seat. He'd never meant to bring this shit down on Savannah. Her reputation was critical to her success. Hell, she relied on it almost as much as her skills as a trainer. She had to. She was a woman.

For the life of him, he couldn't figure out why he hadn't understood that from the moment he'd met her. *Fucking dense, LeBlanc.*

Garrick checked his cell phone again, but still no response from Reese. He'd included his email address in the letter he'd sent along with the business plan, indicating it was the best way to reach him.

Now he was obsessively checking his phone like a teenage girl.

There were too many loose strings and it drove him crazy not to get at least a couple of them tied off. Confirmation from Reese. Determining what the fuck game Bobby was playing. Figuring out how the hell he was *ever* going to get Savannah in bed again when Bobby had sent her into a completely justified paranoid freak-out.

Garrick wrestled with the burning desire to stand up, walk three rows forward, and punch Bobby Kramer in the face. *God, that would feel so damn good.*

Just when he was descending into that happy fantasy, thoroughly enjoying the image it invoked, they crossed the Moncton city limits and Mark stood up at the front of the bus.

"Team meeting," he announced over the din of conversation and the hum of the bus tires on the highway. "Tomorrow morning, nine o'clock."

A general groan went up from the crowd. Garrick dug his fingers into his tired eyes.

Fuck, what now?

Savannah smiled at Mike Erdo as she got out of her car and saw him lingering in the doorway to the arena. She really was going to have to talk to Mark about this escort thing. Poor Mike was standing out in the bitter cold, hanging around like it was his preference to freeze his nuts off for a while rather than moving the five feet it would take to get into the warm lobby.

"Good morning, Mike."

"Morning, Savannah."

She opened the door and held it for him. He hardly even gave her a funny look. She was finally getting these men properly trained. She buried her mouth in her scarf to hide her smile.

It was almost nine o'clock so they went directly to the meeting room. She stepped through the door and had the worst kind of déjà vu. Maybe she was turning into a pessimist, but she'd bet this meeting wasn't going to be any more fun than the last.

Bobby's glare sure was reminiscent of the last time around. What was new was the little smile, the crinkle in the corners of his beady little eyes.

Just when she'd thought he couldn't get any creepier.

Working her way to the front of the room, she murmured a quiet thank you to Mike when he stepped into a row to sit with Alexei. She continued on, putting her hand on Rhian's shoulder to get his attention. He started to stand but she pressed down and nodded at his long legs. Sighing, he swung them to the side and let her slide past him.

Garrick did the same without being asked.

Yes, the training was definitely starting to take.

She sat next to Garrick, not bothering to check if Bobby was still smirking at her. She could feel his stare on the back of her neck.

"Any idea?" she asked.

"Not a blessed one," Garrick replied.

Mark looked over his shoulder from the front row, purposefully catching Savannah's eye. Her stomach clenched.

Rhian and Garrick muttered various colorful curses. "Did you see that look?" Rhian whispered.

She nodded. Garrick sighed.

Mark stood.

"Ladies and gentlemen," he began, stepping to the front of the room. "Yesterday the EHL and Edwin Lamont received what is considered to be a reasonable bid for the team."

Murmurs rippled around the room but Mark continued, slicing through the noise.

"It will take a while to sort out the paperwork, and the league will have to approve the purchase. Nothing is final until that happens."

Savannah looked at Garrick and he shrugged, his narrow gaze and full attention focused on the team's manager. A new owner could mean their jobs were all saved, at least for a while longer. But instead of pleased, Mark appeared to be somewhere between uneasy and nauseous.

Garrick sat forward. "Who's the buyer?"

"My dad," said a familiar voice from the back of the room.

With dawning horror, Savannah and everyone else in the room turned to see a triumphant Bobby being congratulated by his friends.

Savannah barely heard a word of the rest of the meeting. Rhian looked like he'd swallowed something sour and Garrick appeared ready to commit murder.

She wished she had some comfort to offer them. To offer

any of her colleagues as everyone quietly fled the room.

She stood on wooden legs, only vaguely aware of Garrick and Rhian trailing her into the hallway. Neither said a word when she walked right past her door and continued on to the lobby.

The game wasn't until seven that night. Normally she would have stuck close, spent the day working on fitness plans, checking in with her players. Today she strode back out into the cold air of the parking lot.

As the door swung closed, Garrick called, "Savannah—"

"Leave her be, man," Rhian said.

She wanted to turn back. To fling herself into Garrick's arms and cry all over him. But it was too late.

At least she hadn't gotten attached. Much.

Garrick cursed under his breath as Savannah drove out of the lot. Thanks to Bobby Fuckhead Kramer, she hadn't felt safe for a month, and now this.

His hands curled into fists. For his professional reputation—not to mention his criminal record—he needed to avoid Bobby for a while.

"I'll be back," he said, though he didn't move.

Rhian stared out at the parking lot like he might drive away too. "Yeah. I'll see you in the gym later?"

Garrick nodded, not really sure what the hell he was going to do, but vaguely aware that he did have to come back to do his conditioning, his stretches. Ice. Heat. Go through the routine of a game day and get out on the ice. He had to play, and play well. He owed Moncton and his teammates that much.

And he might as well enjoy it while it lasted.

He was the only person who might actually lose his job faster than Savannah, if only because Bobby would want to keep her around so he could assault her again at his leisure.

That thought got Garrick moving. Jamming the door open,

he jogged to his car.

Fuck, he had to do *something*.

He fished his cell phone out of his pocket and checked his email automatically, belatedly realizing why he had not received a message from Reese Lamont about his business plan.

He allowed himself to feel humiliated by his own stupidity and wide-eyed optimism for thirty seconds while he started the car and drove out of the lot. Then he pulled up the contact he'd programmed in only a few days before and hit SEND.

It only rang once. "Yes?"

The first time Reese Lamont's personal assistant had answered the phone like this, Garrick had thought it was strange. Mysterious and aloof. Now it just irritated the shit out of him.

"Garrick LeBlanc for Mr. Lamont."

"Yes, Mr. LeBlanc. He is expecting your call."

Garrick blinked. He used the few seconds he was on hold to pull into a Tim Horton's and throw his truck into park.

"Garrick?"

"Mr. Lamont."

A pause. "That mad, are you?"

Garrick considered his response carefully. "Not mad. Disappointed."

Reese sighed audibly over the phone line. "If it's any consolation, I didn't get your business plan until after the offer was in to me and the league. In truth, I didn't expect anyone to offer this much—neither did the league. Turning it down would make me appear insane."

Seemed like a trivial concern from somebody who was rumored not to have left his house in a decade. Garrick fought his anger and held his tongue, focusing on what Reese had implied. "Do you want to turn down the offer?"

"Honestly? Yes. Robert Kramer is a bastard. A dirty,

crooked bastard."

Garrick blinked. "He is?"

"Aren't you from Moncton?" Reese asked. "I would have thought you'd at least heard the rumors."

"Well, yeah, I've heard talk," Garrick said, "but mostly just that he's an asshole. I've never heard of him actually being in trouble with the law. What do you mean by *dirty*?"

"Letting drugs run through his bars, letting all manner of transaction take place in his OTB shops. Money laundering. Underground clubs. Did you know his second cousin owns most of the strip clubs in New Brunswick and a bunch more in Quebec?"

"Yeah, so?"

"He's sixteen. He opened his first club when he was four. Quite an accomplishment. A cousin on the other side of his family is the CEO of that child's corporation."

"Jesus. Why bother with the ruse?"

"He likes to keep his nose clean. It helps not to have your name on anything when the shit hits the fan. And it's not just bad business. Two years ago, a dancer at the Foxy Lady in Fredericton told the RCMP that there was a vast business operating in the basement of the club. When the Mounties raided the next morning, all they found was empty desks and scraps of shredded paper. The girl disappeared that night and was never seen again."

The hair on the back of Garrick's neck bristled. "Oh shit."

"Yes, precisely. Total shit. So, no, I don't want to sell him the damn Ice Cats, but it's not going to be easy to prevent given my public announcement to solicit buyers and his more-than-reasonable offer."

Garrick put his head back against the headrest and rubbed his eyes hard. "This is bad."

"I'm sorry, Garrick. I truly am."

He didn't know the half of it.

"Look," Reese continued, "I'll do what I can to stall the

process. Drag my feet on the paperwork, be unavailable for meetings. I can't stretch it out forever, but maybe long enough for a better bid to come in."

"And then what?"

"I'll accept it. Quickly. And do whatever is in my power to avoid a bidding war. It may not help. Something tells me Robert Kramer wants the Ice Cats and is willing to pay a premium."

"How much was his bid?" The question was rude but Garrick needed to know what it was going to take to save his team.

The number Reese quoted made him queasy.

Savannah sat at her computer staring at her updated résumé. Closing that window, she read again the job description glowing on her screen.

It was a long shot. A one in a million. She could only imagine the pile of eligible candidates who had already put their names in for consideration. The countless more who would follow.

What the hell? It couldn't hurt to try.

With false confidence, she worked up a new version of her cover letter and attached her résumé in the wizard provided. Her bravado waivered as she stared at the SUBMIT button and fingered the button on her mouse, hesitating to take the last step.

She wanted the job. But she was also shocked to discover she didn't want to leave Moncton. She'd just started to settle in and make friends. She'd miss Rhian. And Alexei and Mike.

Garrick.

She stood, walked to her window, and looked out onto the street. A dark SUV idled in front of her stoop, its tinted windows too dark for her to see in. She peered closer, cupping her hands to the glass for a better view. The SUV drove off quickly.

Jesus. Sometimes the universe sent messages. She listened.

But first she checked the locks on her doors and windows and snapped the curtains closed.

Resolved, she sat at her computer and rechecked everything she'd entered. Seeing no mistakes, she clicked SUBMIT.

She stared at the confirmation screen for a long time.

THE BOSTON BRUINS THANK YOU FOR SUBMITTING YOUR INFORMATION FOR THE POSITION OF ATHLETIC TRAINER. A MEMBER OF OUR CANDIDATE SELECTION TEAM WILL FOLLOW UP WITH YOU IN THE NEXT TWO WEEKS.

Garrick sat with his mouth hanging open, staring at his old friend Jack Chevalier. Jack stared back, his bright blue eyes amused.

The team meeting, the phone call with Reese, Bobby's fucking attitude in the locker room, all followed by tonight's game on autopilot in spite of his intention to play his best. Now midnight had come and gone and he was sitting in Quigley's Bar, around the corner from where he and Jack had grown up.

"Dude, are you the only person in this town who doesn't know?" Jack laughed, running his fingers through his thick black hair and shaking his head.

"I guess I am."

Jack looked around them again, for the tenth time at least.

"Garrick, the guy runs all the books in town. Sports, horses, fights, elections, celebrity deaths. If you can bet on it, he's running a game." Jack paused to search the faces of their fellow patrons again. They'd chosen a bar Robert Kramer didn't own, there was no one sitting in the tables around them, and it was late—almost last call—but still Jack wouldn't stop checking.

"He can't own a fucking hockey team if he's betting on sports or profiting from people who are," Garrick said in disbelief.

Jack gave him the pitying look his naïveté warranted. "Yeah, dude, which is why it's all under the table. He can't exactly advertise that he's making big coin every time his son throws a game."

An anvil landed in Garrick's gut. "What?"

Jack shook his head. "I don't have to tell you it's really not possible for one guy to fuck up a whole hockey game, but he sure does help it along sometimes. Don't you ever wonder why in some games Bobby is as sweet as pie and in others he's starting fights and picking up penalties like it's his job?"

Garrick stared at Jack. Numb.

"It *is* his job, Garrick. He's so far up his dad's ass, so desperate to keep his access to the treasury, he'd sell his own mother as polar bear food."

Garrick's throat was dry, his chest tight. He chugged the rest of his beer, hoping to ease the tension. It immediately tried to come back up again.

Robert Kramer couldn't own the Ice Cats. Not just because Garrick would lose his job. Or because Savannah would have to walk away from hers. Robert Kramer would screw this team, each and every one of the players, the management, the arena staff. The town.

Garrick scrubbed a palm over his face and rose to his feet. He carefully masked the ripple of pain stabbing his nuts as his groin pull reminded him why it was important to stretch after the game and not run straight to a cold bar to sit on a rock hard seat.

"Thanks, Jack. It's been educational."

Jack nodded. "Sorry to be the one to have to tell you. Though, if anyone asks, we talked about beer and hockey. Nothing else."

"Understood. You working this week?"

Jack eyed him. "Yeah, I work every week. It's not like I can afford a lot of vacations. Not to mention I'm not allowed to leave the country."

Garrick grimaced. Jack was a bartender at the Brunswicker Ale House, one of Kramer's many establishments. He'd had the job since getting out of prison five years before and Garrick had harbored the belief that Kramer couldn't be *that* big an asshole if he were willing to hire a con right out on his parole.

Jack deserved a good job. He and Garrick had gone to high school together, and a few short months before what would have been Jack's graduation from Université de Moncton, he'd been caught helping his old man rob a liquor store. Not that Jack had known he was abetting a felony while he sat in his car, waiting for his dad to come out with a six pack. When his dad had come out empty-handed but for the wad of cash and the gun shoved in his belt, Jack had panicked and driven his father away.

They'd been arrested within an hour, long before Jack could do the right thing and call the cops on his own father. A judge decided to make an example of Jack for these fleeting moments of decidedly poor judgment and sentenced him to five years. Since then, Jack had kept his nose clean and tried damn hard not to stir the pot. Garrick wouldn't jeopardize that.

Garrick clapped him on the shoulder as they stepped out of the bar and turned toward their cars. "I might poke around a little. You can pretend you've never seen me before."

"Nah," Jack said. "Stick as close to the truth as we can. I can't help you, but I'm not going to tell you I don't wish someone would take that man down a peg or two. I'd like to see him survive a week in the joint. Fucking idiot. He treats people like they're meat, dumb animals he's forced to deal with."

"You see him do a lot of business?"

"Yeah, sure, but at the Brunswicker it's all on the up and up. The mayor comes for lunch, sometimes with Kramer. We've got a bunch of cops who come in after shift. You know the drill. And anyway, no way I'm going to witness shit and not report it."

Garrick nodded.

"Look, if I get wind of anything, a place to look, a time to be somewhere, I'll let you know. Some of the other bartenders and bar-backs move between properties. I'll see what I can get."

"No, man, not worth it," Garrick said immediately. "I appreciate the offer, but do not stick your neck out on this."

Jack shrugged. "We'll see." He stopped to unlock his truck. "I'll see you around?"

"Yeah. Stop by the house for a beer when you get a chance."

"I'd like that."

Garrick sighed. Jack always said that, and he'd never once done it.

Chapter Fourteen

Savannah sprinted down the long corridor beneath the arena. The sound of her feet striking the concrete a hollow echo. Heart pounding, she ran as faster, gasping for breath, senses tingling. He was getting closer. He was going to catch her soon.

She didn't need to look to know it was Bobby who chased her. Whose big ugly hands were reaching for her as she darted around a corner.

Now she was on the ice, her skates a natural extension of her legs as she pumped them to gain speed, to swing around behind the net in a desperate attempt to put something, anything, between her and Bobby.

Garrick was calling. She could hear his ringtone—*Thunderstruck* by AC/DC. Even as she made the dash for the other net, trying to keep ahead of Bobby, she wondered why the hell he was calling her when she needed him here. Now.

With a start, Savannah sat up in her bed and stared at her alarm clock.

2:12 AM

Flopping onto her side, she groped for her phone and managed to hit ANSWER a moment before the last notes of AC/DC's classic arena jam played out and voicemail took over.

"Hello?" She sounded drunk and tired.

"Hi." He sounded good. Way too good. But tired.

"You okay?"

"Yeah. Just..."

He didn't finish the sentence. Didn't have to.

"Me too. I sent out my résumé today."

"Good."

Perversely, it irritated her that he was so fine with that.

"I hate it," he said after a while, "but I'm glad you did it. You need to get out if this happens."

"When, Garrick. Not *if*. I hate to say it—"

"I know. I'll be gone too. Done with hockey."

He said it calmly, but she knew. For her it was a job change, for him the end of a career.

"You should start your own business. Consulting or something." She rolled onto her back and stared up at her ceiling.

"Yeah?" He sounded less than convinced.

"I'm serious, Garrick. The business plan was great. I had no idea that profits could be invested outside the sport and all that stuff about capital and whatever. You know what you're doing."

Silence stretched on long enough that she wondered if they'd been disconnected.

"Thanks." His voice was a deep rumble down the phone line.

"You're welcome."

"I wish I could fix this," he said.

"No brilliant ideas on that?"

"Sure. I got one. Know anyone who wants to buy a hockey team?"

She sighed. "Would it do any good?"

"Actually, it might." Garrick told her about his phone call with Reese. It wasn't really much of a hope, but it was something. Then he filled her in on the conversation with his friend Jack. Goosebumps sprung up over her arms and neck.

"That's really bad," she said quietly.

"Yeah. It really is."

The next day Savannah sat at the desk in her office and stared at the wall.

Did she know anyone who wanted to buy a hockey team?

No. Maybe. She sighed. Probably not. It was a long shot.

She closed her eyes and plunked her elbow on the desk, her forehead in her palm. She pictured Garrick out on the ice. Sitting in her hot tub. Walking her to her car. She remembered how Alexei and Mike had teased her about the little index card fitness plans she liked to hand out. She was sure she'd spotted an NHL scout at last night's game, taking notes and pictures every time Rhian was on the ice.

She had to at least try.

Picking up her phone, she hit the speed dial on the first of two phone calls she needed to make.

Hours later Savannah was puttering around her office, cleaning up the usual mountain of post-game detritus. She grimaced when Bobby stalked into the room.

Her last appointment of the day. To say she hoped it would be quick and painless was a gross understatement. He caught her gaze with his beady-eyed stare. She had to fight back a shiver.

She'd noticed during his pre-game visit that his usual anger had been replaced with a smug satisfaction that made her want to slap his face. And leave town.

Forcing herself to remain professional, she rolled the wheelie cart loaded with tape, bandages, and various scissors to her table. She turned to Bobby and braced herself, stifling a growl when she saw her chair sat empty. As usual, he stood with his hips against her table, arms crossed, and stared down at her.

Ignore him. Ignore him. Ignore him.

Savannah shoved her scissors in her back pocket and went to work on his elbow. Or at least she tried. He kept his arms tight to his chest, refusing to move his limbs until she was forced to tug them apart and repeatedly reposition them.

It was ridiculous. So fucking stupid she actually smiled. Bobby Kramer was a fucking baby.

"What's so funny?" he asked softly.

She probably should have been concerned by his silky tone, so uncharacteristic, but she was too fed up to care.

"Nothing." She put his arm where she needed it and grabbed her scissors, seriously considering cutting through perfectly good and reusable bindings to speed the process of removing them.

"You're going to learn to respect your betters, Savannah Morrison."

"Hunh," she snorted. She sure didn't see any *betters* right now.

She refused to back away when he leaned into her, his breath hot on the side of her face.

"I'm going to own you. I'm going to own this whole fucking team. You'll come around when you see what I have to offer. What I can take away. Like your job, your reputation. You'll never work in hockey again."

Savannah kept working, even as her blood boiled. She ripped off the last piece of tape, leaning to the side to give herself some space while she tossed it into the trash. Relief flooded her when she saw Mike Erdo in the hallway. His back was to the door, but he was well within shouting distance.

Standing straight, she forced Bobby to back off and stared him right in the eyes. "You're a bully, Bobby. Nothing but a stupid grinder. And I would no more work for losers like you and your father than I would sell myself on a street corner."

Bobby's eyes bulged, his face flushing scarlet.

"Now," she continued, "shut the fuck up and stand there while I finish." She didn't try to disguise her sneer as she looked him over. "You'll never get anything from me, Bobby Kramer. Not. A. Damn. Thing. And you sure as hell don't have *anything* I'm ever going to want."

Bobby's complexion took on shades of purple.

If she'd had any idea how satisfying it would be to tell Bobby to fuck off, she would have done it long before now. The look on his face was priceless. She wished she had phone so she could snap a picture to show Garrick.

She didn't see Bobby's hand come up until it grasped the front of her pullover, fisting in the soft fleece and the sports bra beneath.

She yelped when he yanked her close, his face almost touching hers. "I got something you want. I got it right here."

Bobby had her feet almost off the floor. The strength of his grip tightened her sports bra until it cut into her skin. She sucked air into her lungs to scream and dug her fingernails into Bobby's hand, desperately battling him and her fear.

What little air she'd managed to gather left her in a *whoosh* when he shoved her away and she crashed into her supplies, barely keeping herself and the cart upright. Bobby reached down and her eyes followed, widening with horror.

"This is for you, sweetheart." He shoved his shorts to his thighs and fisted his limp dick, stroking it slowly. She shuddered with revulsion, unable to look away from his hairy groin or his ham-sized hand choking his cock into a response.

Something in her *snapped*.

"That's for me?" Cocking her head, she pretending to stare her fill. She'd have to find a way to bleach her eyeballs later. "Well, then it turns out I *do* have something for you." With the confidence of long practice, she grabbed a roll of tape from the cart behind her.

Then she tore a long strip free and lobbed the heavy roll at Bobby's face.

He caught it automatically, the reflex to protect his face leaving him vulnerable to attack elsewhere. Lunging, she slammed the strip of duct tape across his semi-erect cock and pinned it to one of his big, hairy thighs, shoving the adhesive against the thick thatch of groin hair.

Bobby bellowed, dropping the roll of tape and grabbing at his junk. His fingers pressed the tape around his shaft, catching in the adhesive and yanking the sensitive hairs.

"I'm going to fucking kill you, bitch! Do you hear me!? FUCKING KILL YOU!" His cry echoed off the cinderblock walls.

Footsteps rushed toward them. Mike shouted her name as he barreled into her office. Someone else called for Mark down the corridor.

There'd be a circus in her office within seconds. An entire hockey team and countless staff to witness Bobby's predicament. To see the evidence of her complete loss of professionalism and control.

Oh Jesus, what have I done?

Though it was way too late, adrenaline and embarrassment struck in force. She'd done the unthinkable. She'd made a scene. She'd assaulted a player on her team, and regardless of how richly he'd deserved it, now there'd be questions. Now everyone would know she couldn't handle herself with a shithead like Bobby.

In less than ten minutes, the entire arena would know she'd lost her fucking mind. As it was, they could probably hear Bobby screaming that he was going to end her life with his bare hands.

Dodging Mike, she snatched her bag and coat off her desk and ran.

Garrick sat at the computer in his study, his eyes gritty with exhaustion from staring at reports, analysis, news pieces, and any other data points he could find about well-run, profitable sports teams. He put down the white paper he was working through when he heard the crunch of driveway gravel in front of his house.

He checked the clock. 1:17 AM.

He'd only been home for a half hour, having dashed out of the arena after the game to meet up with Melissa DuPont, another childhood friend who worked for the Kramers.

Another unofficial conversation and the picture was bleaker than ever. Garrick was walking a careful line between collecting information and putting his friends, people he cared about, at risk. What had seemed a vague threat at first now felt like imminent danger. The Kramers, the apparent captains of all underground industry in the area, had interests to protect.

The question was how great a threat they would perceive Garrick to be. He had no idea what he was going to do with what he'd learned, especially since he couldn't tell anyone how he'd gotten it.

He went to the window and saw the sweep of headlights across his barn. When the sound of the idling engine didn't change, when there was no car door opening or closing, he went to investigate.

He didn't get lost travelers or drunken drop-bys out here at his farmhouse, being a solid ten miles outside the Moncton city limits and in the dead middle of farm country.

He flipped on lights as he moved through the house, hesitating when he got to the front hall. For the first time in his life, a frisson of fear rushed through him when he thought about opening his door.

Another reason to hate the Kramers.

He pulled aside the sheer curtain over the front door window and considered rubbing his eyes, convinced he was imagining things.

Savannah.

Something is wrong.

He threw the door open, cursing himself for not listening to the voicemails Rhian and Alexei had left earlier. He'd assumed they were telling him where to find them if he wanted to celebrate their win. He should have known something was up after Rhian called a third time.

Savannah sat in her car and stared at the steering wheel, not even glancing at him as he leaped down his front porch stairs and ran the length of his front walk.

She yelped when he wrenched her door open. Her unblinking gaze and pale face brought him up short. She was frightened. He knelt by her open door, ignoring the bite of driveway gravel digging into his knees.

"Are you okay?" he asked gently.

She didn't answer. He reached out to touch her face, alarmed by the tear stains reflecting the dim blue light of the dashboard dials. When she flinched away, he let his hand drop and rested it on her leg.

She looked back at her steering wheel. "I'm in big trouble."

She was still wearing her game clothes. Had she come straight from the arena? She should have left hours ago. His need for answers nearly choked him but he stomped on it. He'd get there, but first he needed her to turn off the car and come inside.

"You're not in trouble with me."

"Is Melissa still here?"

He blinked, surprised. "She was never here."

Confusion clouded her expression. "I drove around for a while." She glanced at him. "I didn't want to interrupt..."

Garrick's alarm grew. "You've been driving around since the game?"

"I was afraid to go home. There's been this car. A big SUV, sometimes, at night."

Fear churned in his gut. He forced himself not to shake answers from her. "You can always come here."

Some day he'd even ask how she knew his address.

"I heard you tell Rhian you were meeting Melissa. Am I interrupting?"

A piece of the puzzle fell into place.

"Melissa is an old friend who I met for a late supper so we could talk about the Kramers."

The relief she failed to hide was a bright spot in a long and increasingly stressful evening.

He wanted to tell her there wasn't another woman in his life. Hell, he hadn't given any other woman more than a passing thought since he'd met her. Hadn't even managed the passing thoughts since he'd been with Savannah on Cape Breton Island. Now didn't seem like the time.

"It wasn't a date. I'm trying to find as much dirt as I can on the Kramers."

Savannah cocked her head at him. "Why?"

He sighed. "Damned if I know. I guess I'm hoping I can prove they're running a sports book and that Bobby is messing with the games. Maybe I can get the league to block the deal."

He shrugged. His half-baked plan sounded stupid out loud.

"Can I help?" she asked.

"Sure. I learned a lot from Melissa tonight. You want to come in for some coffee and I'll tell you what I know?"

He let go a deep breath of relief when she shut off the engine and pulled the key from the ignition.

He helped her out of the car and kept hold of her hand as he towed her up the porch steps and to the front door. She looked around. He smiled when she shifted her weight back and forth and made the porch plank creak.

"It was built in 1859," he said.

She nodded and followed him through the front door. A rush of satisfaction surged through him when her eyes widened upon seeing the restored foyer and staircase. "It's in wonderful shape."

"Thanks."

"You did it?"

"Sure. I had to have something to do on the off season aside from work Dad's farm and babysit my sister's kids."

"It's lovely. I like how you didn't change things."

He laughed. "I tried to stick to the classic design, though sometimes I wonder why." He made a show of having to hang her coat sideway and wrestle the tiny front hall closet's door shut. "Come on back. I'll make some coffee and you can be suitably appalled at how updated the kitchen is."

His spine tingled in response to her husky laugh as she trailed behind him through the dining room and into the kitchen. She ran her hand over the green granite counter tops before reaching up to touch the glass-front cabinet.

Then she looked at him as if she'd never seen him before. He stood still under her regard. He hoped she'd been expecting a bachelor pad condo and found the antique farmhouse more to her liking.

Her green eyes glowed and the warmth of the house was returning the pink to her cheeks. His arms twitched with the need to hold her.

"Here, I'll get that coffee." He turned to the kettle.

A hand on his back stilled him. "No."

He turned back to her. "You don't want coffee? I have tea or hot cocoa, if you'd rather."

She stepped closer and dragged the thick elastic from her hair, letting it cascade down over her shoulders. "No, thank you."

His pulse sped up and his jeans got considerably tighter.

He gulped. "What *do* you want?"

"You."

Chapter Fifteen

Garrick's eyes darkened to chocolate. Savannah loved how honest he was with his reactions. It was exactly what he demanded from her. She understood why now.

He never hid anything, was never ashamed of the truth.

God, she wanted to rip his clothes off.

Before she could do just that, he was there, yanking her up against him as his mouth locked on hers.

Her tongue met his as he thrust between her lips. Her moan echoed his as his large hand on her ass brought her belly against the hard ridge under his fly. She ground against him, desperate for his touch. His taste.

For the first time in hours, she forgot the feeling of Bobby's hand on her chest, the sight of his flaccid cock. Now, at last, she felt clean. Whole. *Normal.*

She wrapped her arms around Garrick's neck and held on for dear life. Her fingers burrowed through his thick hair as she kissed him back, trying to communicate her relief, her passion.

The world tilted and she tore her lips from his with an undignified squeak. She was cradled against his chest and he was already charging through the dining room and mounting the stairs.

She briefly considered insisting he not carry her. His bad hip, his pulled groin—she was an athletic five feet ten inches...*ah, fuck it*. Who was she kidding? She was enjoying the hell out of it.

He practically ran the length of the upstairs hallway. Through a door at the front of the house they entered a large master bedroom and sitting area. She glimpsed an en suite bathroom the size of her apartment, before he tossed her onto the huge four-poster bed.

Garrick shucked his shirt and reached for the button on his

jeans before she'd finished bouncing.

She smiled. Excellent. They were on the same page.

She couldn't get out of her pullover fast enough. The sports bra followed, and her sneakers sailed through the air as she toed them off. She never wanted to wear the things Bobby had touched again. She might just burn them in the large fireplace she'd seen from the foyer if Garrick would lend her a shirt to get home.

Bare from the waist up, she looked up at Garrick standing beside the bed, stark naked.

God, he was gorgeous.

He clamped a hand around her ankle and dragged her to the edge of the bed. Her heart knocked against her ribs and her body swelled with anticipation. She flat-out loved it when he took charge.

She thought he might try to rip her pants off, but he ignored them. Instead, he bent down to nestle his face into the crook of her neck and shoulder. His lips caressed her skin when he spoke.

"You're beautiful."

She smiled. "We're not going to go through that again, are we?"

He laughed, and she squirmed when he skimmed his tongue over her shoulder. "We will if you don't believe me."

He cupped her breast and flicked his thumb across her nipple.

"I believe I can be completely uninhibited with you," she said. "That I don't have to hold anything back."

He grumbled against her collar bone. "You better not."

"Oh, god," she moaned as he sucked the tender spots on her neck. "I can't hold back. I don't want to."

His lips curved against her skin as he continued to torment her. Her head fell back to give him as much access as he wanted. She blissed out on the clean and powerful sensations coursing through her.

Garrick worked his way along her skin with his mouth, his lips, then teased down over her chest and lingered on one nipple. He tortured it until she cried out, the sensitive bud hardened to the point of pain. She squirmed, telling him with wordless moans and frantic movements that she was ready for more. Ready for anything.

Arching her back and forcing her breast up into the wet heat of his mouth drew a grumble of pleasure from Garrick, but nothing seemed able to make him hurry. She reached for his cock, sliding her hand under his body, but he danced his hips away. When he moved onto the other nipple and showered it with the same exquisite attention, she gave up, threaded her fingers through his hair, and just held on.

The tug of his lips drew a line from nipple to clit. His hand on her hip stilled her thrashing and she groaned. God, he was killing her.

He left her breasts with a tender kiss to each tip before embarking on a slow exploration of her ribs. Her navel. Her tummy.

Each touch of his mouth warmed her, his departure leaving a cool bloom of pleasure when the air reached it. Every brush of his fingers sent beautiful licks of desire along her skin.

One large hand slid beneath her, and with a tug, her yoga pants and panties were peeled away. She'd been ready to divest herself of the damn things the moment she'd hit the bed, but somehow he'd lulled her. Now she waited, content to let him lead at whatever pace. Patience had already proven to have its own reward.

For the first time since his lips had brushed her neck, he left her. Cold air tickled her skin. She opened her eyes to find Garrick staring down at her.

He took his time with this, too, and she let him. A flash of shyness nipped at her as she lay exposed on the bed in the bright light of the bedside lamp, but she fought it back. A woman would have to be blind and crazy not to appreciate the look in his eyes as they traveled the length of her.

She felt beautiful.

He had convinced her after all.

He focused on his hands as he cupped her feet, slid his palms over her ankles and calves and up the outsides of her legs, seemingly determined to touch every inch of her. For one glorious moment, he hesitated, bringing his face close and inhaling deeply as his fingers hovered on her hips. She thought he might stop to taste her. The shine on her thighs and curls made her need obvious. She groaned with resigned delight when he slipped by, his chin barely brushing her hip before he buried his nose in the dip of her waist.

He stroked her flanks, gentling her, while his lips trailed over skin she'd had no idea could be so highly erogenous. Her ribs, the inside of her elbow, the side of her breast. He brushed his face against her in a thousand places, rolling her, urging her to lift her hands over her head and let him have his way.

Everything melted away. Every worry about what was to come of her altercation with Bobby. Every concern she'd ever had about being intimate with a player on her team. Every insecure thought she'd ever had about her sexual desires, her sexual demands. None of it mattered. There was only here. Now.

She gave herself over to Garrick. Wholeheartedly.

Savannah wasn't sure how long she hung suspended in the web of arousal Garrick wove. She felt flushed and swollen all over. Her thighs were slick, her nipples hard peaks stabbing the cold air. She let him move her however he wished, acquiescing to his gentle demands—a touch to her thigh, a tap on her hip.

His hot tongue traced a line from her navel south, and she moaned, long and low, the needy sound cut off by a desperate whimper when he pushed her legs apart, lifting her knees and spreading her open to him.

She came almost the moment his tongue flicked across her clit, thrust from languid satisfaction to pulsing ecstasy in the blink of an eye. Fisting her hands in the sheets, she arched her back and yelled his name.

"Garrick!"

Waves of pleasure crashed over her, having hovered on her shore for so long, now unleashed in a relentless tide. She writhed and he took her higher, his tongue unyielding as it worked the hood, the bundle of nerves beneath.

She plunged back to earth with a gasp when he drove two thick fingers deep into her pussy. Her body vibrating, she joyously relinquished the peak to start the climb once more.

She panted, overwhelmed. She could do nothing but thrust against his tongue and hand. She held her legs higher so he could reach anything and everything he wanted. Everything *she* wanted.

He must have understood, sensed her plea, as soon the rough pad of one finger traced over the tightly clenched muscles of her anus. Too quickly it was gone.

She whimpered shamelessly, trying to find the words to encourage him but too incoherent and inexperienced to know what to ask. She'd always been curious but had never dared. If she'd been too loud, too out of control with plain old missionary sex, what would happen if her fantasies came true and she got to experience things she'd only dreamed about?

But Garrick wouldn't mind. Hell, he'd love it if she lost her mind at his hand. His mouth on her clit, his fingers in her pussy—it was all good. But she wanted *more*, and here with Garrick, it was safe to have it.

The finger returned, brushing over the tight knot of muscles. She jolted at its stroke, even as she hummed her approval. Her mind swirled, confused by the cold licking at her skin, then it clicked. *Lube.*

Around and around, the cool touch edged her hole—her focus, her desire, so singular that she hardly noticed his continued efforts elsewhere. She wanted to ask him what she should do, what he needed from her, but he stopped again.

She groaned with frustration, the sound cut short with a hiccup of shock and pleasure when the pressure returned, firmer this time, a fresh chill to his touch as his finger slowly eased into her body.

"Oh my god!" she cried.

He immediately stopped.

"No! Keep going. God, don't stop." He pushed harder, stretching and filling her, and she sobbed out her pleasure. "God, Garrick. Yes. Yes, please!"

Garrick was close to shooting his load from no more than the uncontrollable twitch of his hips. His cock brushing nothing but air as he stood between Savannah's splayed thighs at the side of his bed.

He'd asked for uninhibited. Begged for it. But the reality of Savannah coming unhinged nearly buckled his knees.

Sucking in desperately needed oxygen, he gathered what little control he had left and slid his finger high into her ass. She bucked against him.

"More!"

God, she was perfect.

He thrust his fingers in her pussy and dragged the finger in her ass back out slowly. Soon his hands were in sync, working in tandem, finding a rhythm in spite of the irregular jerk of her hips.

He moved faster, fucked her harder, and sucked her clit into his mouth. She growled and fisted her hand in his hair hard enough to make his eyes water.

He wanted to howl with joy and pent-up desire.

"Garrick! Yes, god, Garrick! It's too much! Please, just... *please!*"

She was gorgeous, her eyes sightless while her body thrashed around on his bed. With a keening cry, she screwed her eyes shut and came, her back arching high off the bed.

"Garrick!"

It had become his life's mission to hear her scream his

name.

He sucked her clit harder, forced his fingers higher and marveled at the tight clench of muscles clamping down on him. He was light-headed with his need. He had to fuck her. *Now.*

He slid his fingers from her body and eased her back down onto the bed. A final nip to her clit made her entire body jerk. He was so lightheaded with need he almost dumped his bedside drawer onto the floor before he tossed its contents onto the bed beside them.

He tore a foil packet open with his teeth and cursed his shaking hands. The latex was barely rolled into place before he crawled over Savannah's limp body and looked down into her face.

She opened her eyes, her green gaze vague, her little smile deeply satisfied. Deeply satisfying. He watched her face carefully as he slowly eased his aching cock into her tight, hot pussy.

Relief and desire roared through him. Her mouth opened in a perfect "oh" as he slid home. Arms trembling, he held himself above her, perfectly still, and tried to give her time to adjust to his size. In truth, he needed that moment to grapple with the onslaught of sensations.

She undulated beneath him, wrapped her knees around his hips, and let him notch that last magical centimeter deeper into her body.

He shuddered, fighting for control, certain he was going to lose it as she drew him in for a scorching kiss. He wasn't sure when he started to move, his nervous system overrun as Savannah thrust her tongue in his mouth. She pulled him closer until his chest pressed to hers and they touched everywhere, not a sliver of light or space between them. His hips rocked against hers. Her hips rolled up to meet his.

He wanted to have a long, slow, hot fuck with Savannah. Someday. This wasn't going to be it.

He slid his hand down her side, cupped her ass in his hand and forced it up against him as he ground down into her. His face buried against her silky hair and soft skin, the last of his control slipped from his grasp.

Within two thrusts, he was snapping his hips with more force and speed than finesse, pounding her into the mattress. His pelvic bone shoved against her clit with every push. Her legs refused to allow a full retreat, but gave him enough room to run the length of his cock along her gripping walls.

His balls tightened, and the tingle at the base of his spine foretold the unavoidable conclusion. The masochist and the hedonist wanted it to go on forever. The realist thought if he didn't come soon, he'd have a stroke.

He used the last of his strength to throw his hips forward harder, and nudged the end of her passage. She made a startled sound and her limbs convulsed around him.

"Oh my god! Again!" she gasped.

The clamp of muscles dragging over his cock undid him. With an incoherent shout, he buried himself in her heat and the lightening unleashed, rising up out of his balls and storming his entire body with every racking pulse. His eyes slammed shut and stars danced behind his lids. His body shook as the clench of Savannah's muscles urged him to give until he was breathless from the pleasure.

With a shuddering sigh, he collapsed on top of Savannah, hardly having the wherewithal to hold his weight on his elbows as he gasped for air and groped for his sanity.

He finally registered that he was still attached to the earth, his only anchor the long, slow glide of Savannah's hand on his back.

"You okay?"

He laughed. "Yeah." He lifted his head and looked down at her. "You?"

Her slow smile would have been answer enough. "Oh. Yes."

With regret, he shifted, easing back as his cock softened enough to require he deal with the condom. Her face showed no sign of pain, only keen disappointment as he slipped from her body.

"I'll go take care of this and get something to clean us up."

She smiled and nodded, already crawling beneath the sheets.

He came back to find her sitting with one of several objects he'd dumped out of his bedside table resting in her palm. He stopped in the door and watched for her reaction.

He was relieved to see only curiosity.

"Is this what I think it is?"

He shrugged and moved over to the bed. "It depends on what you think it is, I suppose." He tugged down the covers and urged her to lie back on the pillows.

She didn't say anything as he wiped down her mons, her thighs, spreading her legs to wash away her arousal with a warm washcloth. He tapped her side, indicating she should roll away from him, and she looked at him curiously again before doing as he asked.

She jumped when he used one hand to spread her cheeks and gently wiped away the lube coating her anus.

"It's a butt plug, isn't it?"

He couldn't see her face, which, he suspected, was why she'd chosen that moment to ask. It put him at a distinct disadvantage, though, and he was unwilling to take any chances. He tossed the washcloth into the hamper by the bathroom door and rolled her back toward him.

"Yes, it is."

She bit her lip while looking down at the little plug in her hand.

He smiled. "Would you like to try it?"

Chapter Sixteen

Savannah stared at the cone-shaped device, shivering as Garrick's question ran through her mind. *Did* she want to try it?

Yes.

Garrick climbed into the bed and lay down facing her, his elbow planted on the mattress, his hand holding up his chin. He hauled the covers up over them and she was momentarily distracted by the cocoon of warmth he'd created with comforter and quilts and the heat from their still flushed bodies.

"You don't have to answer now." He reached for the plug.

She held it away from him. "No, I want..."

He kicked up one sexy eyebrow when she stumbled to a halt. Crap, what *did* she want?

She gnawed on her lip. "I've never really done any of this before," she blurted out.

His slow smile went a long way toward making her feel less stupid. "You mean anal play? Anal sex?"

She shrugged. "Anal anything," she admitted. "Until you...I mean, until just now, I'd never..." *God, Savannah, spit it out.* "I don't think I realized it would feel like that. I was curious, but always figured it was more for the giver than the receiver. Now I know...*wow* on the receiving part."

His soft chuckle tickled her ear, the glint in his smiling eyes mesmerizing. "I remember what that was like. Learning there was a whole set of sensations no one ever told me about."

She smiled back, curiosity nipping at her. "Well, how old were you when that happened? Because at twenty-eight, I'm feeling pretty lame." And how had Garrick discovered this new pleasure?

Garrick lifted his eyes to the ceiling. She was about to ask what was bothering him when he turned back to her, searching her face.

"I trust you." He said it softly, as if he were speaking to himself rather than her.

She brushed her fingers down his cheek. "You can tell me anything."

He nodded. "I met David in college. I was nineteen."

She failed to mask her surprise and her eyes went wide before she could get herself back under control.

"David?" she said, breathless even to her own ears.

His gaze narrowed and a hint of color bloomed in his cheeks. "Shit. Forget I mentioned it. Please."

He started to roll away from her but she stopped him with a tight grip around his arm.

"*No way*," she said.

He tried to tug his arm free but she held firm.

"No way?"

"Yeah, no fucking way you get to drop that bomb and not give me all the details."

He looked decidedly confused. "What?"

"Are you gay?"

Both his eyebrows up. "Do *you* think I'm gay?"

She grinned. "Hell no."

His lips quivered, a smile almost escaping.

"Okay, it was a dumb question," she said. "Bi?"

"Technically?" He shrugged. "I guess. Though what you need to know is that I'm monogamous. Always."

It was her turn to lift a skeptical brow or two. And not just because he thought she needed to know he was willing to commit. That wasn't where this relationship was going. After tonight, there *was* no relationship and the only place she'd be going was *away*.

"Yes, contrary to my legendary and total pain-in-the-ass reputation," he continued, dragging her thoughts back to their intriguing conversation and away from her disastrous career move earlier that evening, "I'm not a dog, and I only date one person at a time."

"One person?"

"One *woman* at a time, for the last decade or so." He shrugged. "This is Moncton. I'm a local, a recognizable face and a professional hockey player. My love life has spent enough time in the paper and on the news. I haven't touched a man since I left McGill and the relative anonymity of college life and Montreal."

"But—"

"It's fine. The nice thing about being truly bi is that I enjoy men and women equally. I haven't suffered, languishing in the closet for all these years," he said with a laugh. "You know, at least *some* of my reputation was earned."

"You mean the part where you're supposed to be a titan in bed?"

"What do you think?"

"All true." She kept a straight face until he tickled her ribs, making her laugh. She fell into him before squirming away from his tormenting fingers.

"It is true," he assured her.

Flopping onto her back, she looked up into his face. She still clutched a butt plug in her hand.

"I do want to try it," she said quietly.

He stilled. "Yeah?"

"Yes, but on two conditions."

He nodded.

She gathered her courage, reminding herself she was allowed to ask for anything she wanted with Garrick. He wouldn't make fun of her. The worst he could do was say no.

"I want you to do it too."

"Do what?"

She drew her arm from under the covers and brought the

plug back into view.

"Oh."

"Do you have another?" she asked.

"I do."

"Well?"

"Okay. Condition one can be met," he agreed slowly. "What's the second condition?"

She took a deep breath. "I want you to tell me about what you've done."

"What I've done?"

"With David. With other men."

His brows drew low over his eyes. "Why?"

"Because it's hotter than hell." She reached for his hand and drew it under the covers and over her belly. "Ever since you said you knew what these nerve endings were all about from personal experience, I've been trying not to roll over and beg you to have your way with me." She dipped his fingers between her legs and dragged them through her swollen folds and the pool of thick cream.

"Jesus," he murmured.

"Unless that's the name of one of the men you've been with, leave him out of this." She gasped as his fingers flexed and the rough pad of one finger flicked over her clit. "Just start talking."

Garrick stared down at Savannah and tried to pry his tongue from the roof of his mouth.

The old adage about being careful what you wished for ran through his head. He'd insisted, no, *demanded* she be herself with him. Always. He'd just never imagined that prim, buttoned-down, straight-laced Savannah Morrison was a kinky seductress who'd been sent to this earth to rock his world.

Holy fuck.

With a shake, he tore loose from his paralysis and did the

first thing that came to mind. He kissed Savannah as if his life depended on it.

She met his tongue with equal aggression, her moans loud. Her body arching to press the plug still resting on her sternum up into his chest reminded him of the promises he'd just made. Of his confession, the details of which he was now going to share. He never spoke of David to anyone, hadn't in years, but somehow it was all rushing back. Savannah made it easy. Safe. Fun. *Hot.*

With a shudder, he broke free from their kiss and let himself drown in her sultry gaze.

"You're sure you want to do this?"

She spread her legs wider and used her grip on his wrist to thrust his fingers farther along her wet slit. "Do I feel like I'm not sure?"

He smiled and swallowed hard.

"David was the first," he said slowly, trying desperately to order his thoughts while he flicked his fingers along her swollen labia and over her clit. He enjoyed her rapt attention even as her body twitched and writhed.

She didn't say anything. Didn't ask questions, just let him decide where to take them.

He told her how they met, how he'd been so shocked to find himself attracted to another man. She never looked away from him as he spun the tale, even when he rolled away to yank open the second bedside table drawer and retrieve a packet of wipes and another, slightly larger and differently shaped plug.

He paused in his story when she gave it a curious look, switching from his history to her education. He wanted this to be good for her, and a little information could go a long way toward safety and confidence.

"Men have a gland in them," he said, pointing at the curve in the larger butt plug, "and if I put this in right, it will hit that gland."

"That's good?" she asked.

"Very good."

"Will you put it in yourself?"

He watched her closely. "If you want, I can coach you through it, but you have to be careful."

She shivered. "I want to see you put it in yourself." Her whisper was rough.

Now *he* was shivering. *Shit.* She was going to make him come just telling him all her wonderful dirty thoughts and wishes.

Clamping down on his spiraling need, he sucked in a deep breath before continuing. "Yours," he said, pointing to the plug still on her chest, "is a classic design. The widest part will stretch you as open as you'd have to be to take my cock."

She hummed quietly and he reached down to give his balls a tug. She was killing him.

"We'll push past that until your muscles lock the cone in your body, and the anchor" —he pointed to the long narrow foot— "will make sure it doesn't get pulled all the way in."

Her eyes widened and he lifted his plug to distract her. "Mine has the same thing, see?"

She nodded and he waited while she looked her fill. Soon her eyes flicked away from his plug and up to his face. "How long were you and David friends before something happened?"

"Not long. I wanted him right away." He reached for the lube and popped the cap, taking her return to the story to mean she was ready to proceed. He searched her face for any sign of concern or resistance. "We were out one night, a little drunk, riding the high of nerves and flirtation that I wasn't sure was real or imagined, and we stumbled back to my dorm room to discover my roommate wasn't there."

He smiled at the memory as he lowered himself to lie on his side facing her. "As soon as the door shut behind us, I felt like my feet were nailed to the floor. The look in his eyes..."

Savannah's eyes traced his neck and shoulders where

goosebumps rose on his skin. He squeezed lube on his finger and continued. "I don't remember if he said a word. I just remember watching him come toward me, seeing his hand come up to touch my face, and I thought I was going to either pass out or vomit. Eventually, I started breathing again, which helped, until he kissed me. Then I was sure I was going to pass out from the blood rushing to my dick that fast."

He laughed as he ran his hand over his hip, the covers shifting with his arm. Savannah's gaze followed the movement, narrowing before she sat up and tossed the bedding to the footboard.

"I want to see," she said.

For the first time in longer than he could remember, Garrick found himself a little embarrassed in a sexual situation. Not even when he'd come in his pants with David that first time had he felt this unsure.

"I, uh..."

Savannah leaned in and kissed him, running her hand over his arm. Encouraging him to go on. With a sigh, he slid his finger down his crack and traced the lube over his hole.

She switched to nibbling along his neck and out to his shoulder. He opened his eyes, not at all surprised to find hers already open and fixed on his ass. He took a deep breath before wriggling the tip of his finger inside his body.

"Was that the night you discovered anal sex?"

He laughed. "No. God, we were so young, we ended up slammed against the wall, humping each other like the couple of teenagers we were."

She smiled. He worked his finger against the tight muscles, his body responding eagerly to his own caress. Shit, he'd done this recently enough that it wouldn't take much to get him there.

"So when did you learn?"

"Soon after that," he said with a chuckle, easing his finger free to add more lube, then thrusting it deep. He heard her whimper when he added a second finger. God, if she thought it *looked* good, what was she going to do when she felt it?

The image that popped into his mind was so enchanting he had to shake his head to dislodge it. He returned to his story.

"David was more experienced. He'd had an older boyfriend in high school. Taught him what no Sex Ed teacher had ever dared to mention."

"Such as?"

"That you have to stretch the muscles, soften them to prepare for penetration," he said through clenched teeth as he spread his fingers, his belly clenching at the hint of pain and the flood of pleasure. "If you don't, you can get hurt."

She looked away from his hand to meet his gaze. "I've heard it can hurt."

"It can, but not if you do it right. The problem is that people aren't patient." Even as he said it, his own patience reached its limit and he drew his fingers from the heat of his ass and picked up the plug. "It will take longer for you. I'm more..."

She smiled at his hesitation. "Ready?"

"God," he groaned, his hands shaking as he coated the plug with lubricant. She watched him carefully. "I can't honestly believe I'm about to do this."

Her eyebrows winged up. "You've never done this?"

"Not with an audience. Not while telling said audience about an ex-boyfriend." He brought the plug behind him and took a couple deep breaths through his nose before pressing the tip against his anus. "I've never actually told *any* woman I've dated about the boyfriends."

Savannah's startled gaze flicked to his face, but his expression must have told her what she was missing. She immediately looked away and watched in slack-jawed awe as he shoved the thick plug against his straining muscles.

The stretch turned to burn and he stopped, enjoying the high, his eyes closed against the well of pleasure. Hovering there, he felt the edge begin to dull. He gave the anchor another gentle nudge and eased the plug the rest of the way into his ass.

Oh shit, that was good. Grunting, he clamped down around the neck, the anchor doing its job, the kick of his hips bouncing the tip of the plug against his prostate gland. His breath left him in a hiss, and for a few seconds, all he could do was breathe and try to get himself back under control.

"God, that looks like it feels good," she murmured.

He opened his eyes, her flushed cheeks and swollen lips tempting him. "It does."

When she continued to stare at him, he smiled, and for a moment, she looked mildly alarmed. *Good.* Perhaps it was her turn to recall the old adage about being careful what you wish for.

He tipped her off her elbow and onto her back on the mattress. With a groan, he rolled to his knees between her spread legs and stared down at the bounty before him. Her thighs glistened, her labia flushed and swollen, legs parted to reveal all her secrets. Including the tight pucker of her ass, coated with her own juices.

Not that he'd rely on those. He grabbed the lube and plug and put them within reach. His every movement sent a shocking reminder of his own stretched ass roaring up his spine. The spacey high of arousal rang like a bell in his skull.

He tamped it back, forcing himself to focus. He had to get this right.

Savannah stared up at him, her face flushed, her hands fisted in the sheets. She looked ready. And nervous. He remembered what a heady combination that could be.

"It wasn't until about a month later that David and I really started to try some of this stuff," he said. "We'd frotted like dogs every chance we got, eventually getting to the real exploration with our mouths. Tongues."

Savannah bit her lip, her cheeks flushing pink. "Did you?"

"Did I what?" He carefully cleaned his hand and applied fresh lube.

156

"Did you suck his cock?"

The question made him pause, his balls drawing up tighter. God, this was hotter than he'd ever have imagined. "Yes."

"Did you like it?"

He looked at Savannah, emboldened by her unabashed arousal at his revelations. Her unequivocal acceptance. "Yes. I love it."

She smiled, almost shyly, if such a thing were possible at this point. "Me too."

Their gazes held and they had a moment of perfect communion. Never in his life did he think he'd bond with his girlfriend over *that.*

Chapter Seventeen

Savannah looked down her body at Garrick kneeling between her knees, his eyes laughing. They both liked to give head.

Life was strange and wonderful sometimes.

Maybe there was something wrong with her that she was so freaking turned on by the thought of Garrick with another man, but she didn't care. For one crazy, decadent, uninhibited night, she wanted to indulge in any damn fantasy that felt good for her and her lover.

Based on the steel pike waving at her from between Garrick's legs since he'd shoved that ginormous plug in his ass, he was enjoying the hell out of their evening too.

It was *all good*.

She wasn't even nervous about what was to come next. Well, that was what she was telling herself, even as her heart galloped in her chest. The expression on Garrick's face as he'd pushed his plug home had been pure agony and ecstasy all rolled into one. She was both terrified and desperate to experience it herself.

Garrick cleared his throat, dragging her attention away from his erection and the drop of pre-come she was dying to taste hovering there at the tip.

"David was the one that broached the subject first," he said, bringing them back to his story. His eyes dropped as she spread her legs wider.

"We were in his bed one night, me on top, frotting against him, our cocks sliding between our bellies and against each other now that we'd introduced lube to the equation." He smiled a little, flexing his broad shoulders. "Then his hands were on my ass, his fingers digging in and pulling the cheeks apart. I remember thinking, 'Where's his other hand?' and then I felt his finger pressing against my hole."

As he said it, she felt it too. Only it was Garrick's finger, also lubed up, pressing into her.

She bucked against him, gasping at the dark thrill. Before when he'd touched her like this, she'd been in the throes of passion, on the brink of orgasm. This time was more real—entirely about the wealth of sensations rolling up through her body from her clenching ass.

"He got one finger in me before I knew it and I stopped moving, trying to figure out what the fuck I thought of that."

She smiled slowly. He winked back.

"That night he gave me a blow job I will never forget, his finger high in my ass, thumping my prostate. I came so damn hard, I lost all sense for a few minutes."

She made a mental note. She wanted to recreate that for him. Soon. Just as soon as he stopped tormenting her ass. His finger felt thick. Wonderful. Then he started to move, thrusting it in and out of her. She could do nothing but roll her hips in counterpoint, trying to force him higher. She needed *more*.

"Before long, we were both working each other's asses any chance we got." His finger moved faster, twisting, the drag of his knuckles making her whimper. "First one finger, then two."

His second finger brushed along wildly sensitive skin and instinct made her clench.

Garrick didn't stop his gentle thrusts. His free hand came up and coaxed one of her legs up until her thigh almost touched her chest. She grabbed her knee, holding herself open when he let go.

The angle of his thrusts changed, sending new zings across her body. She watched, fascinated by the play of muscles under his skin, by his broad shoulders and brute masculinity as he loomed above her. He was an athlete. A thickly built hockey player. With a big plug in his ass. And loving it.

She had no idea why that was so fucking hot, but it was.

He took her hand and drew her arm above her head. "Hold onto the headboard. Relax. I'll tell you what's happening. What to do."

She nodded and gripped the thick wood above her head. Her other hand held her leg bent tight to her body. He twisted his finger on each thrust and retreat, pressing up and down, pressing everywhere. Her eyes fluttered closed and she sighed. *Bliss.*

The second finger slid in, thrust deep then held still. She moaned, her eyes screwed shut, her back arched, and she rode out the stretch. For a single second the burn was pain before it melted into something dark and hot. Something she'd never felt before but couldn't imagine living without.

Garrick was patient with her while she tried to collect herself, her breathing hectic, her eyes fluttering open long enough to see how carefully he watched her face. She tried to smile but thought maybe she'd failed when his brows drew together. *Shit, please don't let him stop.*

She let out a deep breath and forced her muscles to go lax, only then noticing her spine was arched above the bed, her back tight in response to his wicked gift. She settled back down onto the mattress and wriggled against his hand, pleading for more.

The still silence that followed was torture. The slow drag of his fingers as he pulled them from her body then sank them back in was heaven.

"David knew what he was doing. His hands were magic," Garrick continued, his voice deeper. His thrusts were gentle, even and relentless. She couldn't stop the sounds coming from deep in her chest.

"We didn't have any toys, didn't even know what a butt plug was," Garrick said with a laugh. "Hell, we were kids, working on mostly instinct and just barely enough information." He paused when he pushed particularly high into her body, spreading his fingers apart. The stretch was intense, coaxing desperate sounds from the back of her throat.

She floated there, not even aware if he was talking for a long time. Her body gave in to his encouragement, her muscles easing, opening to him. When he withdrew his fingers from her body, she was bereft.

"No!" she gasped.

"It took us a good two months to work up to it," Garrick said. "But eventually, I was begging him to fuck me. God, I wanted to know what that was like so damn bad."

She imagined a young Garrick pleading with his lover to fuck him in the ass and her little hole fluttered in sympathy. The quivering edged into a clench when the lube bottle brushed her cheek and coolness flooded her ass.

Something else new. She wondered if he would explain it. Then again, it seemed fairly self explanatory.

"He wouldn't do it until I could comfortably take three of his fingers," Garrick said as a new pressure bloomed against the ring of muscles guarding her ass. It was the plug. It felt huge.

Relax. Enjoy it.

If asked even two weeks ago if she could, she'd have said no way.

But it was easy.

"I started fingering myself before I'd see him, desperate to convince him I was ready."

He thrust harder and she groaned, burying her face against her arm. She didn't want him to stop. Not easing the plug into her or his story. The image of him fingering himself would be burned in her brain forever.

"Finally he couldn't hold back anymore."

Garrick pushed again, pumping the plug against her in gentle waves. The little shoves rocking her body on the bed soothed her. Her arm clamped on the headboard was a counter balance that allowed her to set the pressure. The pace.

He wasn't making progress nearly fast enough, to her mind, so she started pushing back.

"He made me get on all fours. The first time, it's better that way. The angle is better, especially if you're not both sure of what you're doing."

The image Garrick painted in her head made her pant—his ass tipped in the air, waiting for his lover.

"And then he worked and worked, until I was sure I was ready, and then he still worked me some more."

Savannah thought she might lose her mind. When she was sure the plug was going to go all the way in, that it couldn't possibly get any wider, it would stretch her tighter still and then Garrick would ease back.

"I was begging him, pleading with him to fuck me, sure I would blow the minute his thick cock slid home. Finally he knelt behind me and I felt the press of his cock and the cold lube."

Savannah's pussy clenched with need, her body aching with emptiness. Groaning, she used all the strength she had left and forced herself down on the plug. With a spine-arching zing, pain bloomed and the plug lodged farther into her, opening her. She hung there, her moan echoing in the room.

She never wanted it to end. So close. So big. Her hips twitched against the sensations and the plug slipped all the way into her body, her muscles clamping down around the neck.

For a long stunned moment she lay frozen, staring at the ceiling, the only sound her panting breaths.

"How's that feel?" Garrick asked in a low voice. His wide-eyed gaze was riveted to her ass.

She let go of the headboard and her leg and sat up. Her eyes bulged and she squeaked, her weight bearing down on the plug lodged even more deeply into her body.

"Easy, now." Garrick wrapped his hands around her upper arms. She wasn't sure if he was holding her still or holding her up.

"Oh, wow."

He chuckled. "Good, oh wow?"

"Uh yeah, oh wow. But I'm not sure I can move again. I feel

so...full. It's strange. Different."

"Good strange and different?"

"Fucking amazing strange and different."

He grinned before leaning in to capture her lips with his own. The kiss was slow, making her already spinning head feel like it was going to roll right off her shoulders.

He pulled back, kneeling before her, his knees wide, his ass not touching the bed.

"How do you keep your shit together, feeling like this?"

He groaned. "If you so much as breathed near my dick right now, I'd blow."

She laughed, stopping suddenly when her shaking body did fascinating and unspeakably erotic things with the plug jammed in ass.

She looked up at him, breathless. "Please."

Savannah probably didn't even knew what she was asking for, but Garrick had about a thousand ideas on how to give it to her.

His thighs shook when he tried to move across the bed and he stopped, planting his hand on the mattress. Head bowed, he tried to pull himself together.

Fuck, he was a mess. A big, happy, fucking mess.

Forcing himself to crawl to the head of the bed, he shoved pillows against the headboard, turned and eased himself down onto his ass. He fisted his cock brutally and squelched the overwhelming need to bounce on that fucking plug until he came. When he finally had his weight on the mattress, the plug forced high inside him, he released his stranglehold on his junk and opened his eyes.

Savannah's eyes sparkled with amusement.

"It's really not funny," he grumbled. Next time he'd let her fuck herself with the butt plug and then put one in him and see how she felt when it was over.

God, just the idea had him grabbing his package again, giving his sac a sharp tug.

She laughed. "Oh yes, it is. Look at us. When was the last time you had this much fun?"

"Never," he answered immediately.

Her smile faded a little. "Me either." She carefully got to her hands and knees and struggled toward him on shaky arms and legs. She stopped when her forehead was pressed to his. "Thank you."

"For what?" His eyes closed against the picture she made on all fours above him, her breath hot on his cheek.

"For trusting me. For being someone I can trust."

He smiled, nodding against her. There were few people on earth he had told about David. About who he really was. No matter how it turned out with Savannah in the long run, he would always be grateful for this and that she was one of them.

He pressed his lips to hers, pouring his emotion into the kiss, and hoped she understood.

She responded in kind, and the slow slide of tongues quickly turned frantic. If her body felt half the chaos his was battling, they were running out of time. Hands unsteady, he ripped open another condom packet and sheathed himself.

Wrapping a hand around her hip, he guided her over his legs to straddle him, their kiss never ending, not even easing up a little as she lowered herself and trapped his cock between them. Her pussy soaked his belly with her arousal.

He really, *really* wanted to hurry.

He fought that back. When she lifted herself away and wrapped her long, hot fingers around his cock, he grabbed her wrist.

"Go slow. You'll be tighter with the plug in."

She bit her lip, her brows drawn together, and nodded. Carefully, she lowered herself until his painfully sensitive head furrowed through her thick cream and lodged against the entrance to her body. With a whimper, she slid down the length of his shaft, taking him deep.

Fuck. She was tight, tighter than ever. The plug narrowed her channel down to an exquisite wet fist.

"Oh my god," she gasped.

He wanted to pound up into her but held himself in check. She had to set the pace, but he'd be damned if he didn't encourage her along.

Gently, he rubbed the pad of his thumb over her clitoris as the fingers of his other hand tapped her plug, nudging it into her body and against his cock.

"Oh shit!"

"Garrick!"

His bellow of surprise mingled with Savannah's cry. Head thrown back, her face a mask of ecstasy, her pussy clamped down on his cock as her orgasm roared through her. He fought hard to hold back, his hands clenched on her hips so tightly he feared he'd leave bruises, though Savannah didn't seem to know or care.

With a gasp, she jerked upwards then plunged, taking his cock into her unbearably tight body with a grunt, her weight forcing him down on the mattress and slamming his plug against his prostate. Then she lifted, his cock running the length of her clenching channel. Her narrowed eyes homed in on his face, and she took him deep again.

And again.

His hands on her hips guided her, urging her down on his cock over and over as he slammed up into her and she bottomed out and shoved him down onto his plug.

The tension in his balls was unbearable, the need for release painful, swelling, and huge, almost frightening in its intensity. He gasped her name, begging her for relief. Release.

Her hands fisted in his hair, her forehead pressed to his as she rode him hard, granting no mercy. He pulled her cheeks apart and shoved at her butt plug in time with their thrusts. Three hard jolts. She screamed, her back bowing, and fell onto him. Stars exploded in his head as his cock shoved deep into her body, clenched in her tight channel as she came. The plug in his ass jammed against his prostate so hard his vision grayed out.

His orgasm rolled up and over him, his voice hoarse as he cried out. Wave after wave boiled up and out of him. Their bodies rocked with the power of their release and forced the tip of his butt plug to rub over his prostate time and again, until he thought his climax might be endless, his sanity in question.

Savannah went completely lax in his arms and he barely had the wherewithal to catch her. They rolled together and collapsed on the heap of pillows beside them.

Neither moved for a long time, but the little smile on Savannah's face told him all he needed to know.

Chapter Eighteen

Savannah woke to see the sun bright behind the curtains in Garrick's room.

Shit. She panicked, sitting up and pulling away from the large warm body curled around her back. Then she remembered there was no game today. And while she should be at work, it wasn't as though she'd be particularly missed this morning. That was, if she still had a job.

Sighing, she snuggled back into Garrick's chest and tried to figure out what she was going to do.

She had enough pride and dignity left to go back to the arena and hold her head high. Not that she looked forward to being fired, but at least she would do it like a grownup with some ethics.

She cringed. *Ethics*? Duct taping the johnson of one of your players probably failed to meet the guidelines set out in the Athletic Trainers Code of Conduct.

"I can hear you thinking from here," Garrick said softly behind her. His hand stroked across her belly.

She sighed. It was past time for her to confess. She rolled to face him. He kept his arms around her.

"I'm probably going to get fired today."

He lifted a distinctly skeptical eyebrow. "You are?"

"Yeah. I am."

His skepticism was lost by the time she finished telling him about her incident with Bobby and the ensuing tape job. Now he looked positively murderous.

She didn't tell him that of all the possible fallout from her inevitable termination, what stung the most was she would have to leave Moncton and say goodbye to Garrick.

He lay beside her quietly, digesting her story, presumably unaware of how hard he was gripping her hip and shoulder.

She'd have fresh bruises to match the ones from last night.

She smiled. Remembered. Craved more. Good lord, she was sex-addled.

Oblivious to her rising arousal, he pursed his lips. "You really *are* god's gift to tape."

She laughed. "Yeah, that's my special talent."

"Not your only one," he said with a growly voice that made her want to pounce on him.

"Too bad duct taping dicks isn't a job qualification for a good sports trainer. There's no way Mark can ignore this."

"He sure as fuck can't. Bobby assaulted you last night!"

"Garrick, the only person who knows that for certain is me. It's he-said-she-said. And he's a player, with a contract, whose father is going to *buy* the team. I'm fucked."

"Don't say that."

"Mark has to fire me. Hell, I don't blame him. I'd fire me. And so would you."

"You might be surprised. Why don't you call Mark and ask?"

"Because I'm not a chicken."

"What?"

"Because I'm not a chicken. I'm not calling. I'm going to the arena and I'm going to face it head on."

He nodded and rolled out of bed. "Let's go, then."

He stalked into the bathroom, naked and perfect and not one bit shy about it. As mornings went, the view was unsurpassed. Too bad the rest of her day was bound to be a downhill experience.

Garrick followed Savannah into the arena parking lot, intentionally putting his truck a few aisles over from where she parked. They'd already gone to her apartment for her to change out of his t-shirt and sweats. The burnable clothes Bobby had touched were piled in his laundry room, waiting for his kitchen woodstove, while the fleece was in the trash.

She marched into the arena, her head high, as if it were just another day at the office. He could only imagine what she was facing—the stares, the results of the gossip overnight, her possible termination. It made him mental to be stuck in his truck.

She had to face it alone. No back up. No generating new rumors about their relationship by walking in together. He understood the reasons, even if he hated the outcome.

After fifteen minutes, he got out of his truck, thankful no one had seen him sitting there. His phone was in hand, at the ready to pretend to be stuck on a call as a possible excuse for loitering in his car. He was about to shove it into his coat pocket when it started to buzz.

He didn't recognize the number.

"Garrick LeBlanc," he answered, using his best *this better be good or I'm hanging up* voice.

"G."

Jack had called him that since they were kids. Garrick knew Jack's cell number. This wasn't it.

"Where are you?" he asked.

"Pay phone. Not important."

Tension knotted in his belly. "Please tell me you're being careful."

"The Sugar Shack," Jack said impatiently.

"What?"

"The Sugar Shack. On Robinson."

"What about it?"

"I don't know, I just thought you'd like it there. Have a drink. Enjoy the atmosphere." Sarcasm dripped from every word.

"Okay, thanks for the tip. I'll check it out."

"Now *you* be careful. Good luck. I'm done."

Jack meant he was done helping. It was nothing but a relief

to Garrick.

"Thanks," Garrick said, not sure Jack heard him before he hung up.

Garrick stood in the cold wind of the parking lot and mentally kicked himself again for asking Jack about the Kramers. If Jack got into trouble, lost his job, it would be Garrick's fault, and the son of a bitch was way too proud to let Garrick help him. Garrick had tried before.

Sighing, he shoved his phone into his coat pocket and went into the arena. He forced himself to walk slowly around the long outer corridor. Eventually he found Rhian, Mike and Alexei standing outside the trainer's office.

Garrick smiled and wondered if she even knew they were there. Ready to do battle, from the looks on their faces.

Savannah's army.

He stopped to say hello and pretended shock and awe as Mike related the events of the previous evening. The look on Rhian's face over Mike's shoulder was comical—he knew Garrick was full of shit since Garrick had called him and asked him to keep an eye on Savannah while he was stuck in the parking lot.

He didn't have to fake his surprise when Mike got to the part where he and Alexei had seen and heard enough to back up Savannah's story. It wasn't just he-said-she-said after all.

Thank god.

The door opened and they turned to watch Mark stalk from Savannah's office, shaking his head at them loitering outside the door. He didn't say a word, just marched down the hall toward his office.

Savannah was the next to come out, stopping short when she saw them.

"Vell?" Alexei's question—without the thick Russian accent—was on the tip of everyone's tongue. Garrick didn't think he was the only one holding his breath.

"Aren't you guys supposed to be in the gym?" Savannah

170

asked with a smile. "As your trainer, I expect you to stick with our agreed-to fitness plans."

Mike smiled. "Still the trainer, huh?"

Savannah's smile faded into a grimace. "For now, anyway."

Rhian broke protocol and hugged Savannah. Garrick almost laughed at her alarm as she stared at him over Rhian's shoulder.

Setting her back on her feet, Rhian beamed down at her while Mike and Alexei patted her back and arm hard enough to almost knock her off her feet.

"Oh, well, thanks. I, uh…"

Garrick grinned at her complete loss of words. The guys laughed and turned for the locker room and the gym beyond, leaving them alone.

She stared at their backs as they disappeared around the bend. "They stood up for me."

"I don't know why you sound so surprised."

She shrugged. "I thought you were my only friend."

Garrick grinned. "I'm not your *only* friend, I'm your *best* friend."

Savannah rolled her eyes. "And not too cocky or anything."

He tried not to read too much into the fact that she didn't deny it, but his heart leaped in his chest. Jesus, he was like a teenager with his first crush.

Then he pictured them in his bed, hardly able to move because of the butt plugs lodged in their asses, about to fuck until they lost consciousness.

Okay, no teenagers here. So maybe he was like a grown up with his first…

Shit, the first word that popped into his mind wasn't *crush*. It was a hell of a lot scarier than that.

Savannah cocked her head. "You okay?"

"What? Oh, yeah. Sorry. Just remembered something."

Her cell phone saved him from further explanation. The

ringtone caught his attention. Who in her life warranted the Olympic Anthem? A stab of jealousy almost made him ask, but his brain caught up with his caveman instincts in time to save the day.

"I better get that," she said as she backed through her door.

"Will I see you later?"

She paused. The call went to voicemail. "After your workout? Do you want me to look at your hip?"

He checked the corridor, relieved it was empty. So much for his brain outdistancing his baser urges. "No. I mean, yes. If you would help me with my stretches and check out my hip, I'd appreciate it."

"Okay, see you then."

He checked again. Still clear. "What are you doing tonight?"

She hovered in her door, biting her lower lip.

Shit. Please don't let me be back to square one on convincing her we can be more than friends.

"Nothing." She moved into her office and tilted her head, indicating he should follow. "I usually spend no-game nights at home catching up on sleep."

Certainly a goal that wouldn't be met if he got his way. He waited, though, hearing the unspoken "but" in her sentence.

"I guess..." She looked up at him. "I don't feel safe at home. Alone."

Amazing how the urge to punch Bobby in the face could spring up at any time. "Come stay with me."

"I don't know. My reputation is already in tatters."

"I live in the middle of nowhere. No one will know." He understood her need for discretion, but they could do this. He was sure. "Park behind the house. I'll cook you dinner."

With her nod, hope—and a few other things—sprang to life in Garrick.

Savannah sat at her desk three days later and stared at her

phone in shock.

She was a good interviewee. She was comfortable having conversations with people she didn't know, she was passionate about her sport, and she knew her shit.

But never in her life had she had a phone interview like this. In the course of an hour she'd spoken with three people, all of whom should have been intimidating as hell, but had proven to be kind, easy to talk to, and—if she wasn't delusional—impressed with her knowledge and experience.

The results of which meant she was going to Boston for an in-person interview with the Bruins.

If she hadn't been sitting in her office, she would have leaped from her chair and whooped like a loon. This was *it*. The dream. The brass ring. The NHL.

Gathering the papers scattered on her desk, she tried to compose herself and focus on more immediate tasks. They had a game tonight and her players would be arriving shortly.

With a sigh, she checked her schedule, knowing whose name would be first.

Bobby Kramer.

And Mark, or whoever was assigned to play chaperone tonight.

For a moment she hoped it would be Garrick. Just as quickly, she forced that hope aside.

The last three nights in his house, in his bed, had been mind-boggling. The sex was incredible. By all reasonable standards, she should be sated. Replete with vigorous and gymnastic loving. But she wanted more.

And then there was the time out of bed. The quiet meals expertly prepared, the heated debates between two news junkies, the quiet cuddles on the couch while they zoned out to their common addiction—cop dramas.

She remembered her first impressions of Garrick. God, she'd been dead wrong. Even more galling, she had pigeonholed him. A hockey player who'd had the unfortunate impulse to ask her out, and she'd socked him into the role of jock, philanderer, and jerk. With the exception of his athleticism, he was none of those things.

Though, he had quite thoroughly lived up to his reputation as a titan in bed. And then some. Indeed, he was forcing her to revise some beliefs she'd always held about love, lovers, and sex.

In her experience, there had been only two kinds of lovers—selfish and generous. Now there were three—selfish, generous, and Garrick.

There was something wholly unique about him. Selfish lovers focused on doing what they needed to get some relief. Generous lovers focused on what *she* needed to get some relief.

Garrick was certainly generous. She smiled at the zing tickling up her spine from the ache in her bottom. Very generous. But it was more than finding relief. Or release. Or anything as simple as meeting some goal—hell, *imperative*— that sprung to life every time she was near him.

At times he'd stopped their headlong rush into the abyss to do the most unexpected things. Like rub his soft nose, just the tip, smooth like velvet, down her rib cage, twisting from her shoulder blade, tucking under her arm to the sensitive flesh over her ribs, and dipping into her waist and over the bump of one hip. The trip was slow. His touch firm. Just the memory of his smile made her shiver. Eyes closed, lips curled. It was so soothing and erotic. But it was not for her benefit. At least, not hers alone.

She'd felt...cherished. Stupid word, like he might write her an ode, which would be completely mortifying if it weren't somewhere between extremely unlikely and impossible.

But he *was* sweet. And he did something like that every time they were together. He wasn't courting her. What would be the point when she was already sprawled naked beneath him in his bed? She was writhing, begging with word and deed for him to do as he pleased. And what seemed to please him were these simple acts of...affection.

She'd cared for lovers before. Heck, she'd been in love with Doug in college. He'd been a good lover, often generous, sometimes selfish. She'd been selfish sometimes, too. But Doug had touched her just for the pleasure of the connection, to simply enjoy the touch. *Hadn't he?*

Sitting there, staring at her corkboard, she couldn't remember a time Doug had touched her like that. Nor a time she'd touched him with nothing more than the need to express her feelings, how she cared for him. They'd been young. Driving toward release, maybe even thinking about the next one after that.

Garrick was different.

Which royally sucked since she had to leave town. Soon. She'd already arranged to go to Boston next week after they got back from their three-day road trip.

Some distance would help clear her head. She had to stop her growing addiction to Garrick before it really took hold. Three days on the road would help, being in the hotel and not his house. Living with the team and not just each other. Then Boston. Three days on her own, with no Garrick, no mind-numbing sex, just her career and future to hold her focus.

Because Bruins or no Bruins, she was leaving Moncton and the Ice Cats.

And Garrick.

Chapter Nineteen

Garrick snapped awake at seven a.m., as was his habit, and smiled. Savannah lay curled against him, warm and naked in his bed, her head ducked beneath his chin, her breath a tickle on his chest. She'd slept burrowed under the covers, snuggled into him, every night for a week.

He was quickly getting used to it. Aw hell, he *was* used to it.

He'd be a fool to get any more attached. The thought of Savannah moving away already caused a tug of panic in his chest, and she was leaving for an interview in Boston in just a few hours. He'd have to learn how to live without her again.

Not that she was *with* him now. As far as anyone knew, she slept at her apartment and he in his house. Friends. Work colleagues. Not lovers.

It was how it had to be but it still rankled. He wanted to take her to dinner, see a movie, hell, go grocery shopping with her. He wanted to be *normal*.

He huffed out a silent laugh. That was never going to happen. Even if he did manage to yank the team from the Kramers' clutches, there would be another owner, another manager, another team full of men who might be fooled into believing the worst of her. And then there were the Bruins. Perversely, he wanted her to land her dream job, even if it meant she'd be gone for good.

Sighing, he looked down into her face, rubbing his hand along her smooth back. He wanted to haul her up against him and not let go.

Good god, he was becoming the caveman she'd accused him of being.

Savannah murmured in her sleep and arched into his touch as his palm skimmed over her ass. He stopped to rub one cheek, her silky skin warm, the crease at the top of her thigh too great a temptation for his roaming fingers.

She blinked up at him. "Good morning."

Her voice was rough, and he recalled how she'd shrieked for more as he'd fucked her against the shower wall last night, quick and hard. How they'd taken that shower to clean up from the long, slow, shattering sex they'd had in the kitchen after their three-day road trip. He'd only meant to kiss her, but the next thing they knew she was on the table. Then they both had ended up there, enjoying a second course of dessert directly from each other's bodies.

The sight of whipped cream and chocolate sauce would likely give him an erection for the rest of his life. He anticipated awkward trips to Dairy Queen with glee.

She smiled at him, and he couldn't resist her sweet lips. Their kiss was slow, an awakening of body and mind. Arousal built, swirling around them as they lay facing one another. The scent of her swelling body reached him from the warm cocoon of covers and tangled limbs. The blood surging into his cock felt thick and hot, his heartbeat ponderous in his ears.

The perfect way to wake up.

He urged her thigh up over his hip and she hooked it high against his ribs, opening herself to him.

He drew a finger through her slit, gathering sweet cream on his finger and delicate moans from her lips. He traced her clit, once, twice. Her languid movements became jerky, and her hand fisted in his hair.

He pulled her chest to his, enjoying the stab of her hard nipples against his flushed skin, the press of her soft breasts. He nudged his hips forward and found her wet heat with his swollen cock.

Shit. *No condom.*

He jerked back, sympathizing with her low moan of disappointment as he groped behind him for the bedside table. Damn it, after a week he should have known to have one at hand any time they were in the house together.

She touched his chest, bringing his attention back to her. "I'm on the Pill. I haven't had condomless sex in years and have been checked out more than once since."

He stared at her, somewhere between shocked and elated. "Are you sure?"

"Are you safe?" she asked with a gentle smile.

He smiled back. "Very. I've never done this before."

"What?"

"I've never had sex without a condom in my life. Ever. Not with any man or woman. And you know from my physicals that I'm clean."

She bit her lip. "Are *you* sure?"

He'd never been more certain it was the right time, place, and person in his life. "Yes. Very." He kissed her again.

She moaned and rolled her pelvis toward him.

He dragged her against him so their bodies touched from chest to belly to knee. His tongue delved into every corner of her mouth and surged his hips forward. His eyes rolled back in his head as his swollen crown slid through her silky cream and notched against the entrance of her vagina. He thrust forward slowly, sinking to the hilt into her hot, tight, welcoming body.

Fuck.

Their kiss ended with a gasp. Her eyes fluttered open and she pinned him with her deep green gaze.

"How is that?" she asked with a mischievous twinkle in her eye.

Words were lost to him, along with the ability to reboot his now stalled-out brain. She was beautiful. Hot and wet and clenching around him in torturous pulses. This gift, her trust, was more then he'd expected. He hadn't understood. The intimacy was shattering.

He wanted to tell her he would miss her, that he was sorry she would be gone from his bed, his life, even if just for the next three days. He had no idea how she'd react to that, and while his brain was scrambled, there was enough of it still functioning to keep his mouth shut.

He showed her instead with the stroke of his hands and thrust of his hips. He rocked hard, surging into her again and again, rejoicing in the hot slide against his skin, the silky drag along her satin walls. He wanted to imprint himself on her. Make her think of him, *feel* him every moment she was away.

He drove deep, holding himself there and grinding against her, his cock pressing her tight walls, his pelvic bone digging against her clit.

"God, Garrick. Yes!"

She was, as ever, Savannah. Vocal. Demanding. Perfect.

Her hand slid over his hip to his ass, her questing finger on the hunt. He loved her generosity. Her attention. But he had other plans.

Wriggling away, he pulled his cock from her body. He laughed at her groan of disappointment. It ended with a sharp grunt when he rolled her to her tummy.

As soon as he knelt between her thighs, she brought her knees under her body, lifting her ass into the air. He plunged deep again.

"Fuck!" he cried, shocked by how good it felt. He didn't know if he'd ever get used to the sensations running along his cock. She was tighter at this angle, his shaft running along the front wall of her pussy as he drove into her in long, hard thrusts.

"Yes, Garrick! Harder!"

He switched to short, sharp shoves that jabbed at her g-spot. The intensity of that rub on his bare skin, the head of his cock stroking her soft heat over and over, made his head spin. She threw herself back at him, begging for more, shouting out her pleasure.

He thrust his hand under a pillow to retrieve the bottle of lube they'd left there the night before. Fingers unsteady, he popped the lid and poured some down the smooth crease of her ass. He hissed through his teeth when it slithered over his cock where their bodies were joined. He used two fingers to draw some back up, along with her juices, and circle the tight pucker, listening to her litany of moans and shouts of praise while trying to maintain his rhythm.

She was close. He could feel it in the clench of her pussy on his cock, sense it in the jerk of her hips.

He wrapped his hands around her ass, his fingers almost reaching her hips. Tucking his thumbs against her anus, he tugged her cheeks apart and pressed in. Her body gave in to his demands, her muscles still pliant from their play over the past week. Last night. With barely more than a nudge, both thumbs slid deep into her body.

Savannah buried her face in the comforter and screamed, shaking with the strength of her climax.

The clamp of her muscles on his cock was unbearable. His balls drew up close and his spine tingled with the desperate need to come.

He bit his cheek, hard, wishing he had a third hand to yank his sac from his body and force his orgasm back. The ripples continued to flow down his shaft, her body milking his, begging for his release. He groaned long and low as he fought it with every ounce of control he had left to him.

He refused to be dragged over the edge.

Savannah flew over the edge with abandon.

Her face buried in the bedding, she howled as her orgasm ripped through her. The feeling of Garrick stretching her ass wide while he fucked her, rubbing over that perfect spot, was too intense. Her heart galloped in her chest, in her ears, almost drowning out the sound of Garrick's muttered curses.

He hadn't come. Sometimes with a condom she was so overwrought during her climax that it wasn't until the first huge waves had passed that she could tell. But with no condom, she'd been looking forward to the burn of his come filling her. She *wanted* that.

Ready to make him give it to her, she leaned back into his grasp, forcing his cock deeper and grinding her hips.

"Fuck, Savannah," he gasped.

That was the idea. She was about to try again when his thumbs pulled her ass open. The stretch was breathtaking, the burn too delicious, wider than she'd been the night before with his three fingers shoved high. *Christ.* She smashed her face to the mattress, her hands fisted in the bedding, and rode the edge of pain and delight.

When he slowly eased his thick shaft from her still quivering pussy, she thought she would cry with relief.

At last.

His hands left her body and she whimpered. *Just relax.* She was right where she wanted to be, her chest pressed to the bed and her ass tilted in the air, shamelessly offered up for Garrick to do with as he wished.

And if he didn't wish to finally put his long, hard, thick cock in her ass, she was fully prepared to beg.

She heard the sound of the bottle cap snapping back onto the lube, and she closed her eyes, sighing. Whatever he was going to do next was going to be good.

The silken head of his cock tickled along her ass before coming to rest against her anus. She smiled. She looked up the curve of her back and into Garrick's face.

Sweat trickled past his temples, his brow beaded with it. His expression was fierce, the aching point where their bodies met his sole focus.

One big hand slid up her back, soothing her, and she murmured in response, arching back against him.

His scowl was ferocious as he wrapped a hand around her waist and held her still. Chest muscles twitching, hands shaking, he slowly pushed forward.

There was a moment, a single second of hovering pain and pressure, then the head of Garrick's cock popped into her ass and her eyes fluttered closed.

Perfect.

In spite of her best efforts to relax, the ring of muscles

guarding her entrance clenched around him, tearing a grunt from them both. It felt incredible, the stretch endless.

He rocked, slowly, and her body moved with his. His hands worked in counterpoint so that each roll forward eased him a little farther into her body. The sense of being filled, of being full, washed over her. Garrick talked about the high. Now she got it. She was drunk on sensation.

He had to be almost all the way in. The burn increased with the girth of his shaft as it neared the base. She felt every centimeter, every vein and ridge as they eased into her body.

Heaven. Better than she'd guessed. Better than anything Garrick had ever described in all the times she'd made him detail his liaisons with other men. The sensations were unlike any others—even the plug. Because this wasn't some object. This was Garrick. This was absolute trust.

More cold lube flowed over her ass, his fingers and cock working it around and into her, his thrusts getting stronger. More and more of Garrick's cock wedged into her and she wondered if he might nudge her heart, he was so deep.

His hands locked around her waist, and with a final hard shove, he seated himself fully within her, her ass stretched farther than ever before, holding him tight in her body.

She came.

Her muscles clamped down on the thick shaft invading her body and she moaned, her empty pussy clenching as the waves rushed over her. She wanted to scream, to howl and cry out her pleasure, but the sheer force of her release, the fascinating power of this dark passion, held her unusually silent.

"Are you okay?" Garrick asked, his voice raw.

She nodded. He didn't move.

"Yes. God, yes, Garrick."

His hands resettled on her waist and he slowly drew his shaft from her, her body clinging to him, desperate to drag him back in, to regain that fullness.

He didn't disappoint.

He fucked her with long, deep strokes, nearly pulling himself from her body with each retreat before slamming home until their thighs met, his balls rubbing her sensitive ass and perineum.

For once she did little to help, content—no, *ecstatic*—to simply lie there and take him, her mind thrilling to the rush. She'd thought he'd introduced her to new sensations before, with his fingers, his toys. His tongue. But there was more she had to learn. She lay with her cheek to the bed, her eyes half closed, and wondered how many more things he might be able to teach her.

His rhythm faltered. She waited for his climax, but he held it off. Buried in her to the hilt, he curled himself down over her back.

Soft lips cruised down her neck, panting breaths hot on her skin, his teeth sharp when they sank into her shoulder blade. Rather than bring her back from the edge, it sent her closer to toppling over it again.

"Are you okay?" he asked. His hips rocked against her ass, evoking yet more bliss.

"God, yes. This is...it's so much more...I can't..."

He laughed against her neck. "Yeah, that's how I remember it too."

The image of Garrick's face smashed to the bed, a huge cock jammed in his ass, feeling what she was feeling, made her shudder. Her sphincter clamped down on his shaft and held him deep within her.

He whispered a heartfelt expletive. "You ready to go on?"

Holy shit, was she *ever*. She nodded. "Please."

She expected him to lift his big body up off hers again, but she wasn't prepared for him to wrap his arms around her ribs and lift her with him.

He brought them both up onto their knees, his sliding between hers as she came down on his lap. Her weight drove his cock deeper, higher than it had been before.

"Garrick!"

His answer was to punch his hips upwards, shoving into her. His arms around her waist and across her chest to held her upright as he drew out as far as he could, then thrust up again once more.

How did he do it? How did he know all the ways to drive her wild?

She moaned. Shouted. Cried out his name. Words of praise spilled from her with every thrust, her body singing with zings of electricity with every retreat.

She was so enthralled, she didn't feel his hand move until he thrust two thick fingers deep into her pussy.

"Oh god. Yes, please, do that too!"

Garrick thrust mercilessly into her ass, into her pussy, and she clenched his cock, his fingers, and rode him harder. Faster. Running headlong into the ecstasy she knew waited. So close. So, so close.

Garrick's arms tightened, a low growl vibrating in his chest as he shoved her down onto his cock, hard, and ground himself up into her. His shaft swelled, her sensitive entrance stretching as he gasped for breath and she lost the ability to breathe altogether.

The first pulse of his come was warm in her ass. His shout of pleasure rang in her ears. Her body convulsed as her orgasm welled up and out of her, thrumming across her nerves, rippling over his fingers, and clenching his shaft.

The pulses in her backside went on forever, his groan sounding almost painful, eventually choking off his breath.

They fell together, his arms still around her, his cock still lodged in her ass as they collapsed, euphoric, spent.

It was a long time before coherent thought returned, and with it the fervent wish she didn't have to get on that plane to Boston. She would rather spend the day right here, slowly floating back to earth just so they could take the trip back into the stratosphere once more.

That thought alone prodded her out of bed and into the shower. On to the airport. She stood, waiting for her flight, and with a sinking heart, accepted that she missed him already.

Chapter Twenty

Garrick sprawled face down across the sheets, the comforter tangled around his waist. The sun streaming in through the open curtains warmed his bare back. Savannah had crawled out of bed after their lovemaking and accused him of trying to make her late for her flight. Her smile had said she didn't mind in the slightest.

He'd briefly considered following her into the shower, but had known where it would lead. As much as he hated that he would sleep alone in this bed for the next three nights, he was glad she'd made her flight and would have an opportunity to show the Bruins what she could do.

He had a good feeling about this interview, even if it made him nauseous to contemplate what it would mean when she got the job.

He rolled onto his back and stretched, his back cracking, his hip twinging as he arched his body up off the bed. He smiled. No way in hell he was going to tell Savannah their lovemaking was exacerbating his hip pain.

He didn't see the note on his bedside table until he stood to go into the bathroom. His name was written in Savannah's tidy penmanship across the front, the folded paper propped against the vibrator he'd left out to dry after cleaning it the night before. He smirked, tickled by her shameless humor. She'd come a long way from the woman who was afraid to make noise when she was aroused, who was ashamed of her own enthusiasm.

He plucked up the note and opened it as he walked across the cold floor, stopping in the middle of the room as he read.

DUNCAN MORRISON 202.266.2360

CALLUM MORRISON 303.405.1105

YOU ASKED IF I KNEW ANYONE WHO WANTED TO BUY A HOCKEY TEAM. THEY'RE EXPECTING YOUR CALL. GOOD LUCK. ~ S.

Garrick blinked, hardly believing his eyes.

The Morrison brothers were two of the hottest properties in the NHL. He barely resisted the urge to smack his own forehead. She'd told him all her brothers played hockey. He just hadn't realized she meant some of them played hockey *professionally*.

Now he knew who was assigned the Olympic Anthem ringtone on her cell phone. Callum, goalie with the Colorado Avalanche, had a silver medal. He and Duncan, who was a winger for the Washington Capitals, had a good chance of going to the next games, too.

And if he wasn't mistaken, one of her other brothers played in the WHL in Vancouver. And there was an infamous legend about another Morrison leading his team at Harvard to a championship before leaving the sport to pursue his Ph.D.

Garrick staggered back to the bed and sat down hard.

Did Savannah's brothers want to buy the Moncton Ice Cats?

Hope surged. Tossing the note down on the mattress, he bolted into the bathroom to take a quick shower then threw on his workout clothes. He grabbed the paper again on his way to the kitchen. He had to get his fitness routine done or his trainer, not to mention his groin and hip, might never forgive him. But in the meantime, he could leave a voicemail or two.

He nearly swallowed his tongue when Callum picked up after two rings. "Hello, Garrick. You being good to my sister?"

"Uhhh..." Garrick floundered, totally unprepared for one of his heroes to answer his call, let alone address him by name. He stumbled for a response, unsure what Savannah had told her brother but one hundred percent certain that revealing anything would land him in the doghouse. Possibly for life.

Callum Morrison chuckled. "I can tell she's got you well trained already. Join the club. Six bothers, and not one of us would dare cross her. She's damn bossy. But I bet you know that already."

Garrick was glad Callum couldn't see his face heating. "She

likes to think of it as persuasive."

Callum's laughter boomed down the line. "Oh man, she's got your number. Though, look at me talking to you about buying some damn hockey team. I guess she *is* pretty persuasive after all."

Garrick's gut clenched. "If you have some time, I'd like to talk to you about that very thing."

"I bet you would," Callum said, a smile in his voice. "Give me a second to figure out how to conference Duncan in on this damn phone and we'll talk about what's possible and what's not. You got numbers for us?"

"I've got some."

"Savannah says you're good with numbers. That you've got the chops for the business side of this thing."

She did? A flush of pleasure warmed Garrick and eased the roiling nerves in his gut. "I have a business plan."

"We've seen it. That's why we're talking. Hold on while I get Duncan."

The following night, Savannah sat in the owner's box at the Boston Garden, watching the Bruins play for a sold-out crowd. The noise was awesome, the fans roaring as the team fought for a win in a closely matched game.

Re-crossing her legs, she smiled and thought of Garrick. As she'd thought of him every time the gentle pang zipped through her body from her still-sensitive ass. He'd effectively ruined her plan to focus solely on her interview while she was in town. Her smile widened and she intentionally sat back in her seat, enjoying another zing.

All eyes were pinned to the ice, following the action as it moved the length of the rink and back. She, on the other hand, had spent most of the night with her gaze riveted to the interim trainer. His job looked fast-paced, hectic even, and exactly the same as working with the Ice Cats.

She could totally rock this job.

Her interviews had gone well and she'd left each meeting confident and energized. She knew her stuff. They knew she knew her stuff. She'd played down her name, never mentioning her connections, though prepared to be honest if someone asked. No one had. They either had no idea, or knew for certain and didn't need her to confirm it.

Regardless, she didn't see that as an obstacle. And if it was, it was small compared to the bigger hurdles she had to clear to get this gig.

Like the fact that she was young. And a woman.

She couldn't change either of those things, so it boiled down to whether or not the management gave a damn.

The previous trainer had been a year older than she was now when he'd started, and he'd been with the team for the almost two decades since. A genetic degeneration of the spine combined with a recent car accident had made the job too painful and dangerous for him. His interim replacement—the assistant trainer, who had a good, if relatively short history in sports medicine and training—seemed competent.

The sound of a whistle yanked her attention back to the ice. One of the Bruins was down and within seconds the trainer was on his way.

Savannah immediately knew two things about the assistant trainer—he was nervous and he'd never been a hockey player. He looked damned uncomfortable out on the ice.

As if the fates had heard her, the trainer stopped short by his player's side and promptly lost his footing, landing on his ass instead of taking a knee. Savannah winced as he caught himself with one hand. She'd bet his right wrist wasn't feeling too good right now. Probably sprained. No doubt adrenaline and embarrassment got him back on his knee and over his player to triage the injury.

Fortunately, the player got up on his own and easily skated back to the bench. The trainer rose more slowly, cradling his hand in the crook of his other elbow as he walked back to the tunnel. As soon as he got there, the coach looked up at the box and reached for the phone.

Savannah wasn't surprised when the phone on the bar promptly rang. A vigorous round of swearing behind her confirmed her suspicions. The assistant trainer was out for the game.

She jumped a foot when a hand landed on her shoulder. She smiled tentatively at the strength-and-conditioning coach, with whom she'd been sitting for most of the game.

"I need your help."

She suppressed the urge to gulp and squared her shoulders. "What can I do?"

"I'm in for the rest of the game and I've got a handle on most of it, but the team doc and I suck at taping and that shit. You'll probably just be keeping me company, but you should come along in case I need you to keep me honest if someone needs a patch up."

Savannah rose from her seat slowly, her dignified carriage somewhat diminished by the huge grin on her face.

"Let's go."

Garrick stared at the huge LCD screen above the Sugar Shack's bar. For the love of Christ, Savannah was on the bench at the Bruins game.

He'd asked the bartender to switch to the game in some vague attempt at solidarity, knowing she was there and hoping by some miracle he'd catch a glimpse of her in the sweet seats she'd texted him about earlier.

But on the bench? Well, okay, standing *next* to the bench in the tunnel, watching the game from ice height, which was close enough.

He'd seen their trainer go down, but what the hell happened after that, he couldn't imagine. Still in her interview clothes, she clearly hadn't gone to the game prepared to work. She wouldn't show up at the Ice Cats arena, let alone go out to the bench for a game, without her hair up, her shapeless pullover, and those yoga pants. Garrick was almost certain this would be the first time anyone in high-heeled, knee-length leather boots and a plum-colored skirt suit had ever worked the bench of an NHL game.

Smiling, he dug his cell phone from his pocket and texted Savannah.

Having fun?

The TV cut to a commercial. Garrick caught the bartender's eye and ordered another beer. He'd been here for two hours and this was only his third. At his size, with his metabolism, he was sober as a judge.

His phone buzzed and he looked down to see a text from Savannah.

WOOO!

God, she was so going to get that fucking job.

It was just as well, since even with her brothers throwing in a good portion, it wasn't enough to outbid Robert Kramer. Garrick thought he could pull together another chunk of the bid from his own savings, matching the Morrison brothers' stakes, but they still needed a fourth to make a go at it. It was a damn good thing he'd been lucky with his investments over the past decade. As much as it freaked him out to think of life after hockey, some part of him had known all along the day would come.

Sighing, Garrick paid his tab and picked up his beer, sorry to miss the rest of the game. He'd have to watch it on DVR later.

He'd been trying his hand at detective work all night, hoping to see something—a transaction, a shady character doing shady things, *anything*—if he hung out at the bar. After two hours, he accepted his plan sucked.

He wandered through the restaurant, ducked into the back room to watch some pool, and flirted with a couple women who he might once have found interesting, but now left him totally cold. When one put her hand on his chest, he actually felt skeeved out.

He was going to have to figure some way to get the hell over this when Savannah left. For now, he was quite happily monogamous.

And there was the masochistic truth.

By the time another hour had passed, he'd stood in every corner of the Sugar Shack, checked every booth and alcove, even looked behind the damn jukebox. The only things anyone might take exception to at this fine Kramer-owned establishment were the warm beer, cheesy music, and sticky floors.

Garrick laughed at himself, wondering when he'd become such an old fudd.

The only area of the building he hadn't inspected was the back hallway. He'd made it to the men's room once, but there was no way he was going to get inside the ladies' room. Even if there hadn't been a line, which there inevitably was, getting arrested for being a pervert didn't rank high on his bucket list.

The back hallway continued beyond the bathrooms, with three more doors lining the way to the emergency exit, which the sign claimed was alarmed. He circled around three times to see where those doors might go, but every time he made his way into the hall, the same guy was leaning against the wall, appearing to all the world as if he were waiting for his girlfriend in the ladies' room. He was young and had hair so light blond, it appeared almost white. If he hadn't been built like a professional wrestler, Garrick might have believed he was just some dumb kid.

When Garrick stepped into the corridor for the fourth time in an hour, Blondie stood away from the wall and watched him carefully.

Chucking his beer bottle in the trash can outside the bathroom door, Garrick ducked into the stench of the men's room one last time, resigned to waiting a few minutes before leaving the Sugar Shack for the night.

As clandestine missions went, he had managed an epic fail.

He washed his hands, giving an inordinate amount of

concentration to the task. The other guys probably thought he had OCD but after four trips into this bacteria farm, all he wanted to do was go home and shower.

The door from the hallway squeaked and he glanced up into the mirror. His guts clenched when Blondie came in, followed closely by another thug in matching black t-shirt and cargo pants, and none other than Robert Kramer.

Oh shit.

Garrick rinsed his hands and shook the excess water off as if he hadn't a care in the world. At least two other men were in the room with them, so he calmly reached for some paper towels and turned toward the door.

He didn't bother to act surprised to find the Goon Squad behind him. He wasn't that good an actor. Instead, he moved toward the exit, trying to follow the guy who'd just zipped up and run from the urinal and out the door without washing his hands.

Blondie clamped a hand on Garrick's left arm. He stopped, lifted an eyebrow and gave him his best face-off stare. Goon Two grabbed Garrick's other arm and yanked him back toward the sink.

The stall door opened to reveal the last of the innocent bystanders and Garrick's only hope of a witness. Garrick tugged at his arms, trying to free himself. No luck. The man in the stall stared wide-eyed at his struggle, then bolted from the bathroom as if it were on fire.

Fucking chicken.

"Let the fuck go of me," Garrick barked, fighting harder. He almost knocked his captors off their feet, but the bastards held on. Goon Two wrapped a second hand around Garrick's arm.

"No, Mr. LeBlanc. That's not how this is going to work." Robert Kramer's smooth voice cut through the room, his vowels oddly rounded. Garrick almost rolled his eyes at the bogus British accent. Was this guy for real? Garrick had researched Robert Kramer thoroughly. He had been born not forty miles from where they stood, had barely finished high school here in Moncton, and had lived here every day since.

Robert Kramer was about as British as Garrick's left nut.

The grips on his arms tightened. The goons appeared to be enjoying their roles as enforcers. Garrick wished them luck. He wasn't going to make it easy.

He threw himself at Blondie, checking him hard and sending him staggering into the stalls, his arms wheeling. He caught himself on a partition, narrowly avoiding crashing onto the floor beside the toilet. Garrick shuddered just thinking about touching the floor in this place. Blondie wasn't nearly so bothered. He was already up, thrusting up his sleeves to reveal a Canadiens tattoo on the inside of his forearm.

Oh good, Garrick thought gleefully, *a hockey fan.*

With another hard check, he forced Goon Two into the sinks, his ass almost landing in a basin.

Blondie grabbed the back of Garrick's shirt and hauled him away before he could check his friend again. Garrick threw himself back and slammed his head into Blondie's face.

A satisfying crunch echoed off the tiled walls, followed by a howl of pain. Goon Two grabbed Garrick's right arm again and Garrick narrowed his eyes, prepared to prove that any hockey player worth his salt can punch equally hard with either arm.

"Stop!" Robert Kramer's sharp command brought both goons to a halt. "Outside."

Did these knuckleheads have to be addressed in single word commands to ensure comprehension? He spun to fight Blondie off again, but Robert Kramer's words stopped him cold.

"Mr. LeBlanc, I suggest you cooperate, or I'll see to it that these two visit Ms. Morrison upon her return from Boston."

Fuck. Garrick's blood turned to ice.

He wanted to rip Robert Kramer's fucking lungs out. Instead, he took a steadying breath and walked out of the men's room, not bothering to check to see if he was followed.

He turned to go back into the bar, but a hand shoved him

toward the back door.

Well, at least I can finally check out the rest of the back hallway.

One door was labeled Supplies, and another had a brass clasp and sturdy padlock securing it. The third door had no sign. No padlock. And if he wasn't mistaken, would allow for a pretty good-sized room between the bathrooms and the alley out back.

Another hard shove sent him stumbling and his shoulder crashed into the mystery door. It shook from the impact, but held. Damn it. He should have thrown some extra weight into it. He seriously considered trying the knob.

He jumped back when the door popped open and a middle-aged man poked his head out.

He immediately spotted Robert Kramer. "Everything okay, boss?"

Robert Kramer shoved Garrick farther down the hallway. "Go!" he hissed at his goons, but not before Garrick got a glimpse of the room beyond. It was set up like an office, the furniture handed down from the 1970s. Faux wood laminate—*sexy*. The light from the filthy windows high on the wall was weak, the glass covered in what looked like sheets of standard white copier paper. There were at least four desks, all with sleek computers, some with multiple monitors.

When Robert Kramer turned, Garrick pinned his gaze to the exit and let the goons move him along. They slammed him into the release bar, shoving the door open with enough force that it crashed into the brick wall and bounced back. No alarm after all. Garrick jumped down the single step and into the alley behind The Sugar Shack.

The sour smells coming from the dumpster were eye-watering. The snow banks were high in places, partially obscuring their position from the busy streets on either end of the block. He shook himself free from the goons and stood his ground.

"Mr. LeBlanc," Robert Kramer drawled. He stood in the

door, no doubt intending the step up as a means to look down on Garrick. Guess he should have considered Garrick was a good eight inches taller than he was. Now they were eye-to-eye.

"I'm not sure what brought you here tonight," Robert Kramer continued, "or what you thought to accomplish."

"Just getting a drink," Garrick said blandly.

Robert Kramer got to the point. "Stay away from my business, Mr. LeBlanc. I'm not going to warn you again. If I find you snooping around, I will see to it that Ms. Morrison pays the price. Do I make myself clear?"

Garrick shook with the desire to launch himself at Robert Kramer. God's honest truth, the only reason he didn't was because he wouldn't stop once he started.

"Why the fuck don't you man up and come after me? What kind of asshole threatens innocent women?"

"The kind of asshole who knows what threats work. Take me seriously, Garrick. Ms. Morrison's safety depends on your good behavior. Everyone is vulnerable sometime. Somehow."

Garrick had never been more keenly aware of that fact than at this moment.

Chapter Twenty One

Savannah was tired. Way down, deep-in-her-bones tired. She staggered off the airplane, relieved the Moncton airport was small enough that she would be able to grab her bag and drag her ass to her car within a matter of minutes.

When she'd arrived in Boston, a quarter-mile concourse hike to an escalator had delivered her down into traveler hysteria to retrieve her bags. But then, in Boston, she'd been walking on air, on her way to interview with an NHL team.

She still couldn't believe all that had happened. The entire trip had been exhilarating. And exhausting. Normally a game by the bench was her idea of the perfect night out, but then normally she knew the people, the team, the details.

The coaching staff had been curious but welcoming, the players friendly. A few had commented on her outfit, which she acknowledged had been highly unusual for the circumstances. Heels and a skirt at a hockey game. Maybe she'd start a new trend.

For now, she forged down the concourse toward baggage claim. The first time she heard her name called, she shrugged it off. When she heard it a second time, she looked up and found Garrick jogging toward her.

A slow smile spread across her face. Clutching the shoulder strap of her carry-on, she took off at a run. When she was within a few feet of Garrick, she dropped her bags and threw herself at him.

He caught her against his broad chest and held her tight, her feet off the ground. Her arms coiled around his neck, her face buried against his skin, his pulse to her lips.

She didn't care who saw. She had to leave this city, to get away from the Kramers. Right now, all she cared about was celebrating her crazy trip to Boston and being held by the one person who really, truly understood.

"Hey there, beautiful," Garrick murmured into her shoulder.

He sounded surprised. Pleased. Sexy. She smiled against his neck. "Hi."

"Good trip?"

She lifted her head and he let her slide down his body, her feet touching the floor gently. "Awesome trip."

"You're going to get that job."

She grinned. "From your lips to god's ears." She cocked her head. "What are you doing here? I have my car in the lot."

Garrick shrugged. "It's a long story. I had Rhian drop me off, so we can take your car home together."

She wanted to ask why, but figured standing in the middle of the airport wasn't the time. Quickly, they retrieved her bag from the carousel and her car from the parking lot. As soon as she settled into the passenger seat, more than happy to let Garrick do the driving, her burst of energy disappeared and she slumped against the seat, her eyes sliding shut.

Before she knew it they were back at the farmhouse. She dragged herself from the car and up the front stairs. Garrick grabbed her bag from the trunk and, with a start, she realized she hadn't even gone to get it.

She stood on the porch and watched him unlock the door, feeling a bit useless. "I'm sorry, I should have—"

He cut her off with his kiss. His hand cupped her face as he walked her backwards over the threshold and into the front hall. He pushed her to sit on the long bench, his lips never leaving hers. Dropping her bags at their feet, he hovered there, kissing her gently, their noses bumping.

Her heart kicked in her chest. His firm lips nibbled at hers, his thumb stroked over her cheek, but he never took the kiss deeper, even when her lips parted in a silent plea for more.

Eventually he drew back, toed off his sneakers, and knelt before her. "I missed you."

This should have been a terrifying admission, but her brain

was overruled by her heart.

"I missed you, too."

He kissed her again. She ran her hands through his hair before dragging her fingertips against the first hints of stubble along his jaw. He slipped off her boots, his palm rubbing and warming her arches before skimming back up her legs.

"Oh, that's good," she moaned as he massaged one foot.

His grin held more than a hint of the devil. "I've never understood foot fetishes. But seeing your face when I do this..." He forced his thumb up into the ball of her foot, right in the spot every high-heeled shoe in the world could make feel bruised and weak. She gasped and arched her back, her eyes narrowing with pain and pleasure.

Garrick shuddered. "That was hot."

She smiled. "If doing this turns you on, feel free to develop any kind of foot fetish you want."

He laughed, moving to the other foot and eliciting more moans of ecstasy. When she couldn't take it any longer, she cupped his face in her hands. She'd hardly leaned forward before he captured her mouth and thrust his tongue past her lips.

The kiss was carnal. God, she'd missed this. Him.

She fisted her hands in his hair and wallowed in his taste and her soaring arousal as he attempted to eat her alive. She tugged the strands tangled in her fingers, making him grunt. She was desperate to feel his skin against hers. Every inch of her body cried out for him.

Tearing her lips from his, she buried her face in the junction of his neck and shoulder and absorbed the scent of pine, lemon, and spice. Garrick.

Hands clumsy, she went to work on the buttons of his shirt. It needed to be gone. All his clothes needed to be gone. She got the shirt open and off his shoulders just as the last button of her jacket sprang free with the help of his nimble fingers. They both shucked their top layer, panting, before their lips came together once more.

It was a challenge to get a man naked when she didn't want to separate her mouth from his, but damn it, she was going to try. She maneuvered his t-shirt until they only had to back off for a second to pull it up over his face.

Garrick forced her skirt up over her hips and slid his fingers over the tops of her stockings. A determined tug yanked her panties down her legs.

She laughed as her undies flew through the air, then he cupped her ass and hauled her to the edge of the bench. Their bodies would have made contact, finally flush to one another, but she was still wrestling with his damn fly. Stupid jeans. If they didn't look so goddamn gorgeous on him, hugging his magnificent ass like a lover, she'd burn them.

Now she was pinned, her breasts pressed together between her elbows, her hands slipping into soft denim to cup Garrick's thick shaft and tight sac through his boxer briefs.

She tugged gently and he gasped. The slow curl of one side of his mouth sent a zing of pleasure right through her.

His lips returned to hers for a peck, then cruised over her cheek, licked and nibbled their way down to her ear, and drew the lobe between his teeth. He sucked the tender flesh with quick pulses before carefully scraping his teeth over it. God, that was exactly what he would do to her clit. Her hips twitched at the memory, the aftershocks of those world-tilting orgasms rising to the surface.

He used his teeth and lips to draw one bra strap over her shoulder and made his way to the soft flesh cupped beneath. She shivered when his soft stubble abraded her nipples before he latched onto the aching peak and sucked it hard. He kissed a path across her chest, over her collar bones, along her shoulder, nuzzling countless places on her body, awakening them.

How does he do that?

With a herculean effort to gather her wits, she ignored his big hands kneading her ass, his lips torturing first one, then the other nipple. She shoved his jeans low on his hips, dragging his underwear with them. The moment his cock sprang free, she wrapped her hands around it and sighed.

Veins tickled her palm as she tugged her hands up and over his shaft. She wasn't gentle. She wanted him to feel her. The corners of his eyes tightened with every yank under the velvet crown. Yes, this was how he liked it. Just a little rough.

Garrick tore his mouth from her, his chest heaving. "Stop. You have to stop. I don't want to go yet and...*oh shit*..."

She smiled. Smug.

He grabbed her wrists and pulled her hands away from his body. "Let's go upstairs."

Pants barely clinging to his hips, he leaped to his feet and dragged her up from the bench and across the hall. He looked as flushed and needy as she felt. When they reached the bottom of the stairs a few short paces away, he kissed her again. She met him enthusiastically, trapping his erection between their bodies so it traced a warm line of pre-come across her belly. She wished she could lick her own stomach.

Then again, why bother when she could go straight to the source? Upstairs was too freaking far away anyhow.

She shoved him back. Hard. He caught himself a second before his bare ass landed on the third stair. His cock bobbed against his stomach. More pre-come pearled on the tip as she stared down at him hungrily.

She tore her gaze away from so much temptation to stare at his beautiful face. His warm whiskey eyes had transformed to rich dark chocolate. Her pulse thudded in her ears, throbbed in her clit. God, that eye-color-changing thing was sexy. It wasn't just about sex—it was about emotion. Affection.

Her heart stumbled in her chest even as she fell to her knees on the bottom step and wrapped her lips around the head of his cock. His shout of ecstasy was sweet accompaniment to the bitter splash across her tongue. She closed her eyes in concentration and bliss, tugging his pants down over his knees and forcing his legs apart. She relaxed her jaw and took him as deep as she could, her hand around the remainder of his shaft, and set a steady rhythm. Her tongue lapped at the head with each upward suck, her hand twisted for each downward spiral.

She wanted him wild, shouting her name. She wanted to do to him what he was always doing to her. To turn him inside out.

His hips bucked, his breath heaved. She sucked harder, worked her tongue faster, forcing deep moans from his parted lips.

"Savannah!" His cry was hoarse, almost a question.

She loved the sting of his fingers tangling in her hair, tugging it from the confines of the clip and bracketing her head. The tight clench spoke of his control, and how close he was to losing it. That was what she wanted. Garrick undone.

Running her free hand down her belly, she slid her index finger along her slit and through the thick cream, careful not to bump her clit and distract herself. When she'd gathered enough lubrication, she slipped her hand beneath him and touched her finger against his anus, tracing the warm moisture around his hole before pressing in. No resistance. She eased past the outer ring and deep into his ass.

With a strangled grunt, Garrick went into overdrive. His weight suspended by his elbows on a higher step, he shoved his ass down on her finger then forced his cock up into her mouth. He wouldn't last much longer at all. She twisted her finger, searching for his prostate. No way he would get through that without emptying himself in her mouth. Down her throat.

It was what she wanted. More than just about anything on earth at that moment.

The last thing on earth Garrick wanted to do at that moment was come in Savannah's mouth.

"Stop!" He forced his hips back against the stairs, away from her mouth and her questing finger. "No. Stop. Please, Savannah. Stop."

The please must have gotten through. She lifted her head. Her swollen lips hovering above his straining cock almost undid him. And her finger, still lodged in his ass, wasn't helping. Jesus.

She was never what he expected. He'd demanded she let herself go, be free with her passion, and still she surprised, delighted, and shocked him every time they touched.

He stared at her glowing face and his chest ached. The image of the Kramers or their goons touching her tore at him, his ribs squeezing painfully, forcing the air from his lungs.

He would stop his inquiries. His stupid investigation. He would let the Kramers have the Ice Cats before he let anything happen to Savannah. If she didn't end up in Boston, she'd land somewhere else. Her talent was too great to go untapped for long. But wherever she ended up, that place could not be Moncton. She had to leave and he had to let her go. He had to keep her safe.

Heart pounding, he gently pushed her arm away and unwittingly distracted himself from his worries. Nothing could have stopped the groan of self-inflicted, agonizing frustration as her finger eased from his wildly sensitive hole.

He lay sprawled on his stairs, panting, and tried to regain his focus. He attempted a shaky smile. "No fair, you trying to finish me off. I'm not done with you yet."

Her shiver delighted him. The goosebumps raced across her arms and flushed chest. He pulled her to him. Kissed her again. Slowly. Thoroughly.

He swallowed past the ache in his chest. He was going to miss her, but she was here now. And she would remember him. If nothing else, he'd do his level best to make sure of that.

She whimpered when he ended their kiss, and he grinned at her bemused expression. Yes, she would remember him.

Jumping to his feet, he forced her back a step before he tackled her. Holding her against his chest, he twisted and they tumbled to the floor, landing with her on top so that he broke her fall. She squealed with laughter but immediately put her hand over his sore hip.

Fuck that. His career in hockey was over as soon as the Kramers took control of the team. It didn't matter. Certainly not more than this.

He rolled fast and pinned her to the floor. She moaned as his cock jammed up against her slick folds, the head bumping over her swollen clit. Her legs caged his hips. Garrick closed his eyes and counted to ten.

He'd had some vague idea of torturing her the way she had him on the stairs, but her heat, the moisture coating her thighs beckoned him. He couldn't wait.

Thrusting his hands under her ass, he settled on his knees, lifted her hips clear off the floor, and eased ever so slowly into her. He wanted to take, to thrust and plunge and hurry, but he held back. His arms trembled as he stretched her tight walls, his mind torn between staring at his shaft slipping into her body and watching her face.

With a final urgent shove, his body came up against hers, his balls nestled to her ass.

"Garrick!" She rocked against him. She was beautiful, her face flushed, her eyes ablaze and sightless as she practically purred. "Please, Garrick. Please now. Hard."

In only three days, he'd somehow forgotten how much he loved this. How it made him a little crazy to hear her demands for more. She'd learned to ask for what she wanted. From him. Of him. She could have it all. He'd deny her nothing.

The thought alone sapped the last of Garrick's control and he thrust hard and fast, pounding into her, their bodies sounding dull thumps as they crashed together. He wanted to pull her into his body. Keep her there forever, even when he knew he couldn't. He couldn't stop wishing for it.

He fell over her and pressed his face to hers. Their noses rubbed. She moaned louder against his lips, in time with his thrusts, as if his cock forced each sound out of her body.

Her orgasm bloomed quickly, and her muscles clamped down on him, yanking the tingle and fire up out of his balls to the base of his spine before it exploded over him. Release snapped his head back and ripped a guttural shout from his chest as lightning flowed down his cock, blinding him to everything but the sensations running over his body and the dull ache in the vicinity of his heart.

Chapter Twenty Two

Savannah climbed out of her car into the bitter wind of the arena parking lot. Mike Erdo waited by the back door. Sighing, she tugged her coat up around her face and jogged toward him. How many more times would she have to go through this routine before she left town? In spite of her now constant escorts and the strain of feeling watched and threatened at every turn, she was going to miss the Ice Cats and Moncton.

Two months ago she'd felt like a visitor. Now she felt entrenched. Which was foolish, of course, because she had to get the hell out of town as soon as possible.

Garrick had told her about Robert Kramer's threats. In the two weeks since her return from Boston, she hadn't been alone more than the fifteen minute drive from Garrick's house to the arena. And often not even then. This morning Garrick had an appointment at the bank that he was being very tight-lipped about, so he'd sent her ahead with the promise that Mike would be waiting. And here he was.

"Good morning, Savannah."

"Hey, Mike. Thanks for waiting out in the cold. You could have stayed inside."

Mike glanced back at the glass doors before gazing out over the cars. His eyes narrowed. She fought the urge to look behind her.

"What is it?"

Mike shrugged. "Didn't recognize the guy or the car. I made sure to wave hello, though. A couple times."

Savannah smiled weakly. "Thanks." She held the door for Mike.

He smiled as he walked past. "Don't mention it."

He waited patiently while she unlocked her office door, and leaned against the doorjamb once she went in.

"Are you going to work in the gym today?" he asked.

She squashed the pang of irritation at not being able to sit in her office alone for five minutes. It wasn't Mike's fault.

She grabbed the files, folders, and pencil box from her desk. "I am if it's okay with you?"

"Sure. Alexei will be waiting for you so I can go change."

She was about to protest that she could spend five minutes in the gym with some of the players that weren't on her personal security detail, but the words faltered when Bobby shoved past Mike and into her office.

The genuinely pleased smile on his face was chilling. "Good morning," he said. His smirk was more arrogant than usual, which was really saying something.

"Good morning," she replied, barely keeping her tone civil.

Mike took up position behind her left shoulder. They'd long ago stopped trying to disguise their purpose for hanging around her all the time. At least to Bobby. Bobby eyed him, his disgust plain, before turning his beady eyes and smarmy smile back to her.

"You're here early."

Was this an attempt at small talk or was there was a threat hidden in there somewhere? Not for the first time, she wished she'd succeeded in convincing Garrick to continue his investigation into the Kramers. She had to leave Moncton no matter what, but they still didn't deserve the Ice Cats.

"This is my usual start time, actually." She sounded remarkably reasonable, considering how badly she wanted to punch this man in the nose.

"Huh. I guess you don't even have time to watch the news over breakfast, then?"

"Uh, no." *The news? What the fuck is he talking about?*

"Too bad. Interesting stuff this morning."

She gave Bobby a blank stare, but he kept smiling at her. She forced back a shudder of disgust and tried to move things along. "Did you need me for something?"

For a moment, Bobby looked confused, as if he'd forgotten why he'd come to the trainer's office. Then he traded in his smile for his usual angry sneer.

"Yeah," he bitched, "my fucking elbow hurts."

They were back on familiar ground. It was almost a relief. "Did you ice it last night and again this morning?"

Bobby scrunched up his face and rocked his head back and forth. "No, I didn't ice it last night," he said in a snotty voice, casting a derisive look at Mike. "Unlike your loser friends, some of us have lives and go out after the games."

Savannah held her tongue.

Mike felt no such compulsion. "Some of us are professional athletes and take our responsibility to the team seriously."

Bobby opened his mouth, but Savannah cut him off. "Go ice it and do the stretches. If it's not better, I'll adjust your program for today."

He stared at her, his eyes narrowing. Mike moved closer.

"I'll be back." Bobby stomped toward the door.

Savannah resisted the urge to roll her eyes. Barely. She kept her polite smile fixed in place and waited for Bobby to leave. As soon as he disappeared into the corridor, her shoulders slumped.

Garrick drove into the arena parking lot an hour later, his mind jammed with figures and interest rates and business plans. He was so preoccupied, he almost didn't notice Rhian slamming out the back door and running toward his car. When Rhian's headlong charge finally registered, Garrick ditched the SUV in the first spot he came to and leaped from the car.

"What?"

"We've got a problem. A big one."

Rhian was not particularly given to hysteria, so his wide eyes and urgent tone were downright alarming.

Garrick grabbed Rhian's arm. "Is she okay? What happened?"

"She's fine. At least, she was when I left her with Alexei a few minutes ago. She's not going to be for long, though."

"What the fuck are you talking about?" Garrick's blood pressure was reaching critical levels.

"Come on. I'll show you."

Garrick sprinted after Rhian into the arena and to the gym, where Mike waited for them, his eyes glued to the TV. Before Garrick could ask, the newscaster spoke.

"Local businessman Robert Kramer and the EHL announced today that he will be the new owner of the Ice Cats. The deal, submitted just weeks ago, has been approved by the league."

"Fuck." Garrick's stomach dropped. Reese hadn't been able to stall them for long. How the fuck did Kramer get the league to act so fast?

"Maritimes TV went to the streets to see what fans and the players thought of the news..." Garrick tuned out the news program. Rhian and Mike looked at him with pity. He wondered briefly if they were sorry Savannah was leaving or that he was going to be out of a job.

He needed to find Savannah and see if she was okay, but stopped dead in his tracks when he heard Bobby's voice booming from the television. *"Yeah, I'm pretty pleased that the Ice Cats will be owned by a local, especially since it's my dad."*

The sycophants surrounding Bobby all laughed at this great joke. Garrick wondered if they'd all been lobotomized before they fell in with Bobby or if it was a free service his father offered so his son would have friends.

The newscaster, clearly clueless about what kind of idiot she was dealing with, moved on to particulars. *"Do think there will be a lot of changes to the team?"*

"Well, I think the real talent is safe and the old dead weight can be sure they'll be cut loose, which is long overdue."

Garrick grimaced. No question who he was talking about there.

"And the management?"

Bobby laughed, a grating, malevolent sound.

"Well, we'll see," he drawled. *"I can tell you this—sleeping with half the team won't be enough to secure your job, especially if you're a lousy trainer to begin with."*

Garrick choked on a lungful of stale, sweaty gym air. A stunned silence followed, both in the gym and on the news program. Before the reporter could recover, Mike shut the TV off and hurled the remote against the wall, shattering it.

A small whimper came from the corridor. Heart plummeting, Garrick spun to see Savannah standing in the door, her mouth hanging open, her eyes wide with horror.

"Savannah..." What the fuck he could possibly say? There were no words, no apology, no comfort he could offer her that would undo Bobby's slander. Her worst nightmare come true.

Savannah stared at the blank television screen. A strange ringing in her ears numbed her to the concern in Garrick's voice. Shock prevented her from reacting to the stricken looks on everyone's faces.

Garrick reached for her, but she snapped out of her stupor and dodged his grasp. The buzzing in her head subsided enough for her to hear him and the others call her name as she swung around Alexei, her unwitting escort to the gym. Before they could stop her, reason with her, try to get her to wait, she took off at a dead sprint down the hallway.

Footsteps thundered behind her, proof that Garrick, Alexei, Mike, and Rhian followed. She ran faster. Ran past the stunned stares of the coaching staff, the other players, the front office workers, as she made her way to Mark's office.

She didn't ask to be admitted. Hell, she didn't even knock. She threw his door open and staggered to a stop in front of his desk before slamming it shut behind her.

Mark leaped up from his chair. "Savannah! What's wrong?"

She sucked in a deep breath and fought back the shakes. The tears. *Fucking adrenaline*, she cursed, determined to shut it down. She wasn't going to let anyone, not Mark, not Garrick and the others, and certainly not Bobby Kramer, see one fucking tear.

"I quit."

Mark's mouth fell open. "What?"

He glanced at his desk when the phone starting ringing. Then his cell. The lines for the rest of the office started lighting up as well. Her heart cracked open a little further with every goddamn ring.

"I quit," she restated. She needed for it to be done, for this nightmare to be over. "Two weeks and I'm gone. Less, if you'll give me a decent reference." She prayed he'd let her off the hook. She didn't know how she'd survive the next two weeks. How she'd ever work in hockey again.

Her knees turned to jelly and she waivered, clenching the back of a guest chair to steady herself. Mark came around his desk.

"No!" she barked, and he froze.

She could stand on her own. She *would* walk out of this arena on her own two feet, of her own volition, her head held high.

And then go someplace quiet and dark and curl up in a ball and cry her damn heart out.

"Answer the phones. Turn on the news." She pointed to the screen mounted on his wall. "You'll have your answers."

He glanced back at his phone before he looked at her again. "Are you sure?"

Was he asking about the answers or her resignation? It didn't matter. The answer was the same.

"Absolutely."

Mark said nothing.

Turning, she calmly opened his door and marched out of his office, her molars clamped so tightly they hurt. The pain and her focus were the only things keeping her lips from quivering. The guys were waiting for her but quickly moved out of her way to fall into line behind her. Their support was important to her. Meant so much. At that moment, though, she wanted to tell them to leave her alone. She wanted to screech at everyone to just *leave her the fuck alone.*

She walked faster. Head high, she strode back to her office, ignoring the looks. She didn't know if they were staring because of her mad dash past them five minutes before or because they'd seen the news. It didn't matter.

Soon Moncton would all be a bad memory.

Garrick didn't remember the game that night. Sitting rigidly on the bench in the locker room afterwards, he tried to tune out the tension around him and focus on getting himself dressed. He didn't bother to shower. He'd do it later. At home. Right now he needed to get Savannah out of this fucking arena and back to his house. Away from all the stares, the snickers, the pitying looks.

The usual post-game joking, the ribald humor and inevitable comparisons of that night's performance on the ice to various sexual talents or lack thereof, was completely absent. He'd never been in a quieter locker room. Everyone was strung tight and giving everyone else a wide berth.

Which was wise. Garrick was holding on to his temper by a thread.

Taking three slow, deep breaths, he stared hard into his locker and told himself to just leave. He stood, yanked on his coat, shoved his laundry in his bag, and nodded goodnight to Rhian at the next locker. Rhian and his other friends had been running defense off the ice, keeping everyone else away. He'd thank them for it when he was sure he could keep his shit together. Right now, a single word might lead to the uncorking of what he was trying very hard to keep bottled inside.

He promised himself he could make it to Savannah and then to his car without losing his mind.

He broke that promise when Bobby and three of his stupid friends stopped to face him over the bench.

Bobby's smile was enough to send Garrick over the edge all on its own. But of course, the asshole had something to say.

"Think long and hard before you fuck with me again."

The crack of his fist hitting Bobby's ugly fucking face was the single most satisfying sound Garrick had ever heard. The shiver of impact and pain racing up his arm felt even better.

Yes!

Bobby flew over the bench, fists flying, and Garrick welcomed it. He felt the hits, given and received, and plunged in for more. Swung harder. He used his arms, fists, knees—hell, even his head—to impress upon Bobby how much he fucking hated the son of a bitch.

Bobby's cronies didn't jump in and Garrick could only assume they were being held at bay. He didn't bother to check as he hurled Bobby to the cement floor and fell on top of him.

Garrick was having the devil of a time seeing out of his right eye, but he felt no pain. Bobby put up a good fight, but he was under Garrick now, at his mercy, and Garrick had none to offer. Some distant part of his brain warned him there were no refs, no one to declare the fight over. He swung again anyway, laying into a still struggling Bobby, ignoring the punches to his ribs. Someone grabbed Garrick and lifted him almost completely off Bobby. He threw his arm back and got himself free.

He landed with one knee on Bobby's chest and watched Bobby's pal Greg's eyes widen. A second later Rhian sailed over Garrick, planted one foot on the bench and hurtled himself at Greg and another of Bobby's fan club. All three hit the floor with a sickening thump.

Then all hell broke loose.

Chapter Twenty Three

Savannah crossed her arms over her chest and stared at the four men sitting side-by-side on her table. She was prepared to give them another stern lecture, though they'd already had at least one of those. They couldn't have missed it, either. The entire arena had heard Rick screeching at them. Who knew a grown man, let alone a big bad hockey coach, could reach that octave? She'd barely managed to dart out of his path as he stomped out of the arena, muttering about fucking arrogant, brainless idiots.

And they were that. She lifted a brow and refused to respond to their wide, shameless grins. Two of them couldn't even see out both eyes, for Christ's sake, and yet they were obviously delighted with themselves.

Rolling her eyes, she turned to her supplies and brought out another box of gauze. She'd already gone through three that night—*after* her post-game work—thanks to the brawl Garrick had started in the locker room.

She'd made these four wait to go last. They'd also been the last to be released from Rick's tender care, so their ears were likely still ringing. Bobby had fled the arena without a backward glance, but his buddies had come by to be patched up. She'd also taken care of all the others who'd ended up taking shots to various body parts in their efforts to break up the fight—which included, but was not limited to, Mark, Steve, members of the janitorial staff, the head scout, several of the front office workers, and at least a dozen players.

Half the team's administrative staff had come running to her office as soon as word of the fight had escaped the locker room. Mark had been with her, trying to talk her down from the ledge, but he'd taken off to the locker room, demanding Sheila stay with her. She'd protested, but Sheila had shut her down.

"No way am I leaving you alone for one second."

It was, Savannah reflected as she stuck scissors in her pocket and looped rolls of tape over her fingers, nice to discover she had more support than she'd expected. Too bad she found out just in time to leave.

She shook her head. No point dwelling on that any more than she already had. Every minute standing by the bench tonight had been torture, her focus on the game only possible through sheer willpower and years of training. And for the first time in her life, she'd hated it. The noise. The crowds. The cameras. It was Bobby's most unforgivable sin yet, and god knew that list was long.

Sheila hadn't left her side during the brawl and break-up. Not until these four had shown up and Savannah had decided to let them in to see her. She was glad for their company, though in no mood to admit it. And it wasn't like Mark was in any condition to play escort with his lip split, his ribs bruised, and his pants torn in an exceedingly awkward place.

Yep, there was going to be *hell* to pay.

Bracing her hands on her hips, she gave each of them a stern look in turn. God, it was hard not to let her lips twitch. They were a freaking mess. Garrick was still bleeding over his eye, Rhian had ice packs on his head and groin, and Mike had a black eye that was very nearly swollen shut. Alexei, by some miracle, had only sustained scraped knuckles.

No amount of stink-eye was making a dent in their glee. Fortunately, she knew just how to wipe those grins off their faces.

"You do realize that now the entire city of Moncton thinks they know which half of this team I'm sleeping with, don't you?"

Their stunned expressions were extremely gratifying.

"That's what I thought." She shook her head, went to Alexei, and cleaned his cuts with antiseptic. "How are you going to play like this?"

He shrugged. "It's not so bad. I've played with worse."

If he could make it through the fight with only scraped knuckles, that was probably true.

She moved on to Mike, cleaning his abraded knuckles and then inspecting his eye. "You're probably going to miss a game because of this. You won't be able to see properly for a few days at least."

Mike smiled. "Worth it."

She sighed, totally exasperated. "Really? It doesn't change anything."

Rhian laughed. "Sure it does. Bobby won't be mouthing off again anytime soon."

"And not just because he's missing a couple more teeth," Mike added.

Savannah stopped in the process of breaking open another ice pack and turned her eyes heavenward, praying for patience. She. Would. *Not.* Laugh.

She gently lifted Mike's shirt and prodded his bruised ribs. She grimaced when he sucked in a breath.

"Think they're broken?" she asked.

"Nah. Not even close."

Throwing up her hands, she stood back and planted her fists on her hips once more. She should chastise them. Rail about their stupidity. The risks. But damn it, she just didn't have it in her.

She sighed, then smiled. Begrudgingly. "Thank you."

Their grins faltered, replaced with momentary surprise, before beaming even wider.

God help her, she'd been around hockey players too long. It had been an incredibly foolish thing to do, but she was actually flattered.

Mike and Alexei hopped off the table. She squeaked when Alexei wrapped his huge hands around her face and kissed her on each cheek, then on the first one again, loudly, before releasing her.

"You're welcome."

With that he turned and left.

Mike shrugged. "It's a Russian thing." He kissed her cheek too, though more gently and only once. "But you *are* welcome." He ran to catch up with his friend.

Savannah watched them go, bemused.

Turning back to Rhian and Garrick, she sighed again.

Garrick had yet to say a word. He was still smiling at her. Grinning like a fool, in fact, after Alexei's hearty kisses.

Rhian gingerly slid off the table, still holding the ice packs to his head and his crotch. He winced when his feet hit the floor.

"You sure you're okay?"she asked gently. Groin injuries were one thing, but there was little she could do about the results of a shot to the nuts.

Rhian shrugged, bringing on another wince. "Yeah, the head bump is already better. And getting kneed in the junk sucks, but it will fade." He looked back at Garrick. "Next time you're in that foul a mood, I'm leaving my cup on until I get home."

Garrick laughed. "I didn't do it!"

"No, Steve did."

Savannah's eyes widened at Rhian's accusation that her assistant had maimed him, and he laughed too.

"It was completely by accident when he was trying to pull me off the pile. It's a long story."

For the first time since she'd started with the Ice Cats, Savannah was glad her office wasn't in the men's locker room.

Rhian stepped forward and she smiled, tilting her cheek to his kiss. Garrick's brows lifted—well, at least the one that still worked—as she willingly accepted Rhian's affection. At this point, why not? Her plan to be the queen of all-business-no-play wasn't working anyway. In fact, she wasn't going to miss it at all.

Her smile faded. No, the hard part now was telling Garrick she'd quit. That she'd be leaving as soon as she could pack up her shit and go. She'd already called her parents to let them know she was coming home, her tail tucked firmly between her legs, goddamn it, until she could find a new position.

"I'm sorry about everything, Savannah," Rhian said softly.

"Thanks, Rhi. I'm sorry too."

With a nod to Garrick, Rhian left, shutting the door behind him. She almost called out for him to leave it open, but she let it go. She and Garrick would be locking up in a few minutes anyway.

Turning to Garrick, she cocked her head and studied his swollen face. The bleeding over his eyebrow was down to an ooze, his left eye was swollen almost completely shut, and his upper lip distended to the point it should have been comical.

"How bad is the stuff I can't see?"

Garrick's smile slipped. "Not bad."

She frowned. "That wasn't very convincing."

His shoulders lifted, about to shrug, but froze. He grimaced as he slowly let them fall again. She tugged up his shirt before he could object.

She cringed at the florid bruises across his ribs. With a gentle touch, she traced the continuous path of purple skin until it disappeared beneath his waist band. Then she studied his stony face.

"Your groin?"

"Fine." He said it quickly enough that she believed him.

"Your hip?"

He sighed and met her eyes.

"How bad?"

She was almost glad he couldn't shrug. He twisted his lips in a humorless smile. "Bad. Hit the floor first, with most of mine and Bobby's weight on it."

Shit. She didn't ask if it was a season-ender. A season-

218

ender would be a career-ender, and they both knew it. Buying time by collecting more supplies, she swore she'd get him back on the ice to finish this season, if it was the last thing she did before hauling ass out of town. Garrick had earned her loyalty. Hell, he'd earned her devotion. He deserved the right to wrap up his career on the ice with dignity. Doing something as stupid as picking a fight to defend her honor was not nearly a good enough reason to blow that.

She went to work on what she could fix, cleaning up his face and hands and applying butterfly bandages to the cut. He sat patiently, barely making a sound except to suck in a breath when the sting of antiseptic caught him off guard. She ignored the way he stared into her face, his gaze disconcertingly direct when she leaned in to do the close work on his forehead.

Stepping back, she took stock. He wasn't even close to presentable, but she'd done her best. He'd taken some painkillers a while ago, but she doubted they would do much good. She could send him to the hospital for something more powerful, but he'd refuse.

"God, Garrick. What the hell were you thinking?"

His warm brown gaze captured hers, and Savannah's heart lurched. *Chocolate.* He towed her close with one hand fisted in her fleece, until she stood between his knees.

"You know what I was thinking?" he asked, his voice low and gruff.

She fought the sudden urge to clap her hands over her ears and run from the room, even while part of her was still desperate to wrap his battered body up in her arms.

"No," she said. "You had to know it wouldn't help. That it might make things worse."

"Yeah, I knew that. It didn't matter."

"Why not?"

"Because you're my friend," he said softly.

"Oh, well..." She smiled, touched and uncertain what to say.

"And I love you."

Everything in the world came to a screeching halt. Her heart, her lungs, *everything*.

"No." Her denial was firm. Reflexive. Desperate. "You're confused. We're friends." She grasped for any explanation, for an excuse. A way to make him take it back. "You've never had a woman friend before, right? You're just confused."

Garrick looked at her like she was crazy. That was exactly how she felt. This was *insane*.

"It doesn't really matter if you believe me or not. I am in love with you." He said it calmly, certainly, his chin jutting forward.

God, when had this all gotten so out of control? Her heart pounded as if she'd sprinted to this disastrous end.

"Garrick, you *can't*."

His good eyebrow arched. "Why not?"

Tears pricked at the back of her eyes and for once she did nothing to stop them. "Because I quit. I'm leaving the Ice Cats. Moncton."

You.

Garrick wrapped his fingers around the edge of the padded table, ignoring the sting of his shredded knuckles, the shaking in his hands.

She was leaving him. Already.

The first time in his entire life he'd ever said those words to a woman and it had all gone wrong within ten seconds. That had to be some kind of record.

He'd been stunned to learn something could feel so good, so *right*, when he'd finally figured it out. It had been true for weeks, possibly since she'd climbed into Reese Lamont's limo and lost all control in his arms. That was when the funny kick had started beneath his ribs, the insatiable need to be near her had taken hold in his gut.

Friendship. Love. It was all tied together in Savannah.

And so he'd told her. Only to have it dismissed and handed back to him on a plate of *no thank you* with a side of *have a nice day, I'm leaving*.

He sat motionless, trying to find his way through the emotions—fear, anger, love, sadness.

A tear slowly tracked down Savannah's cheek.

In the time they'd known each other, she'd been assaulted, harassed, stalked, insulted, and had her reputation savaged on television. She'd never cried. Not until he'd told her he loved her.

He brushed the drop from her jaw as another began its slow path down the other cheek.

"I didn't mean to make you sad," he said, his voice gruff. He was dangerously close to losing it. He swallowed hard.

She closed her eyes, freeing two more tears. "I can't stay."

"I know you can't. It doesn't make it any less true."

Savannah's tears came faster. "I don't know what to say."

Garrick tried not to flinch. No doubt now about whether she might say it back, regardless of how ill-fated their relationship.

"You don't have to say anything." He carefully eased off the table and to his feet.

It had been one hell of a day. He needed to go home.

She stepped back, rubbing the heels of her palms across wet cheeks and under reddened eyes. He carefully tugged the rolls of tape from her hands, pulled her scissors from her back pocket, and tossed it all on her work tray.

What few reserves he had left were draining quickly. His body hurt, but it was small compared to the ache in his chest and the increasingly loud pound of his pulse in his head.

"Let's go." He kept his eyes down, as if he had to watch his step.

She didn't move and he looked back. Fresh tears already slid down her cheeks.

"Do you want me to go back to my apartment?" she asked.

Garrick sighed. He was hurting and a little pissed off about it, but he wasn't an asshole and he hadn't lost sight of what was most important to him. Even if it wasn't reciprocated.

"I need you safe. Please come home with me."

She nodded. "Okay." She went to her desk, threw on her coat, and grabbed a few files. "We need to get you in the bath and then stretch out some of that damage."

If that was what it took to get her home again, for however long he could keep her there, he'd take it.

Chapter Twenty Four

Three days later, Savannah opened her eyes as the last ring of Garrick's house phone faded away. She lay in a wash of warm sunlight, sprawled across Garrick's huge bed, feeling decadent and spoiled. It had to be after ten o'clock. She smiled into the pillow and stretched all her aching and love-bruised parts. She hadn't slept this late since college.

The house phone rang again. She ignored it. Again.

Garrick was *definitely* feeling better and he'd proven it last night, twice. And once more this morning. His torso still looked like something out an episode of CSI, but his face was almost back to normal and his hip, thank god, was doing far better than either of them had expected after the fight. In fact, after thoroughly ravaging her this morning, he'd left for the arena and practice. Mark and Rick had told him to stay home another day. She and Garrick thought he'd be back on the ice for tomorrow night's game, though probably not for as much time as he'd normally play.

Savannah chuckled, thinking how much that would piss Garrick off. He'd be back where he belonged within a week.

And so, sadly, would she. She forced the thought aside, knowing full well it would crawl back to the top of her mind before long. It was always there, hovering.

Connecticut. Mom and Dad.

In the meantime, she didn't have anywhere to go. In fact, she didn't have anywhere she *could* go. Garrick, the sneaky bastard, had caught her at a low moment this morning. Or maybe it was a high moment? Her muscles had still been quivering with post-orgasmic joy. Her head still swimming with the rush of pleasure that had only just roared through her body. And her body still stretched with his thick cock jammed in her to the hilt as they lay gasping on the bed. Of course she'd promised to stay home today while he was out. How could she *not* have pledged to sleep in and relax and worry about packing later that night?

Truth be told, she hadn't been worrying about packing much at all over the past few days. Instead she'd devoted herself to helping Garrick mend and sending her resume to every professional sports team and college or university athletics department she could find. She'd had some nibbles, but nothing firm.

Mark had graciously let her out of her contract without forcing her to trudge through two weeks—let alone the balance of the season—humiliated at the hands of the Kramer family. The head trainer from the Université de Moncton had agreed to help Steve until her replacement could be found.

She had Mark's promise to put a positive spin on her sudden departure to anyone who called seeking reference. One scandal in the far reaches of New Brunswick wasn't certain to spread across the entire sport, but it wouldn't shock her if it did. Scouts, management, players—it was a business of networks, travel and keeping track of who was doing what. Once a rumor caught on the wind, it could travel far and wide in little time.

Her best hope was to jump to a new gig as quickly as possible. And regardless of how long her hunt lasted, she couldn't stay in Canada. She'd been granted her Canadian visa through a sponsorship—the Ice Cats—and there weren't many opportunities for new sponsorship in the area. She'd looked.

The phone rang again and she eyed it. It was like Grand Central Station around here today. She still didn't answer it. It was Garrick's phone. What if it was his mother calling? Or his sister?

She'd spend the day finding a moving service. The Ice Cats had paid for her relocation up here, but she was on her own to get back to Connecticut.

She'd told her parents and brothers what had happened, figuring it was better to hear it from her on their monthly Skype call than through the grapevine. She'd barely convinced them not to come to New Brunswick and inflict untold damage on the Kramers. Garrick had sat across the kitchen table and outside the view of the camera, silently cheering her family on the whole time she'd been trying to contain seven enraged hockey players—her dad being the worst in the bunch, much to Garrick's entertainment.

She rolled to the edge of the bed, loving and wincing at the various aches and pains Garrick had left behind. Staggering to her feet, she shuffled toward the bathroom. She was about to close the door behind her when her cell phone buzzed on the bedside table. Sparing it a glance, she shrugged and gave in to the call of the shower first. Whoever it was would leave a voicemail if it was important.

Garrick sat in his car and stared down the alleyway behind The Sugar Shack. His phone buzzed again and he checked to make sure it wasn't Savannah. Rhian. Sighing, he shoved the damn thing back into his pocket.

It was late morning, almost noon, and the bar wouldn't open until five. He'd been watching the back door for a couple hours now, noting the people coming and going. The beer delivery seemed routine. The driver genuine. The bar-backs hauling all the cases and kegs inside were just a couple of college kids working their asses off, from the looks of them. Nothing nefarious from what he could see.

But he hadn't imagined that back room, and there was definitely something more going on in the Sugar Shack then just prepping for a night's work. Robert Kramer had come and gone once this morning, not long after seven people—none wearing the Sugar Shack's uniform of a black t-shirt and jeans—had arrived, each stopping to knock on the back door before quickly being admitted by someone Garrick couldn't see. He'd bet his left nut it was one of the thugs he'd tangled with on his last visit to the Shack, and he cursed the placement of the dumpsters that had forced him to plant himself at this end of the alley. The view from the next street over would have been closer to the door and he'd have been able to see who was acting as doorman, if it weren't for those damn dumpsters.

Not that he had any idea what he would do with the information. Hell, he didn't have anything even approaching a plan. All he knew was he'd woken up this morning to Savannah's soft body curled into his, her smooth ass cheeks wriggling against his morning wood, and he'd known complete and utter happiness, followed by mind-erasing bliss.

Then he'd returned to reality. And the rage.

He wanted the Kramers to *pay*. Savannah couldn't stay, and he wouldn't ask her to even if he thought she would. She had worked too hard to chuck her career for some soon-to-be-retiree. She was starting her career just as his was coming to a stuttering halt.

He couldn't change any of that. But goddamn it, he was going to do his level best to see the Kramers didn't get their heart's desire—the Ice Cats—either.

It only seemed fair.

Not to mention, it felt damn good to channel all his anger into something, and if successful, that something would be good for his friends, his teammates, and his hometown. The Kramers owning the team would be a disaster. Preventing it would be just.

Maybe if he succeeded, the rest of it wouldn't hurt so damn much.

He caught a brief flash of color, movement, in the corner of his eye and he brought his head around quickly, his hand reaching for the ignition as he scanned the sidewalk and the street behind him. Nothing.

When, after five minutes of scanning the street, nothing and no one had materialized, he let go of his key and relaxed back against the seat. Glancing at his watch, he sighed. Staking out an alley was boring as hell, and already he was imagining things in his rearview mirror. It was going to be a long day.

Fortunately, he *could* sit here all day and no one would miss him. He'd mentioned to Rhian he might be back to work today, but Mark and Rick had told him he should wait another day or two. Not that he listened to them. Savannah felt he was ready and he trusted her opinion above all others.

He'd left his house this morning with every intention of proving Rick and Mark wrong. Of proving to Bobby Kramer he wasn't down or out of this fight. It would be satisfying to return to the ice before Bobby. Rumor had it he had a couple more days of recovery, at least. Garrick had been halfway to the arena, his mind churning with thoughts of the Kramers, when he'd turned his truck for the city instead.

The only good news about his renewed obsession with the Kramers and their dirty dealings was that while he was focused on that, he couldn't think about anything else.

It was a welcome respite. He wished he could drag it out, keep his crusade alive until Savannah was done packing and had left Moncton forever. Unfortunately, the league was eager to proceed, and Garrick had to act fast if he was going to make this work.

He considered the odds of him being able to slip in the back hallway and get pictures of the room he'd seen. Only, the bar didn't open for hours. Maybe he could sneak in the back when some of the staff or back office workers started to come and go.

He glanced at his watch again. The five minutes that had passed since he'd last checked the time might have been the longest five minutes of his life. Settling deeper into his seat, he told himself to relax and keep his eyes on the door.

His phone started in again and he yanked it from his pocket. Rhian. He never should have told him he'd be back today. At least it wasn't Savannah. She was going to be pissed if he left her trapped at the house all day and night. Maybe he'd call Rhian back later, when he would be off the ice after practice, and see if he'd go keep Savannah company. Maybe even take her to her place to pack.

Yeah, making that Rhian's job suddenly seemed like a great, if totally cowardly, idea.

Savannah took a long, leisurely shower, and let the hot water and Garrick's soap—a smell now forever branded in her memory—work its magic on her sore body. When her skin had finally pruned to the point she could no longer feel things with her fingertips, she shut off the water and wrapped herself in one of his big, fluffy towels.

She loved this house. He'd made it a home. One she'd been more comfortable in than any other since she'd left her parents' home to go to college. She brushed out her hair and took the time to dry it thoroughly. It had been her routine to tie her wet hair up into an unforgiving knot each morning. Now that she was unemployed, she relished having the time to blow it dry and the freedom to keep it loose around her shoulders.

By the time she stepped back into the bedroom, she was ready to tackle another round of job hunting online. She scooped up her phone and pressed the button for voicemail.

"Hello, Savannah. This is Brian with the Boston Bruins Human Resources Department. I'm pleased to be calling you regarding an offer for the Head Athletic Trainer position here in Boston. Please call me at..."

With a low growl, Garrick yanked his phone from his pocket and hit the answer button. "Dude, shouldn't you be at practice?"

Silence stretched until Rhian's low voice replied, "Shouldn't you?"

Shit.

Thinking quickly, Garrick put the phone to his other ear and turned to keep an eye on the alley. He'd seen four big men go into the bar a few minutes ago and hoped something interesting was going to happen.

"No. I decided to sit it out one more day," he said, cringing at how inauthentic he sounded.

Based on the long pause, Rhian didn't buy it. "What are you doing?"

"Nothing." He fought the urge to bang his head against the steering wheel. He still lied like a fourteen year old. "I'm home."

"Yeah? Why aren't you answering your phone?"

"I was in the shower," he said.

"For the past three hours?"

"Dude, what are you, my mother?"

Rhian didn't say anything and Garrick scowled at his own reflection in the window. The kid sure knew how to make him feel like a jerk.

"It's nothing, Rhian. Just some shit I'm looking into."

The back door swung open and the four men came out again, moving swiftly to the SUV parked at the other end of the alley. Garrick shifted in his seat, craning his neck to see their faces. He considered starting up the truck and following them, but let it go when they quickly pulled away and drove toward the highway.

Too late now. He was trying very hard not to be irritated with Rhian.

"Garrick—"

"Look, I have to go." He tried to sound like he was just busy and not pissed about sitting in his freezing cold truck for another couple hours because Rhian had forced him to miss his first attempt at tailing the bad guys. "I'll see you tomorrow."

"Garr—"

He hung up on his friend. He felt pretty bad about it too, but there was no way he was going to tell Rhian a damn thing. Not that he didn't trust the guy—hell, Rhian was the only one on the team who knew about him and Savannah, and even *she* was cool with that—but dragging him into this mess would be the worst thing Garrick could do.

His phone vibrated again and he shoved it back in his pocket, stretched his cramped legs as best he could, then settled back to watch the dirty alley do nothing some more.

He really needed to work on his plan.

Savannah sat at the kitchen island and stared out the back window at the barren winter fields, trying to wrap her head around the fact that she was due in Boston in a week.

It had to be the single biggest moment of her professional career. A top ten moment in life.

So why did she feel like crying?

She was so lost in her thoughts, she didn't think anything of the sound of a car crunching over the gravel in the driveway, the slam of the heavy car doors. She heard these sorts of noises all day while in town. When the doorbell chimed, she started, sloshing hot tea over her hand.

"Damn it!" she yelped, shaking the scalding liquid from her skin.

Who would be stopping by Garrick's house in the early afternoon on a weekday? She paused by the bottom of the stairs, unsure what to do. All the little hairs on the back of her neck prickled, standing at attention as goosebumps zipped across her skin.

Her pulse kicked up a notch as she studied the silhouettes of two large men through the sheer curtain on the door. Who were they? Could they see her?

Another man stepped up to the door, bending over the knob.

Three men?

The jiggle of the door and the soft scrape of something being inserted into the lock kicked her flight instinct into high gear. Forcing herself to move slowly, she eased her weight over the creaky floorboards as she backed toward the dining room. She considered her options. Her shoes were upstairs. Her car keys too. She couldn't risk getting trapped up there.

Her cell phone was in the kitchen. She took another step in that direction and peeked into the dining room to see if anyone was looking in the window. No one was there.

They must all be too busy picking the lock.

Her best option was to run for her phone, then maybe to the basement to lock herself in Garrick's ancient root cellar. The idea was terrifying, but maybe they wouldn't search that far and would assume she wasn't home.

She froze when the blare of a car horn came from the street. The crunch of driveway gravel was clear to her this time.

Standing in the wide doorway between the hall and the dining room, she could see the front porch out the large dining room windows. When the horn roared again, closer this time, a fourth man stepped from his position against the front of the house.

Jesus. How many of them are there?

Praying the new guy didn't turn around, she slipped around the dining room table and flattened herself against the front wall of the house. She stayed there, listening for voices, some clue about who they were, how many were out there, and why they'd come. Or been sent? She dared a quick peek to see who was out on the porch. And who was in the car making a damn racket.

She couldn't decide if she wanted to laugh or cry when Rhian leaped from his car and waved to the men on the porch. She couldn't hear what he said, but she could guess from his grand gesture and broad smile, it was a friendly greeting.

She eased farther into the window, now able to see two of the strange men in profile. She'd never seen one of them before, but the other looked vaguely familiar. A friend of Bobby's, maybe? Regardless, they appeared nonplussed by their welcoming committee and eager to avoid introductions.

At some signal, they moved off the porch and down the stairs. When they neared Rhian, Savannah considered running for the phone and dialing 9-1-1, but stayed rooted to the spot and watched the scene unfold.

Rhian kept his smile in place as he continued to talk to them, seemingly unaffected by their approach, shrugging as he waved at the house. The men marched past him, their smiles vague, exchanging looks that ranged from concerned to confused as they climbed into their black SUV and drove away.

Now she remembered. She'd seen one of the men in her neighborhood. Just as she'd seen that SUV parked in front of her condo.

She ran into the front hall and threw open the door just as Rhian jogged to the top of the porch stairs. Launching herself from the stoop, she threw herself against him and wrapped her arms around his neck.

"Whoa." Rhian caught her and held on. "You okay?"

"I am thanks to you."

Rhian set her on her feet and urged her back into the house. "Well, I'm not sure how long it's going to take that pack of morons to call into home base and get sent back out here. Get what you need and let's go."

Savannah didn't question him. In less than three minutes she had her shoes and coat on and was bolting down the porch stairs with Rhian right behind her.

Thanks to the adrenaline overload, her brain didn't fire on all cylinders again until they were on the highway to Moncton. "How did you know to come out to the house?"

"I didn't."

Jesus. That had been a really close call. "What's going on?"

"Nothing," he said. "I don't know." He sighed. "Well, maybe something. I feel stupid, since it's not like I'm his keeper, but Garrick said he'd be at practice today and he didn't show."

"He didn't?"

Rhian glanced at her. "So he *was* supposed to come in?"

"Yes. If he's not there, I have no idea where he is."

She pictured the men on Garrick's porch and her blood ran cold, panic fluttering in her chest.

"He's fine," Rhian assured her.

"How do you know?"

"I finally got the S.O.B. to answer his phone a while ago.

That's why I came out to see you. He's up to something, and I'm afraid it's either stupid or dangerous."

She debated brushing it off, keeping Rhian in the dark, but she needed his help. "It's probably both."

Rhian's bark of laughter made her smile. Her amusement was short lived when she glanced at the dashboard clock. "You should be at practice."

Rhian shrugged. "I'm glad I'm not."

"I'm glad you're not, too, but we need to get your ass back there."

He glanced at her. "Why?"

"Because we don't want the Kramers to think you showing up at the house was anything but coincidence." The more she thought about it, the more desperate she was to get Rhian back to the rink. She and Garrick were toast, but scouts were still looking at Rhian.

"Do you know where Garrick's friend Jack works?" she asked.

Rhian didn't comment on her rapid change in subjects. "Yeah, sure. He's over at the Brunswicker Ale House."

"Is it open for lunch?"

Rhian shrugged. "I think so."

"Great. Could you please take me there?"

She held her breath and prayed he would go along. That he wouldn't fight her when she insisted he leave her with Jack.

If Jack is even there. If they're even open.

She was grasping at straws, but somehow she'd figure out how to thread the right ones together.

Chapter Twenty Five

Garrick hunkered down behind the cold funky dumpster and lamented his change in scenery. He might get a better look at the back door from here, but he wasn't sure if that would net him anything but a burning desire to never, ever smell rotting chicken fingers and beer this closely again.

Peering through the small space between the corner of the dumpster and the wall, he rested his shoulder against god only knew what and prayed his hip would forgive him. It was cold and there was no way in hell he was sitting anywhere, let alone in the puddle of fluid that hadn't frozen on a twenty-five degree day.

He could stay here undetected for some time, provided no one took the trash out. And then, he just might be desperate enough to steal it if he thought it came from that damned back room. That is, if he could get his aching legs to spring up and make a run for it.

He grimaced at the image of him hobbling down the alley. His adolescent delusions of being the next James Bond were definitely a thing of the past.

The creak of the back door yanked him from his musings and he sank lower, praying the crates at his back were as sufficient cover up-close as they'd seemed from the street. A hand appeared on the release bar across the door, followed by a thick arm and a familiar Canadiens logo. A head of white-blond hair appeared in the door as one of the back office workers left.

The door swung shut quickly and Garrick sat perfectly still. A middle-aged woman hurried down the alley and out into the street. If she'd noticed him, she gave no indication.

It was two thirty. Early to be going home when you come in at nine. He wouldn't have pegged Kramer as the kind of boss who offered flex hours.

He scanned the alley again. He'd walked the block three times, circling the alley to search for any sign of cameras or surveillance. The windows were still covered, and they faced a brick wall on the other side where some enterprising architect in the 1950s decided windows to an alley weren't necessary.

If the smell were any indication, that architect might have been right.

Clenching his teeth, Garrick shifted his weight again and accepted he wasn't going to be able to stay where he was for long. Maybe he'd follow the next worker to leave back to their house.

And do what?

Savannah took up residence at the bar of the Brunswicker Ale House, having convinced Rhian that she was just going to ask Jack to help her figure out where Garrick might be and that they would call Rhian as soon as they had a plan.

In other words, she'd lied.

Within a minute of sliding onto the stool, Jack came to take her order.

"Hello, gorgeous. What can I do for you today?" he asked with a playful wink and flirtatious smile as he passed her the menu.

She smiled back, intrigued to meet Garrick's old friend. Somehow Garrick had failed to mention Jack Chevalier was drop-dead gorgeous.

Black hair, blue eyes, pink cheeks and long, sooty lashes that should have made him look like a girl, especially with those cheek bones. He obviously had a gift for charming the ladies, his face giving him unfair advantage, his outrageous flirtation sealing the deal. She ordered her drink automatically, enjoying his lingering look. *Wow.*

"I'm Savannah," she said in a low voice, praying the name would mean something. She had no idea if Garrick had told his friend about her, but she knew he'd talked to Jack about the

Kramers. What she didn't know was where else Jack might have sent Garrick to investigate. She needed a place to start searching.

Jack's smile faltered but he kept wiping down the bar. He didn't so much as glance at her, but she sensed she had his undivided attention.

"Can you help me?"

Her heart fell when he tossed the rag into his workspace behind the bar and walked away. Damn it.

She was racking her brain for what the hell her next step should be when he came back, set down her Diet Coke and crossed his arms on the bar.

"What can I get you?" Another big smile. His piercing blue gaze pinned her.

Her face might crack from the wide smile she slapped on. "A tuna melt, no tomato, please."

"Anything else?"

"Any idea where he might be?"

He shook his head. "Fries?"

She tried not to let her frustration show. "Yes, please. With vinegar, if you have it."

"I do. I'm not sure I have what else you're looking for, though."

She nodded and looked down at her hands clenched in her lap. His laugh brought her head up again. He was a marvelous actor, his eyes shining with amusement. She wondered if that was something he'd been born with or had to learn. The idea of that pretty face in prison gave her a chill.

He leaned in close, as if she'd said something funny and he was going to whisper his presumably naughty response in her ear. "How long has he been missing?"

She turned her face toward his, her nose almost bumping his ear, their cheeks brushing. "He's not, really. We're not sure."

Even an actor as talented as Jack couldn't disguise his

dubious look as he departed to help another customer.

When he returned with her food, they began an exhausting back and forth. To anyone watching, they were flirting like strangers who had nothing to lose. He refilled her drink. She ordered dessert. He brought her coffee. It all appeared, she sincerely hoped, perfectly innocent. In reality, she was slowly sketching out her problem to Jack. Her face had burned when he acknowledged he'd seen Bobby's recent television interview, his narrow gaze and muttered curse a small consolation before he returned to his flirtatious act.

Now she was nursing her last cup of coffee. Between her nerves and the obscene amount of food and drink she'd consumed in order to drag out her stay, she thought she might barf. Three o'clock and Jack's break couldn't arrive soon enough.

Her phone sat silent in her lap. Garrick hadn't called. He hadn't answered when she called. Hadn't replied to her texts.

She'd begged Jack to tell her where he'd sent Garrick, but he wouldn't do it, knowing she'd go there alone. He insisted he would use the hour he had between his double shifts and take her there himself.

She thought about texting Garrick where she was. Who she was with. She had no idea if he was even getting these damn messages, but Jack's name and her presence in a Kramer establishment might motivate him to come find her.

But she was also a chicken. She could only hope Garrick would forgive her for dragging Jack into this mess. Jack, like Rhian, was someone to protect, not endanger. She understood that.

But it wasn't enough to override her escalating fear and the need to find Garrick.

Garrick walked around the block one more time, trying to ease the ache in his cold legs and sore hip before sneaking back into the alley and behind that god-awful dumpster. He was coming around the corner, the Sugar Shack's front door halfway down the block, when the SUV he'd seen a while back returned and the same four men piled out.

Garrick eased over to the nearest shop window and pretended great interest in the legion of women either painting toes or having their toes painted. Several of them gave him a strange look and he smiled back, trying to appear innocent.

When he judged enough time had safely passed, he tucked his head down farther into his collar and turned to continue his walk. He was three steps beyond the nail salon's window when he realized he'd made a big mistake.

They were waiting for him.

Oh, fuck.

He ran like hell in the other direction. His boots hit the pavement hard and he winced, regretting that he had let his legs get so cold in the alley and hoping his pounding heart would pump blood back into his muscles quickly.

Taking the corner at a dead run, he pelted full speed down the side street and cut into the alley at the last moment. It was the fastest way to his car.

His sprint seemed to have caught his pursuers off guard and he was gaining ground. He was just beginning to warm up and ease into a long-legged stride when the back door of the Sugar Shack flew open and Blondie, the Canadiens fan, stepped out into the alley in front of him, with Goon Two hot on his heels.

His pace faltered. He looked over his shoulder. Still being chased.

Damn.

Skidding to a halt in the icy slush, Garrick spun, facing the four men first. He'd hardly planted his feet when the first punch landed.

He was no stranger to a good fight. He was a hockey player, for crying out loud, but no one, not even a seasoned brawler, could have done anything but crumple under a pile-on like this.

His head hit the pavement with a resounding crack, though

he feared only he could hear the sickening sound in his head. As his vision narrowed to a thin, brightly lit tunnel, he thought he heard his name and forced his eyes open. The blows had stopped and someone was rolling him onto his stomach, his face pressed to the cold dreck coating the alley.

His stomach roiled and his vision blurred, but not before he saw Savannah standing at the head of the alley, crying out his name.

No!

Savannah stood frozen in horror, the echo of her cry still ringing in the alley, when Jack Chevalier dragged her out of view of the gang of men assaulting Garrick.

She fought against the arms wrapped around her until Jack managed to get them both across the street and behind the cab of his truck. He shook her hard. "Savannah! *Think!*"

She *was* thinking. She was thinking those men were going to kill Garrick. She was thinking she had to stop them. She was thinking that this was a really stupid and typical time for her to figure out just how much she cared about him.

"Savannah, *please.* They'll only come after you, too. Stay here."

Savannah forced herself to calm, to listen to him, because he was right. There was no future for her and Garrick if she got them both killed. With a whimper, she slumped back against the truck and sank to the ground, her forehead on her knee.

Jack ran along the cars parked in front of them, his head low, until he was across from the alley.

"Those are the men," she called to Jack.

"What?" He didn't look away from the alley.

She climbed back to her feet to go see what held his rapt attention, but he ran back to her side at the truck.

"Those are the men who came to Garrick's house earlier. The ones Rhian scared off."

Jack grimaced.

Savannah dug her phone out of her pocket and began to dial 9-1-1. Jack yanked the phone from her hand before she could hit send.

"They might have police scanners." He cleared her phone and shoved it back in her hand.

"So?"

"So, I don't want them to panic. And I don't want them to clear out before the cops get here."

"I need Garrick to be safe."

Jack's expression was sympathetic but firm. "They took him inside," he said as he searched the street.

She didn't know Jack well, but she could tell there was more he wasn't saying.

"What?"

"I don't think he's conscious."

She'd seen his head hit the pavement, so she wasn't all that surprised, but her hand jerked for her phone again automatically. She checked herself when Jack took his phone out and started dialing.

He put the phone to his ear. "I have a friend. A Mountie."

"A what?"

Jack flashed a quick smile. "Royal Canadian Mounted Police."

She pictured the street swarming with men in red jackets on horses. "Like Dudley Do-Right?"

Jack rolled his eyes. "No. Well, yes. But they're like your state police. He'll help us."

Help us what? She paced away from Jack and leaned against the bed of his truck. One man wasn't going to be much help unless he brought a whole lot of friends with him.

The front door of the Sugar Shack swung open and let in their first customers of the night, the neon lights in the window flickering on.

Overwhelmed by helplessness, she turned away and

looked into the jumble of stuff in the bed of Jack's truck. She stared blankly at the mishmash of tools and hardware supplies and an idea flickered to life.

She hauled herself up and over the side of the truck. Jack watched her while he spoke on the phone and desperately tried to convince whoever was on the other end to take action. *Some friend.* Then again, Jack was an ex-con, deservedly so or not. He no doubt had an uphill battle.

Grabbing what she needed, she vaulted back onto the sidewalk and yanked open the passenger door of the truck. She upended her purse onto Jack's front seat, pocketed her Swiss Army knife, and shoved her prize from the back of Jack's truck into the now empty bag. She then slung it over her shoulder and turned for the Sugar Shack.

Jack caught her arm. "Where the hell are you going?"

She looked back at Garrick's friend. "I'm going into the Sugar Shack. You're calling in reinforcements. If you see either me or Garrick leaving that building by some means other than our own volition, call the cops and let the police scanners be damned, Jack."

"You can't go in there."

"No, *you* can't go in there. I don't give a fuck if they recognize me."

"And what are you going to do if they do see you?"

Savannah smiled grimly. "The public will protect me in the bar. And otherwise, I have everything I need."

"Really?"

"You have no idea what I can do," Savannah muttered.

Chapter Twenty Six

Pain exploded in Garrick's head the moment he regained consciousness. It was all he knew, all he could process. It took him far longer than it should have to notice his hands and feet were tied to a chair and his mouth was stuffed with a foul-tasting rag that was further splitting his fat lips. The eye that had only just recovered from the locker room brawl was swollen to the point that the pressure on his eyeball felt equal to the punch that had started it.

Without a doubt, opening his eyes would be punished with additional excruciating pain, but he fought past his desire to slip back into the blessed darkness and forced his one working eye open.

More darkness. Where the fuck was he?

A couple slow, painful blinks brought shapes from the shadows, looming close and above him. Shelves. Boxes. The storage closet?

He turned his head to try to see more, and ruthlessly forced back his need to gag when his head spun like it was trying to detach from his shoulders. His concussion was causing plenty of nausea without the noxious fabric jammed between his teeth helping things along.

He needed to get out of here.

The dull thump of music vibrated through the wall. The bar must be open. He tried to yell, but the gag was effective, his voice a hollow shout that didn't rise above the pounding bass even within the closet. He lost hope that someone might even hear him on their way to the bathroom.

Yeah, he was screwed.

He tipped his head down to examine the binding holding his arms to the chair and winced as his brain shifted inside his skull.

He'd had his bell rung a few times over the years and knew the symptoms. He needed to get his head scanned to make sure it wasn't more serious. Either way, he'd be off the ice for a few days, maybe longer.

But first, he really needed to get out of here.

Praying he didn't pass out, Garrick rocked his chair, using what little leverage he had with his feet taped to the legs to lift and bump his chair closer to the shelves. With each hard thump of impact, his vision waivered and his stomach roiled. He kept at it anyway.

Savannah went straight to the bar, her back to the room, and ordered a Diet Coke.

She scanned the crowd using the mirrors behind the rows of liquor bottles. She didn't see anyone she recognized from the house. Though they'd all been wearing coats, and she'd mostly only seen their profiles. The more she thought about it, the more she worried it could be any of the bigger guys filtering into the bar.

She needed to act fast.

The door to the back hall caught her eye. She'd start there.

She'd taken no more than three steps, her purse on her shoulder and her beverage in hand, when a big guy stepped through the door and leaned against the wall beside it.

Bouncer. A big one. His platinum hair was unusual enough that she was certain she hadn't seen him before. When he looked right through her to the bar, she was convinced he hadn't seen her before either.

Now how the hell was she going to get past him?

Circling the room as if searching for a friend, she skirted the dance floor and made her way to the pool tables at the back. Not surprisingly, she found two men playing a game, both preening for the gaggle of young women sitting at nearby tables. The women were here to watch the show, as evidenced by the empty pool tables around them.

She watched the age-old mating ritual unfold, amused and depressed by the familiar scene. The women were made-up to the hilt, already on the prowl at five o'clock, make-up fresh, heels high, and skirts short. She knew the type. Had walked a mile in those very stilettos, a time or two, when her friends had convinced her to relax and enjoy the hunt for once.

Focusing on a particularly keen-eyed group of young women, she wandered over, standing near enough to hear the women's gossip, their snark so catty it was shameless. Perhaps not so like her and her friends after all. These women were *brutal.*

She edged closer, leaning in until one of the women jostled her.

"Oh! I'm so sorry!"

Savannah smiled broadly and brandished her drink. "No worries, hon."

The woman's eyes narrowed on her but Savannah kept her boozy smile in place. When the woman went to turn away, Savannah clutched her arm and whispered conspiratorially. "Look out for that group of girls over there," she said, waving vaguely with her glass.

"Pardon me?"

"The one there," Savannah said, waving again, only this time more pointedly in the direction of the other large group of women in the room. "One of those bitches said your friend has a bad perm and that she gets her make-up tips from RuPaul."

Savannah had no idea why the latter was an issue, but she'd once seen a girlfriend in college lose her mind over this alleged insult. Worried this alone wouldn't do the trick, she went in for the kill. "She also said your extensions looked cheap."

The woman gasped and Savannah released her arm, staggering back. By the time the woman practically fell on her girlfriends, Savannah was back in the main bar area, headed for clearer ground.

The screech that emanated from the pool room was

spectacular. Everyone in the bar turned toward the source of the noise.

Savannah looked back in time to see the first pitcher of beer sailing over the heads of the two pool players to splash down on the table of women across the way. A hell of a first move, she thought, wincing as a beer tsunami spanned the width of the room.

From there, it was impossible to tell what happened as people rushed to watch the show and blocked her view within seconds. The bouncer with the platinum hair leaped forward, waded into the crowd, and disappeared into the bystanders and the riot beyond.

Savannah ran into the back hall, tossing her purse strap over her head so it lay across her chest and she had both hands free.

The dim corridor was lined with doors. Ladies' Room. Men's Room. Supplies. She was about to inspect the only door without a label when it swung open and a man stepped out. He looked so much like Bobby Kramer there was no mistaking who he was. Savannah dove into the women's bathroom, her hand catching the door handle at the last second and holding it open a crack. She prayed she hadn't been spotted, not sure if Bobby's father would recognize her. She suspected he would.

"Pack it all up and get it the fuck out of here. Now."

The fake British accent confirmed her suspicion. Robert Kramer.

"Yes, boss," replied a voice from the room beyond.

"I'll have the truck here in an hour or less. I expect this office to be up and running in the warehouse on Sylvio by midnight."

At the bang of the back door closing, she sneaked a peek into the hallway and found it blessedly empty. She slipped out of the bathroom and heard the thunk of a deadbolt being locked. The mysterious door at the end of the hallway was once again closed tight. A plan began to take shape in her head, but she had to find Garrick first.

The racket from the bar was still loud, the screeches ear splitting. She forgot all about her pang of guilt, though, when she heard a muffled thump from beyond the door labeled Supplies.

She planted her shoulder against the door, only realizing as her head made contact with the hollow wood that it was locked.

Grateful no one had witnessed that slick maneuver, she backed up and studied the lock, listening as another series of bumps issued from within. She tried the handle, shaking the door as hard as she could, and the thumping noises stopped, replaced by a steady, faint moaning sound. The door was old and scratched. The door jamb was also wood and in serious need of updating.

She was going to be seriously embarrassed if she barged in on some couple getting it on, but she had to check. All those years of breaking into her brothers' rooms were about to pay off.

Selecting the biggest of her Swiss Army knife blades, she jimmied it between the door and the jamb where she felt the resistance of the lock. She worked it back and forth as she shoved her shoulder and hip against the door as hard as she could.

With a soft click, the lock gave way and she stumbled into a tiny room. She caught herself just before she slammed into the shelving filled with cleaning supplies and toilet paper. A sharp grunt brought her head up.

Garrick! Gagged and tied to a chair at the back of the long, narrow space.

He looked like shit, but conscious and in one piece. One eye was almost swollen shut but the wide-eyed stare she got from the other said his mental faculties were in good working order. No question he was processing the sight before him just fine when he started yelling at her through the nasty-looking rag in his mouth.

The vise clamped around her chest eased for the first time

in hours. He was okay.

She hesitated. She wanted to remove the gag but he was hollering like he'd like to bring the walls down around their ears. She couldn't risk him giving her away. And she'd be back in a minute.

She pillaged the office supplies on the shelf above her, grabbed a broom, winked at Garrick, and stepped back out into the hallway, closing the door firmly behind her.

Garrick fought at his bindings like a man possessed. Never in his life had he seen anything more terrifying than Savannah standing in the door with nothing more than a pocket knife, winking at him like a crazy person before going back out into Robert Kramer's lair. With a broom.

What the hell is she doing?

He howled around the wad of cloth in his mouth, sounding a little crazed to his own ears, and promptly shut up. Christ, he didn't want to garner any more attention than they already had. How the hell had she gotten past Blondie? And Robert Kramer was in the building. Garrick had been addled, but he'd heard the cheeseball accent.

That dude was one scary motherfucker.

He fought harder against the ropes and winced as they sawed into his skin. Sweat broke out across his body, his shirt sticking to him beneath his heavy jacket. His respiration rate increased until he risked gagging again.

Before Savannah had appeared, he'd been listening to the commotion out in the bar. The muffled noises were still too distant and vague for him to determine what was happening, but now it was mostly drowned out by what sounded like someone pounding on a door nearby.

Was that Savannah? Had they caught her too?

He yanked his arm harder, on the verge of dislocating his shoulder. Blood trickled down his wrist from beneath the ropes. He kept going.

He'd made some headway when the door swung open again and Savannah rushed to him.

"Are you okay?"

He shouted his answer. She couldn't understand him through the gag. It was probably for the best.

She plucked at the knot behind his head and he gasped as the fabric fell away from his mouth.

"What the *fuck* are you doing here!?" His voice was hoarse, the ridiculous sound compounded by his hugely swollen bottom lip.

Savannah eyed him then the rag in her hand, like she was seriously considering reinserting it in his mouth.

"I'm sorry," he said quickly. "I'm glad you came. Now, please, let's get the hell out of here."

She nodded and fell to her knees, working at the rope holding his right hand with her little knife. "Are you okay?"

"Yes. No."

She stopped and searched his face with her eyes.

"I'm going to be okay. Should see a doctor about the head, but otherwise fine."

"Have you seen your face?"

"Bad?"

She grimaced.

He kept working at his left wrist, ignoring the burn of the rope cutting into his skin. She didn't seem to be getting anywhere either. His right wrist was still pinned. He was about to suggest she work the knot instead when his hand popped free. He went to work on the knot holding his left hand and she started on his feet.

Within a minute, they had him free. He sprang from the chair and stopped, his hand clutching a shelf to steady himself.

Savannah slipped her arm around his waist. "You're not okay."

"No, I am. Everything hurts, but I'm going to be okay."

"You better be."

He wondered if his head injury was allowing him to hallucinate the tender look in her eyes. He wanted it to be true so badly, it was entirely possible he'd conjured the image from some combinations of sheer wishfulness and brain damage.

They staggered to the door. Savannah propped his shoulder against a box of napkins and peeked out into the hallway before ducking back in.

"You ready?"

"Yeah, from here we can go right out the back."

"Not anymore." She opened the door and helped him out into the hallway.

He gawked at the spectacle before him.

Blondie was trussed up on the floor. His hands were bound, his mouth forcibly shut, his feet and calves wrapped to the knee in shiny silver. He struggled against his bindings, but wasn't getting anywhere, as he appeared to be attached to the door leading to the mysterious office like some kind of human crossbar. His bindings were attached to ropes of silver wrapped around the doorknob behind him and the emergency release bar of the back exit. The broom handle, secured in a silver web, was jammed in the release bar of the back door, holding it in the locked position.

Savannah smiled sheepishly and pulled a huge roll of duct tape from her purse.

"But, how…"

"I'll tell you later. Right now we need to get out of here."

He stared a moment longer. "Sweet Jesus, you *are* god's gift to tape."

Savannah grinned.

A fierce pounding shook the back office door.

"Why can't they open it?"

"Aside from the bouncer acting as a wedge?" she asked, as if this were an everyday occurrence. She reached into her purse and fished out a stapler. "I found this in the supply closet."

"I don't get it."

She punched out a cleat and carefully inserted it into the lock in the knob.

He smiled. *Genius.* "I did that to a friend's locker in middle school."

She shrugged. "Still works?"

He laughed then clutched his head. "Shit. I guess it does. Now let's get the fuck out of here and call the cops."

"Everybody freeze!"

As if forced to obey the command, Garrick and Savannah held still. When Jack Chevalier rushed into the hallway with a huge cop at his back, Garrick slumped against the wall, taking Savannah with him.

Jack and Savannah barely caught him as he slid to the floor, his head pounding, his body aching. None of that mattered. Savannah was safe. For the first time in hours, days, *weeks*, he felt like he could breathe. His legs no longer needed to hold him up.

"Are you okay, G?"

Garrick didn't bother to answer.

"Jack, is there an ambulance here?" Savannah asked.

"Yeah, I'll go get the EMTs." He sprang back to his feet. "Grady, can you get G some help?"

"Yeah, come on," Grady said as he led Jack back down the hallway and into the bar.

Garrick watched them go, wondering how the hell Jack was friends with a cop and why that cop seemed so protective of Jack.

He smiled at Savannah weakly. "I think we did it."

"What?"

"Got the sonofabitch."

She gently touched his mangled face. "I knew you were

going to save the team."

"Not bloody likely," snapped an all-too-familiar British accent.

Garrick turned his head too quickly and sent his brain careening around inside his skull. He swallowed back the nausea and fought to remain conscious.

He held on to Savannah and she hauled him back onto his feet while Robert and Bobby Kramer walked down the hallway toward them.

Where the hell had they come from?

Chapter Twenty Seven

Heart pounding, Savannah kept one eye on the Kramers while she hauled Garrick back to his feet.

She almost stumbled when Garrick immediately began walking, hardly having gained his feet before he strode purposefully toward the Kramers and the bar beyond. The cops, Jack, and the public were just around the corner. Unfortunately, that public appeared to still be engaged in a bar brawl of her making, and everyone else was probably trying to break it up.

Jesus, those women really took shit personally.

"Not so fast, Mr. LeBlanc, Ms. Morrison."

Garrick shoved her behind his back so fast her shoulder bounced off the wall. *What the fuck?* She tried to step back to his side but stopped when Robert Kramer pointed the gun in his hand at Garrick's chest.

Her heart lurched and her brilliant rescue plan went straight to hell.

"What the fuck do you want? The place is crawling with cops," Garrick said, his voice hoarse.

She hoped they'd think that was anger. He looked to be barely holding down his lunch. And *was* the place crawling with cops? So far she'd only seen one. Where the hell were Jack and Grady, anyway?

"I know what I want," Bobby said and she snapped her attention back to him.

His still-blackened, beady eyes slid over her body. She wanted to retch.

Payback was going to be a big bad bitch.

She edged away while Garrick tried to block Bobby's approach. Robert pressed the gun to Garrick's ribs and he froze.

Bobby's meaty hand clamped around her upper arm.

Fear unlike any she'd felt before clutched at her chest. She couldn't breathe. Bobby's rage boiled in his eyes, his intent a blatant mixture of sex and violence written across his face. She wrenched her arm free, only to have it captured the moment Garrick grunted and she turned to see the nose of the pistol drilled into his ribs.

This time Bobby didn't let go, no matter how hard she fought him. He got his other arm clamped around her waist and dragged her down the hallway and through the ladies' room door.

Her only consolation was she still had her purse. She'd staple his goddamn eyeball if given half a chance.

As the door shut behind them, she heard Garrick shout her name and she braced, terrified she'd hear a gun shot. Bobby slammed her against the wall, his arm to the back of her neck, her face smashed to the tile. His crotch and growing erection ground against her ass and jammed her hip bones painfully against the unforgiving ceramic.

Her face hurt. Hell, everything hurt, but it didn't matter a damn when his hand worked its way into her waistband. She thrust herself forward, using his weight against him as she plastered herself to the wall. Bobby grunted. His hand was trapped against her stomach. He jerked his arm from the back of her neck, grabbed the back of her pants, and yanked her back.

"Nice try, bitch," he spat into her ear, his breath close, his hand wrenching the button of her jeans open.

She waited, desperate to scream, to vomit, to beg him to leave her alone as the zipper slid down. She held her breath until he pulled his hand from her waistband, and as she'd hoped and feared, lowered himself, eager to press his now rigid erection against her ass.

With a mighty heave, she threw her head back. Pain burst across the back of her skull and she felt the satisfying crunch of cartilage collapsing. Bobby's grip loosened, and she spun around. Howling in pain, Bobby slammed her against the wall with all his weight behind him.

Her breath left her body in a great whoosh, her already sore head striking the tile with enough force to make her see stars.

He pressed his face against her cheek, smearing her with his blood. "I'm going to make you pay for that, too."

God help her, she believed him.

The door opened and noise from the hallway and the bar beyond poured into the room. She prayed it was help coming. Bobby apparently knew better. He held her up against the wall with a straight arm and a tight hand around her neck as his father and Garrick came into the room.

"What the fuck?" Bobby snarled.

"No time for that now, son," Robert Kramer said mildly, locking the door behind him. "We have more company arriving out front. You can finish that once we're away from here."

Savannah locked eyes with Garrick. He stood holding his hands out with Robert Kramer behind him, doubtless with his gun at Garrick's back.

Garrick seemed calm, but then his gaze searched her body, eye lids twitching at the blood on her face, the grip on her neck. When he focused on her mid-section and her open jeans, his eyes narrowed. Bobby was either stupid or not paying attention, because Garrick telegraphed his next move as clear as day.

She punched down on Bobby's bad elbow. He roared as already painful tendons strained. She held on for dear life, forcing his grip from her neck and pulling him off balance as she fell to the floor. Bobby yanked his arm free just as Garrick crashed into him.

She shoved her way out from beneath their grappling limbs and crawled under the sinks. She looked up to search for a clear path to the door and found a gun in her face.

Robert Kramer smiled grimly. "I suggest you ask Mr.

LeBlanc to stop, or I'll shoot you both. I haven't a thing to lose."

She swallowed the lump lodged in her throat and croaked, "Garrick."

The grunting tangle of arms and legs across the room paid no attention amidst the thump of flesh hitting flesh. Carefully, her hands where Robert Kramer could see them, she crawled from under the sinks, stood, and cleared her throat.

"Garrick!"

He heard her. With a shove, he threw himself off Bobby and onto his feet, stumbling back into her. He was in no condition to walk, let alone brawl. She hoped like hell he hadn't just made his head worse.

Not that it would matter if they didn't find some way to get the hell away from the Kramers.

She wrapped her arm around his waist and made a show of clinging to him, giving him a chance to get his head cleared and his legs under him. He curled an arm around her shoulders, holding tight, and tucked her face against his chest. She took the opportunity to refasten her pants.

She was terrified, her hands shaking as she fumbled with the button, but it was somehow better with her clothes on properly.

They were in the women's bathroom in a bar loaded with cops and the backdoor blocked. If they stalled for time, someone would come find them. Jack and Grady should already be looking, shouldn't they?

"What the fuck are you going to do with us?" Garrick asked.

Robert Kramer watched his son drag himself up off the floor. Bobby hadn't looked so hot before she'd smashed his face and elbow. Now he looked like a prize fighter who'd gone ten rounds and lost.

Her gaze darted to the door when someone jiggled the handle.

Hurry up!

Bobby snapped out of his staggering confusion at the

255

noise. With a grunt, he stumbled into the handicapped stall. Only then did she notice the heavy wood door beyond the cubicle wall.

Oh shit. They have a way out.

Garrick's death grip on her arm told her he saw it too. Should they run for the door? Maybe Robert was a lousy shot and wouldn't hit anything vital before they could escape into the relative safety of the hallway.

The muzzle of the gun drilling into her kidney sent her heart rate higher and answered the question for her. Frantic, she scanned the room, the doors, the cubicles, anything, trying to come up with a way to escape. She wiped her sweating palms down her shirt and found her purse still hung across her chest.

They needed a way out and all she had was fucking tape and a stapler.

The door handle jiggled again. Why the hell weren't they breaking the thing down?

If they couldn't get out to the cops, then they needed the cops in here. Now.

Garrick froze when Bobby threw open the door in the stall and revealed a dark hallway. This was bad. There was no way in hell he could let Savannah go through that door. He curled his hands into fists and shifted on his feet. It was hard to find his balance when his head felt like he was on a fucking tilt-a-whirl, but how well he fought didn't matter as much as getting the gun off Savannah and onto him.

It would be a real pleasure to bury his fist into Robert Kramer's face, even if it meant getting shot.

Savannah's fingernails drilled into his arm and he looked down at her. She grabbed hold of him with both hands and let loose a blood curdling scream.

Garrick staggered back, his ears ringing as the sound ricocheted around the tile room, his eyes glued to the gun still pressed to her back. Robert Kramer looked as stunned as Garrick felt, and—*thank Christ*—didn't seem to have an itchy trigger finger.

What the fuck was Savannah thinking?

She stared up at Garrick. "Whatever happens, we are not going through that door. I'd rather be fucking shot."

Who was he to argue?

With what strength he had left, he yanked Savannah to the side, throwing her in the direction of the door to the bar, and lurched toward Robert Kramer.

"Do it again!" Garrick shouted.

She let rip another screech that would make any teenage horror film victim proud. Someone outside this goddamn bathroom had to hear it. The sound brought Garrick to the edge of consciousness, but now he had a gun trained on him and that was working to keep him pretty alert. Bobby barreled through the stall door and charged at Savannah.

She was ready for him. With a quick jerk, she unfurled a foot of duct tape and wrapped it around Bobby's wrist as he reached for her. Bobby jerked back and Savannah followed until his hand slammed into the cubicle wall. It took Savannah less than three seconds to duct tape Bobby's arm to the stall frame securely bolted into the ceiling and floor.

Robert Kramer's mouth dropped open as his son was disabled by nothing more than a pissed-off woman and some home improvement supplies. He swung his gun back toward her as she trussed Bobby's other arm to the other side of the door.

"Get behind Bobby!" Garrick yelled.

Savannah dove under Bobby's arm and into the stall, then plastered herself to Bobby's back. He tried to kick her away and got his ankles taped together for his troubles. Then another piercing wail rent the air. The last note still bounced off the tiles, echoing in the room and his head, when something heavy hit the bathroom door with a loud crack of wood splitting.

Finally!

Robert Kramer didn't seem to know where to point his gun any longer. He looked at the door to their escape route almost longingly, and then at his hog-tied son blocking the way.

The door to the bathroom flew open with a crash, pieces of particle board and the brass lock sailing through the air.

"Freeze! Don't even think about it!" Grady shouted as he barreled through the door, his gun raised. "Robert Kramer, you're under arrest!"

Savannah ran towards Garrick as he jumped out of the way of the good guys, but his foot swung through air instead of finding tile floor. His tenuous grasp on his relative orientation to the earth finally failed entirely. He closed his eyes, knowing the moment his head hit the sinks, or the floor, or whatever stopped his fall first, was going to be bad. Really bad. But he didn't have the will, or perhaps sense, to put out an arm to catch himself.

He grunted when he landed on his ass one second before his head struck the relative softness of someone's legs. The sudden stop jarred his head, shaking his already loose brain. He smiled up at Savannah, then went under.

Chapter Twenty Eight

Savannah stood in the flashing lights of countless emergency and public safety vehicles on the street in front of the Sugar Shack. If only Garrick were there. They'd been separated as soon as the EMTs had found them sprawled on the bathroom floor. She'd been pulled away to give a statement to the various authorities present, while Garrick had been loaded into an ambulance and taken to the hospital.

Her heart had nearly stopped when he collapsed. She was still worried sick, but tried to be patient. She'd been asked to explain at least three times what she'd done with the duct tape, the last time clearly just for the entertainment of the recently arrived brass. Since she had started a bar fight, among other legally questionable transgressions, she played along for as long as she could stand it.

Now she wanted to find Garrick and be sure he was okay.

Turning in place one more time, she finally caught a glimpse of Jack sitting on the back gate of his truck about fifty feet away. Threading through the police cars parked at haphazard angles along the street, she made her way to him and sat by his side.

"Garrick called and asked me to take you home when all this was over."

Why hadn't he called her? She forced herself to smile. "Yeah, a ride would be great. I'm just going to call Garrick before we go, okay?"

"Yeah, okay. I'll wait here."

"Thanks."

She walked back out into the sea of flashing lights and official vehicles and dialed Garrick's number.

"Hey."

She breathed a sigh of relief. "Hi."

He chuckled, though it sounded like an effort. "Thank god that's over, huh?"

"I hear they found another office on Sylvio, over by the airport, and that they're headed to the Kramers' residence right now."

"Good," he said.

An awkward pause seemed to last forever. She wanted to say so much, but couldn't figure out if any of it was right.

"You should go get some rest," Garrick said. "The Ice Cats will be begging for you to come back right away."

She swallowed hard, the tears returning. She couldn't bring herself to say the words.

Garrick's voice cut through the buzzing in her head. "Sav? You there?"

Of all the things she wanted to tell him, this probably wasn't the best place to start. "I got the job."

"What?"

"I got the job. The Bruins. I have to be in Boston in a week."

"That's great," he said, his voice hoarse, but he still sounded like he meant it.

Always so damn generous. She looked out over the flashing lights, pointedly ignoring Jack as more tears rolled down her cheeks.

"You're safe now," he said gently. "You should go back to your place and start packing."

"Yeah." She did need to pack. She had to leave. More silence. It was probably better this way, but when he remained mute, she died a little.

Garrick sighed. "You'll be okay tonight?"

No. "Let me know if there are any issues with your scan, okay?"

"Sure," he said.

She didn't believe him, but she left it alone. She had no right to demand anything.

260

"Goodnight," she choked out, barely disguising her tears.

"Goodnight, Savannah." Garrick hung up.

She stood amidst the hive of activity surrounding the crime scene, her tears unchecked, her breath hitching on silent sobs. When yet another officer looked at her with concern, she stumbled toward Jack.

He held out one arm, and in spite of only having known him for a matter of hours, she gratefully stepped into his embrace and buried her face against his chest.

"Your friend is really stupid," she muttered.

He chuckled. "Yeah, he can be."

"I'm really stupid, too," she said.

Jack wisely didn't comment.

"I got a job in Boston. Now he's sending me away."

"Huh."

"It's the Bruins."

"Wow. I guess you have to go."

That was the problem. Savannah thought about crying harder for a few seconds, then lifted her head and looked into Jack's somber face.

She considered what she knew about their mutual friend. "He's being noble, isn't he?"

Jack shrugged, but his midnight blue eyes twinkled.

She dropped her arms from around Jack's waist and stood back. "I'm ready to go home now."

"And where's that?"

She gave him the address.

"But that's Garrick's house."

"You bet it is."

Jack grinned and got into his truck.

Garrick drove toward his beloved farmhouse as the first pale light of dawn streaked across the sky. Getting home would be a relief, he told himself. He couldn't quite make himself believe it, though.

He rubbed his head gently, wincing when his fingers brushed over the swelling. He'd been cleared by the doctors as having a moderate concussion and given his instructions—rest, sleep, try not to smash his head against anything for a while— and sent home. Jack had come to get him, taken him to his car, and watched him climb in slowly, hovering like a mother hen. He'd offered to drive Garrick home or to follow him, but Garrick had assured him he was fine.

He couldn't have stood another minute of Jack's pitying looks.

Fuck. Maybe he deserved it. He'd done the unthinkable and practically chased Savannah off. But god, it had hurt when she'd said she was leaving for Boston within a week. What else could he do? They both knew she had to leave.

It was her dream job. How could he possibly stand in the way of that?

He scrubbed a hand over his face and stretched his neck, pleased he hadn't experienced any dizziness since leaving the hospital. His head was going to be fine. The rest of him he was a lot less certain about.

Sighing, he considered waiting to call Reese Lamont, but someone ought to warn him his deal had fallen through, and once Garrick got home, he was going to bed. For a week. He hit the speed dial on his cell phone and brought it to his ear.

Reese answered on the first ring. "Lamont."

Garrick was momentarily taken aback. "Reese?"

"Yes, Garrick. Are you okay?"

Garrick didn't know how to answer so he avoided the question all together. "You're going to get a call from the EHL. The deal isn't going to happen."

"I heard. Where are you?"

"On my way home, actually. Long night."

"So I hear. I also heard Robert and Bobby have both been

arrested. Multiple charges."

Garrick grunted, surprised. "You got spies in Moncton, Lamont?"

"In a manner of speaking, yes," he answered stiffly. "Contrary to popular myth, I *do* have friends."

"Don't get your panties in a bunch, Lamont. I know that." Garrick rubbed his eyes.

"Oh yes? And how is that?"

"Because I *am* one."

Garrick stared out the window at the empty road and waited for Lamont to answer.

"Yes, well, thank you. I believe that is true."

Garrick almost worked up a smile at Reese's rigid politeness in the face of Garrick's blatant violation of the guy-code.

"Listen," Garrick continued, "I have most of the money together. I have two partners signed on, we just need to find a fourth. Once we do, I'll make the offer."

"I look forward to it. Though, with Kramer out of the way, are you sure you really want to own the team?"

"Why wouldn't I?" Garrick asked.

"You could play for a couple more years, at least. I figured that's what you'd want."

Was that what he wanted? Two months ago, he'd have said yes, unequivocally. Now he wasn't so sure.

"Garrick?"

"Yes, sorry," he said quickly, embarrassed to have drifted off.

"Why don't you get yourself home safely and then we'll talk about next steps."

Garrick swallowed hard. "Okay. Thanks."

He pulled into his driveway with a sigh, ditched his truck out front and staggered up the front stairs. He steeled himself for the moment that his house, for the first time ever, wouldn't feel the same. That his big, warm home had lost something it needed.

Savannah.

He swung the front door open. Had he bit been hit in the head harder than he thought? Maybe the MRI hadn't shown the damage. Maybe he'd sprung a spontaneous bleed on the drive home.

Because he'd swear to god Savannah was sitting on his stairs, smiling at him.

His hallucination stood and took a step toward him. "Turns out, I couldn't go back to my apartment."

"You couldn't?"

She took another step. "Nope."

"Why not?"

She smiled a little. "Because what I really wanted was to come home."

"Home?"

"Yeah."

His heart beat a little harder, but he shook his head, ignoring the zing of pain. "I don't understand."

Savannah's smile faded, but she took another step closer. "Also, there's something very important that I need to tell you."

"What's that?" A surge of hope terrified him. He'd never felt more vulnerable.

"I love you."

Garrick closed his eyes for a second, staggering under the weight of his relief.

He wasn't sure if he hauled Savannah into his arms or if she hurled herself there. All he knew was he couldn't hold her close enough, couldn't possibly kiss her long enough. Her groan was almost drowned out by his whimper of pain as he belatedly recalled his mangled face. It didn't matter. All that mattered was touching her. Tasting her. Having Savannah back in his arms.

When she pressed closer, he pushed her back.

Shit, wait.

His guts churning, he held her away from him. "You have to go to Boston."

She shook her head.

"Yes, you do."

Her eyes filled with tears. "I know. Of course I do. But this—" she gestured between their bodies "—is important. Just as important as Boston."

He pulled her back into his arms, the relief of having her there far outweighing the pain against his bruised ribs and legs. "It is. We are. We'll figure it out."

She sighed and buried her face against his neck. "I can't believe I fall in love for the first time in my life and I'm about to move five hundred and thirty seven miles away."

Garrick laughed. "Looked that up, did you?"

She leaned back and smiled. "You hadn't?"

"Oh yeah, I had." He grinned down at her. "Now, can you repeat the other part?"

Her hand cupped his cheek. "I love you. My god, I love you so much. I'm sorry I didn't tell you sooner. I've been falling in love with you since that night in Nova Scotia. Maybe before then. I just didn't know what it was. What I was feeling. All it knew was that it scared the crap out of me."

He grinned. "Me too."

Her brows furrowed. "What are we going to do?"

"You're going to go to the Bruins."

"But—"

"And I'm going to finish the season here, then meet you in Boston in March."

Savannah leaned back. "Really?"

He nodded. "Yes. Really."

"What about next season?"

"There is no next season," he said, finding only relief in the words he'd feared for so long. "I'm retiring."

Savannah gripped his arms hard. "Garrick, you can keep playing. Moncton loves you."

He laughed. "Good for Moncton. But they don't love me nearly as much as I love you."

Savannah didn't have any arguments for that. She leaped into his arms, wrapping her long legs around his waist. He gasped in pain and she winced in sympathy, even as he captured her mouth and carried her toward the stairs. No amount of aches and pains were going to stop him.

The doorbell, on the other hand, worked just fine.

Chapter Twenty Nine

As a rule, it wasn't a good thing when someone turned up at his door unexpectedly at seven o'clock in the morning. After the day he'd had, Garrick seriously considered ignoring it. The odds of it being good news were long. And he had so many other things he'd like to be doing right then.

The doorbell rang again. *Damn it.*

With a sigh, he lowered Savannah back to her feet and adjusted the steel bar in his pants, so as not to frighten his unsuspecting visitors. Ignoring Savannah's giggle, he slid his arm around her shoulders and tucked her close as he pulled back the curtain and peeked out to the front porch. When he saw who was standing on the other side of the door, he jerked back.

"Whoa."

"What?" Savannah asked.

Rather than answer, he opened to the door to Reese Lamont and Rupert Smythe.

"Whoa," Savannah agreed quietly.

Rumor had it Reese Lamont didn't leave his estate. Ever. The whole recluse bazillionaire thing more or less required it. The fact that Rupert was hovering at Reese's side, his face creased with worry, made Garrick think this was, indeed, an unusual occurrence.

Garrick snapped his mouth shut and recalled his manners. "Please, come in."

Reese walked into the foyer and shifted uncomfortably, clearly not certain where to look or to sit. In his own home, he'd been the model of social grace, but here he appeared at a loss. At last, his roving gaze alighted on Savannah. "I heard from Mark about your position in Boston."

Garrick racked his brain to come up with a reason this had

lured Reese from his sanctuary, let alone landed him in Garrick's front hall.

"Congratulations," Rupert said, filling the silence.

"Thank you."

"Yes, good luck with that." Reese shifted again, then turned to Garrick. "I actually came to see you. We heard what happened last night and wanted to come sort things out in person."

Garrick nodded. "Okay," he said slowly, wondering what this had to do with Reese's appearance on his doorstep.

"I'd like to propose," Reese continued, "if you're still interested, that we go into a partnership."

He looked at Garrick with a mildly curious expression, as if he hadn't just dropped a bomb.

"What do you mean?"

"You said you had enough to buy three-fourths of the team. I'm willing to sell that to you and your partners, if you still want it. I'll keep a fourth, and the four of us, if you agree, will own the team. We'll draft up a corporation, all that. You know." He waved his hand.

Garrick had no idea. But he could learn. "Really?"

"Yes, really. And I had thought, if you'd be willing to retire from the ice a little early, you ought to manage the team. Obviously, we can let you out of your contract."

Garrick slowly sat on the bench at his back. *Shit.* "I was already planning to retire at the end of this season."

"Excellent."

"And move to Boston."

Reese looked between him and Savannah. "Well, yes, of course. I hadn't realized...but, yes, of course."

Reese's cheeks turned pink and Savannah gave him a small, reassuring smile. Rupert hovered closer.

Garrick's mind spun, then he shot back to his feet and took Savannah's hand, threading their fingers together. "Actually, I can do a lot from there, ownership-wise. We'll keep the farmhouse, and I can visit periodically during the season. I mean, if that's okay with Savannah."

"Of course. I'll be traveling a lot during the season. There will be plenty of time." She squeezed his hand and gave him a bright, encouraging smile.

Garrick looked back to Reese and was alarmed to see his shoulders slump.

"I'm afraid we would be starting with an uphill battle," Reese said. "Mark gave his notice today. Seems the prospect of working for the Kramers was highly unattractive and he went looking. He's been courted away by his alma mater."

"Damn," Garrick muttered. A mid-season replacement would be a nightmare.

"I was hoping you might step in," Reese explained. "But if you'll be leaving between the season and the draft, it might be too disruptive."

Garrick nodded. That kind of upheaval could destroy a team. New players were critical to overall success and decisions had to be made by someone intimately familiar with the sport, the league, and the team.

Rupert cleared his throat. "I'll do it."

For a long time no one said anything.

"The draft?" Reese said, his face pinched with confusion.

"No. Well, yes. And manage the Ice Cats."

Reese's mouth opened but no sound came out. Savannah put a hand on Rupert's arm. "Are you sure? You always seem so...well, nervous around the team."

"Yes, well, it's a silly thing for a grown man to be frightened of other grown men, isn't it?" Rupert's nerves made his British accent particularly prim. "I mean really, they're just athletes, like any other men."

Garrick blinked. Had Rupert just admitted to being afraid of hockey players?

Reese went to his friend. "You don't have to do this. There

is nothing to prove."

Rupert's cheeks colored. "Well, as it turns out, I have something to prove to myself. And I happen to love hockey. You know I tried to talk you out of selling the team to begin with, and now I see I can make an even greater difference." He paused, his beseeching look at Reese morphing into one of concern. "That is, if you'll be all right without me."

Rather than brush Rupert off, Reese appeared to be giving the matter serious consideration. Rupert's determination seemed to melt before their eyes, but before he could rescind his offer, Reese nodded.

"It seems we both could prove some things to ourselves," Reese said quietly. "If you take on the Ice Cats, with Garrick and me and presumably the other owners backing you up, then I'll take over my own business affairs, if you'll promise to advise when needed."

"Of course," Rupert said. "Are you sure?"

Reese nodded. "It's been long enough. If the three of you promise not to identify me to the media or the public, I don't see why I can't move about anonymously. Perhaps I'll get a place here in Moncton. Go to some Ice Cats games."

Garrick exchanged a quick, baffled glance with Savannah.

"Yes, well, we'd better get started then." Rupert clapped and rubbed his hands together. He turned to Savannah. "When are you due in Boston?"

Hours later, the four of them stood from the kitchen table. They'd covered a lot of ground already, including calling Savannah's brothers and securing their agreement, notifying the league, setting the attorneys to work on creating the legal partnership, arranging Savannah's travel and Rupert's move, and debating extensively about what sort of changes they'd like to make first. They'd cobbled together a brunch from what little Garrick had in the house, but now at sunset, they were all tired and hungry.

"Yes, well, I think that settles that. We'll leave you to get some supper and some sleep. You had a long night, and now we've put you to work for the better part of the day," Reese said, moving with Rupert toward the door.

Garrick ushered them out, thanking them, his mind still reeling. *Holy shit.* He was going to own the Ice Cats.

Closing the door behind their guests, Garrick stared at Savannah with wide eyes. She grinned back.

In a blink, his worries about the team and his role faded to the background. Owning the team was going to be fantastic. But it was nothing compared to knowing he'd get to be with this woman.

He was about to prove to her just how much he loved her, when she frowned. "I guess we should go out and get something for dinner."

That wasn't at all what Garrick had in mind, but he *was* hungry. For a lot of things.

"Oh yeah?" A slow smile spread across his face. "Because I was thinking about what we were about to do before we were so rudely interrupted."

Savannah's brows arched. "Oh, were you?" Her eyes widened when he lunged for her. With a squeal of joy, she bolted for the stairs. Her long legs pumped up the steps and to the hallway outside his bedroom. He couldn't catch her before she launched herself onto his bed. With a bounce, she landed on her knees and stripped her shirt off over her head.

That's my girl.

She lunged for him, but he stepped back and stopped her with one hand held out.

"What?" She chucked the rest of her clothes across the room, clearly not interested in any delay. Neither was he, but his priorities weren't completely consumed by his body's clamoring needs. Yet.

"If you stay right there, I'll give you what you really want."

"Hmmm..." she practically purred. "Will you?" Her downright sultry gaze trailed over him and he had to lock his knees to keep himself upright.

"Yes, I will," he promised, watching the goosebumps rise across her ivory skin. Then he pulled out his cell phone and ordered enough Chinese food to feed the population of Belize.

Garrick ordered up a veritable feast. She laughed as his grin, her heart light, and fell back onto the bed. Happiness like she'd never known blazed in her chest, contentedness like she'd never imagined possible warmed her body, and good old-fashioned lust heated her blood.

At last Garrick hung up and tossed his phone on the dresser.

"You *do* know what this girl needs," she teased, her stomach growling with the promise of food. "But I thought we'd already decided there wasn't delivery Chinese in Moncton that wasn't destined to poison us."

"That was House of Lau."

"Hey! They don't deliver!" She was completely over her idea of going out to get food. And hell, now she had plans for Garrick. She didn't want him to go either. Pinned on the bed beneath his hot gaze, there were countless things she wanted from him, and none of them allowed for him to go get supper.

"They do if you went to high school with Brian Lau and you're willing to pay a premium. And boy, am I willing. It will be here in thirty minutes."

She sighed with relief. "You spoil me."

"Every chance I get," he murmured. Fisting a hand in the back of his layered shirts, he stripped them off in one go.

"Shouldn't we wait for the food?"

He grimaced as he toed off his shoes, making quick work of removing the rest of his clothes. "I can't. God help me, I have to touch you. Even if it means I have to pay for the Moo Goo Gai Pan in the altogether."

Savannah's laugh died on her lips as her eyes skimmed over his chest. The bruises were ripe, but they couldn't hide the magnificence. Broad shoulders, the deep curve under his pecs, the bunched muscles of his abs. Perfect.

"Come here." She reached for him.

He crawled over her, settling his weight along hers, his hips cradled between her thighs, his cock nestling in the folds of her pussy. He was hard. She was wet.

Moo Goo Gai Pan be damned. She wasn't in any hurry.

"I love you," she said quietly, carding her fingers through his hair, watching his eyes change to liquid chocolate.

One side of his mouth kicked up. "I love you too."

Their lips met, their tongues exploring one another as though they'd never done it before. As though they had all the time in the world. She cupped his face in her hands, holding him close, treasuring how he pressed her into the mattress. She locked her legs around him. His body fit hers perfectly. She loved his texture. His taste. His scent. His ridiculous fat lip.

He shifted away and she brought her knees higher, opening herself to him, groaning long and loud as he eased into her body. Slowly. Carefully. He fit here too, stretching her, his length just enough to nudge her cervix as he settled deep. Within a few strokes, it would be different, but as they sank into another kiss, it was as though they'd been made for just this. Exactly.

She didn't urge him on, happy to be wrapped around him, joined to him, content to hold him like this forever. She skimmed her palms down his back, into the dip at his waist, and drew her fingers over the swell of his buttocks. She wallowed in the touch of smooth skin, firm muscle, and the rising heat from his body. He eased from her and her breath stuttered, gusting over his chest. His long, slow glide back into her core was so delicious, goosebumps broke out across her body.

"Garrick," she sighed, looking up into his beautiful face. She couldn't form words to tell him what she wanted.

He didn't say a word, his eyes locked on her, his gaze narrow as he shuddered above her.

"Do you feel that?" she asked, unsure how to articulate the depth. The intimacy.

He nodded, stroking, never looking away. She arched beneath him, unable to hold still, her need to be close to him driving her up off the bed and against him.

His strokes picked up speed, the friction unbearably sweet, the power of each thrust lifting her higher. Closer. She brought his face to hers for another kiss and squeezed her eyes shut, moaning into his mouth as he shifted his weight, his knees wider on the bed, his thrusts gathering power. The rock of their bodies, the taste of his tongue on hers, took her to the teetering edge.

The need became too great, their ability to coordinate lips and tongues lost to the maelstrom of passion. They pressed their faces close and gasped, his breath hot against her skin, her moans muffled against his. He was murmuring. Soft words she could barely decipher. Except one.

Love.

Her orgasm rolled up and over her, bowing her spine, drawing a cry from her lips, her chest, her heart, as she arched beneath him. She clung to him as his hips lost their rhythm and kicked in sharp circles.

He sighed her name against her neck as each jerk of his body filled her with his warmth.

With his next breath, he wrapped his arms around her and rolled them to the side. She curled against him, her head on his shoulder, her hand resting over his racing heart.

She wanted to tell him again she loved him. That she'd never made love to another man until that night. Not really. Not as she understood it now.

Her stomach chose that moment to make a noise unlike she'd ever heard before. Then the doorbell rang.

Garrick chuckled and leaped from the bed, tugging on his jeans rather than retrieving the Moo Goo Gai Pan in the altogether as threatened. Savannah lay like a puddle in the middle of the bed. Happy. And content.

She wasn't worried she hadn't had a chance to say what she'd been thinking. She'd have a lifetime to tell Garrick what he meant to her.

About the Author

Samantha Wayland has always dreamed of being a novelist. She wrote her first book as an escape from the pressures of her day job. That fascinating piece of contemporary erotic mystery/suspense with elements of paranormal, international intrigue, and god only knows what else, is safely tucked under her bed, where it will remain until hell freezes over. Since then she's learned a lot about the craft (she hopes) and turned her attention to writing contemporary MM and MMF Ménage erotic romance.

Sam lives with her family—of both the two and four-legged variety—outside of Boston. She used to spend her days toiling away in corporate nerdville but was recently sprung from that hell. Now when she's not locked away in her home office, she can generally be found tucked in the corner of the local Thai place with a few beloved friends (and fellow authors).

Her favorite things include mango martinis, tiny Chihuahuas with big attitude problems, and the Oxford comma.

Sam loves to hear from readers.

Email her at samantha@samanthawayland.com or find her on Facebook (Samantha Wayland) or Twitter (@SamWayland).

Also by Samantha Wayland

With Grace

A man yearning to explore his sexual tastes but afraid to turn up the heat, the woman who loves him but is hungry for more spice...and the chef who craves them both.

When Grace, Philip and Mark find a mobster's flash drive full of incriminating information, they are quickly embroiled in a dangerous situation. They stay together for safety, but proximity ignites the sparks they've long been fighting to ignore.

When three friends dare to succumb to their appetites, they find the perfect recipe for love.

Destiny Calls

Patrick didn't think it would be a big deal to kiss Brandon, his best friend and fellow police officer. Hell, they'd done crazier things to escape a bar fight. But then he had no way of knowing just how hot it would be.

Destiny Matthews is not a woman who is afraid to ask for what she wants, and when she sees her two best friends kissing, she knows just what she's going to ask for. Before she can convince Patrick that he's not as straight as he likes to protest, Brandon is attacked by an unknown enemy.

While they fight to protect each other's lives, they prove time and again that they're even better at protecting their own hearts.

Two Man Advantage
Hat Trick Book Two

Rhian is working his way up the ranks of professional hockey, with the dream of making it to the NHL getting closer every day. He's doing it alone—no family, no friends—and that's the way he likes it. Then he arrives in New Brunswick, and meets the Moncton Ice Cats. Suddenly, he's got friends—and even something that might be an honest-to-god crush.

Garrick is lonely and counting the days until his last season with the Ice Cats is over and he can move to Boston. When his girlfriend suggests he take a lover—as long that lover is a man and Garrick tells her all about it—he laughs it off. But damned if his buddy Rhian doesn't take on the starring role in his fantasies. Good thing Rhian is way too young—and straight—for what Garrick has in mind.

Rhian takes a chance when Garrick's increasingly confusing signals start making sense, and soon discovers he's bitten off more than he can chew. Sex with strangers is simple. Sex with his best friend? Complicated.

End Game

Hat Trick Book Three

Garrick never intended to fall in love with two people, but he has, and now he has to figure out what to do about it. He wants to make them happy, but is afraid he's doing just the opposite. To make matters worse, he's trapped in New Brunswick until the end of the hockey season, while his lovers are both in Boston.

Savannah has no one but herself to blame for practically shoving her lover into the arms of another man. After all, it was her harebrained idea that Garrick take a lover while they are separated for the season. She loves Garrick with all her heart, but how the hell is she going to share him with Rhian? That she and Rhian work together isn't making a difficult situation any easier.

Rhian used to have such a simple life. Now he's in love, his dreams of skating on an NHL team are coming true, and he keeps spotting a familiar face in the crowds. To top it all off, he has to see Savannah every day. He knows she's Garrick's real future, but he doesn't have the balls to do the right thing for all of them and end it.

Then he finds the lump.

www.ingramcontent.com/pod-product-compliance
Lightning Source LLC
Chambersburg PA
CBHW020736250626
47155CB00003B/779